LUCKY LACES

EAGLES HOCKEY #5

ELISE FABER

LUCKY LACES
BY ELISE FABER

Newsletter sign-up

EAGLES HOCKEY SERIES

PROLOGUE

Diana

I FELL FOR A HOCKEY PLAYER.

How could I not?

And, despite my best efforts, the world found out every juicy detail.

ONE

Diana

WE'RE two minutes into the first game of the season and we're down a goal.

This is not where I want my team to be.

But it's part of hockey.

It's not all breakaways and top-shelf goals.

Sometimes...it's fucking up early and clawing our way back.

Tonight, that fuck-up is on me.

I'm the head coach—it *all* comes down to me.

My job, my choices, my...

Fuckups.

Sighing softly, I start to tear my eyes from the jumbotron overhead, from the replay of the shitshow that just happened on the ice. It's changed to a video of the Eagles' mascot—which is, no surprise, an Eagle—striding down a hallway near the luxury suites overhead.

He's probably going to go torture the team's owner, Jean-

Michel Dubois. The notoriously grumpy billionaire is in attendance tonight, and the last time Wings, the mascot, invaded his box, he glared the overgrown bird into submission before escorting him from the room. Meanwhile, his unofficially adopted daughter, Rory, stole the mascot's T-shirt gun so she and his bio daughter, Chrissy, could shoot the prizes into the stands.

The crowd loved it.

Mostly because Jean-Michel *is* grumpy and has little patience for bullshit.

But also because the grump aside, Jean-Michel is a known softie, especially for the women in his life.

So I have a feeling the T-shirt cannon thing is going to become a regular event.

Only as I start to focus back on the ice, the commercial break winding down, the players from both teams slowly moving to their positions at center ice, I realize it's not merch giveaways that are going to happen tonight.

It's heartbreak.

Because right there on a forty-by-thirty foot screen for all to see—

(Or maybe just me).

There's a couple in an alcove.

A couple *canoodling* in that alcove.

And I recognize the tattoo on the man's arm, which is currently looped around a curvy brunette whose face I can't see, his hand splayed, fingers wide as they cup...well, those *curves*.

I don't have an ass, not like that.

Not even if I did a million squats would I have an ass like that—

But that's not the point.

Jason's hand is on the woman's ass and as I follow the

swirling lines of my fiancé's tattoo up his arm, losing them beneath the sleeve of his tee...

My stomach sinks further.

Because the man who is supposed to be mine and mine alone is kissing the woman in his arms like he's going to devour her whole.

He's never kissed me like that. Not even during our most heated moments.

Never.

But he's doing it tonight with another woman—during the highest point in my career.

I'm coaching my first NHL game, and I've busted my ass for fucking *years* to get here.

And my fiancé is sucking some random woman's face.

In the same building I'm coaching.

With twenty-thousand plus people in attendance and who knows how many millions watching at home on TV.

Pain ripples through me, and it's all I can do to stay standing.

He's cheating on me *here.*

Now.

The whistle trills, and I jerk my gaze back to the ice, focus coiling through my insides, frosting over the hurt, but not doing anything for the pure, unadulterated fury filling every cell, every muscle fiber.

It's, unfortunately, not a new feeling for me.

Not just with Jason—but with the other men in my life too.

So, I do what I always do.

The only thing I've ever been able *to* do.

I channel it.

Then I reinforce it with the knowledge that in four-ish hour the asshole who hurt me this way is going to be out of my life.

Forever.

FOUR-ISH HOURS later

"YOU COULD GIVE ME SOME GRACE!" Jason cries, trailing me through the house. "I moved out here for you and I've had a hard time making friends."

That freezes me in place for a second.

But only a second.

Because the idiotic statement sparks my fury, lighting the fuse, sending it smoldering toward explosion.

And it's nearly one in the morning.

The game took three and a half hours and my job doesn't just end when the buzzer rings. There are interviews to give and debriefs to have with my coaching staff, plans to be made for the upcoming games and analyzing what went wrong and right. I need to touch base with specific players who need the one-on-one contact and the training staff to make sure I know the state of the roster's health.

And I have my own work, my own processes and preparations to make.

It takes time, and I'm exhausted.

Though, at least we pulled out the win in a shootout that had the crowd on their feet and the commentators breaking down the replay of Rhodes' filthy move on the other team's goalie over and over again in high definition.

I should be focused on *that*.

Should be focused on the fact that my first NHL game ended in a win, that I'm living my dream, finally at the peak of my career after grinding for years and years, and...

Instead, I'm shoving my fiancé's belongings into a suitcase all while thinking I should have used a trash bag instead.

And he's bitching about how it's hard to make friends.

As a grown fucking man.

I grind my teeth together.

Because, fuck, I don't have the patience for this, the time for this, the emotional bandwidth for dealing with his shit.

Not when I'm so damned...

Hurt.

That word ricochets through my insides like a bullet, wounding, sending blood spurting, and...

I'm tired.

So damned tired.

I shove the last of his clothes inside the suitcase, lean heavily on the hard plastic shell so I can wrestle the zipper closed. That accomplished, I drop it on the floor and straighten, turning toward Jason, who quickly rearranges his expression from outraged to hangdog.

And that right there is confirmation enough.

If I wasn't already done, *that* would have been the straw that broke the camel's back.

I could deal with the toilet seat being left up, the crumbs on the kitchen counter. I could look past the dirty socks on the floor and the fact that he's never done a single load of laundry since we moved in together.

I could put up with the whining that I work too much and the annoyance that I've dared to interrupt his gaming time when I'm home.

I could even pretend to not be bothered by the fact that he's never once bought me flowers.

But *that*—his wounded expression after I saw him kissing someone else on the fucking jumbotron and doing it with a passion I've never experienced—on top of the rest of it?

No.

Just. Fucking. *No.*

I grab the handle of the suitcase and start hauling it down the stairs.

"Baby—"

Through the kitchen.

"Diana, sweetheart—"

I snag his keys from the hook and unlock the door to the garage, still carrying the damned bag.

"Honey—"

I jab at the button to send the metal door rolling up then march into the garage, throwing the suitcase in the back seat of his car then hopping in the driver's side.

The engine rumbles to life.

I reverse out onto the driveway.

Park.

"Baby," he says as I pop open the door.

"Goodbye, Jason."

"Diana—"

"We're done. Just go." I turn away, but I don't make it more than a couple of steps before he snags my arm, yanking me roughly to a stop, spinning me to face him.

"*I* decide when we're done," he says, a look in his eyes I've never seen before.

It's dark, cold, not anything like the somewhat dopey golden retriever I thought I'd been dating.

I shiver, a thread of fear winding through my middle. "Let me go," I order quietly.

He bends so his face is in mine, fingers tightening until the point of pain—

"Everything okay out here?"

We jump, and relief cascades through me at the sound of my neighbor's voice. Ernest is eighty if he's a day, but right now he's shuffling toward us, a bag in one hand, his phone in his other.

"Everything's fine," Jason snaps.

But the distraction of Ernest is enough that I'm able to extricate myself from Jason's hold.

"I'm glad you're here," I say to my neighbor, keeping a watchful eye on—and distance from—Jason as I move over to Ernest. "I picked up that jar of jelly for you"—not a lie, but it's also something that can wait for a time when it's not one in the freaking morning—"want to come in and get it?"

His shrewd gaze tells me he knows exactly what I'm doing, but I'm still relieved when he nods. "Yes, that would be great, missy. I'd love to have some on my toast in the morning."

Jason takes a step toward us. "I—"

"You were leaving, right?" Ernest asks—or rather orders—as he takes my arm. "Don't let an old man keep you." He starts walking, leading me through the garage, pausing at the front and hitting the button to send the door rolling down, waiting for it to fully shut before he turns to me and says on a sigh,

"You're going to have a problem with that one, Dee."

And unfortunately, over the next weeks, I discover...

He's not wrong.

TWO

Hudson

I STARE AT THE TABLET, the drawings on the screen, willing my brain to comprehend them.

It's hockey—something I've done nearly my entire fucking life.

From the moment I could walk, my dad strapped skates on my feet, shoved a stick in my hand, and locked me out of the house so I had nowhere to go except for the frozen rink in the back yard.

So, this shouldn't be complicated.

It *should* be instinctual.

But as much as I stare at the symbols on the screen—at the mix of Xs and Os interspersed with arrows on a drawing of the rink—I can't get them to sit still.

Can't get them to make sense.

This is always the worst part for me.

If I can play it out or if I can watch my teammates do it, then I get it—often in one take.

But attempting to learn it like this? On a piece of paper or tablet, the contents turning into a swirling mass of shapes and arrows, my brain too fucking slow, too fucking dumb to process it—

No.

It doesn't stick.

"Fuck," I mutter, tossing the tablet aside and rubbing my hands over my face, resisting the urge to slap some sense into myself.

That hasn't *ever* worked.

And maybe it's pathetic that I've tried this same shit in the first place.

But it's the start of the season, everyone is picking up the new system, the changes the coaching staff have put in place.

No one seems to be struggling like I am.

So, why can't I fucking get this?

Groaning, I jump up to my feet, leaving the tablet and papers where they are—though I do glare at them as I go into the kitchen and grab a beer from the fridge. I twist off the top, toss it into the trash, and take a long pull.

But it doesn't ease the burn inside me.

Doesn't soothe the ache of frustration.

Not even when I drain the last of the dregs from the bottle.

I drop the empty into the recycle bin—because I may not be able to get the fucking system to make sense in my big dumb brain, but at least I care about the environment—then move down the hall and into my home gym.

To do the one thing I'm good at.

Lift heavy shit.

Get bigger.

Get stronger.

So I can be better on the ice.

I load plates on the barbell, lift it onto my shoulders.

And I start squatting.

But even as sweat breaks out on my skin and my quads cry out for mercy, I don't stop.

I can't.

Because this is the only thing I'm good at.

The only thing I've got.

And sooner or later, I won't be strong enough or big enough.

Sooner or later everyone will see through me.

And then I'll lose everything.

"CHRIST," I mutter as I sink onto the step, chest heaving after having chased Rome up and down the aisles of the practice facility's stairs.

Our captain is a psychopath.

But he's not wrong that this shit is a killer workout.

Though, *he* calls it a warmup.

See? Psychopath.

Likely because he got into the habit of running the stairs at his old team, the San Francisco Gold, and doing beside a woman who moves like liquid lightning. Brit Plantain was the first female player in the league and though she's rumored to finally be retiring (for good, this time) at the end of this season, she is still incredibly talented.

Of course, she's also responsible for this special brand of hell coming to my team.

So, I might need to give her a piece of my mind the next time I see her.

"Christ is right," King says as he collapses next to me. "Why did we think this was a good idea to do before practice?"

"Because," Cam says dropping down next to us, his next

words all but gasped out, *"that* one"—a nod at Rome who's so used to this shit that he's already finished, caught his breath, and is currently smirking at us as he stretches—"is insane."

"Also known as *in shape,*" Rome jokes, his smile nonplussed as he bends his leg behind him and grabs his ankle, stretching out his quad.

Hell.

My quads.

They're toast.

After the workout yesterday and the run today...I'm going to be hobbling my ass into bed tonight.

If I make it through practice, that is.

My stomach starts churning at the thought, all those Xs and Os and arrows swirling through my head like one of those really obscure abstract pieces of art dumbass rich people buy.

Unfortunately, they don't swirl into anything that makes sense.

"Are we getting beers after practice?" Rome asks.

"Isn't Chrissy like eight million years pregnant?" Cam teases, pushing up to his feet with a grunt and starting his own stretching routine. "I'm surprised she lets you out of the house."

Rome rolls his eyes—likely because he's beyond done with being teased about knocking up the owner's daughter.

But hockey is about seventy percent skill and thirty percent giving each other shit, so he's not going to be in for a reprieve from the teasing any time soon.

Especially because he knocked up the owner's daughter.

I grin, having sufficiently caught my breath enough to push up to my feet, and start stretching my own legs.

But my grin fades almost as quickly.

Because...how much shit will I be in for if the guys find out I can't even read a fucking tablet screen?

"Come on, fuckers," Rome grumbles as he turns for the

locker room, calling over his shoulder, "It's almost time for practice."

A practice I'm not prepared for.

Fuck.

"The man is a sadist," King mutters, groaning as he gets to his feet.

"You're just trying to distract us from the fact that you and Rory were caught naked the other day, so you're well on your own way to trying to knock up the owner's other daughter," Cam says.

My brows fly up in surprise.

But worse—for him, anyway—King blushes.

"Dude," I say under my breath, shaking my head, knowing there's no preventing it now.

Because the guys see King's pink cheeks...and the shit-giving commences.

Apparently, he and Rory were caught naked in a supply closet.

Yes, literally.

So yeah, King gets shit all the way to the locker room...and it doesn't stop while we get dressed or even as we make our way onto the ice for practice.

Nor as practice commences.

Lucky for me, the guys are so focused on King—and Rome —and the fact they're dating the daughters of our grumpy, billionaire owner, that me muddling through the drills and struggling with the plays and generally failing all around doesn't hit their radar.

I'm safe. For now.

But when I get off the ice and head for the locker room, I see her.

Diana Connors.

The new head coach of the Eagles, Diana Connors.

The first female head coach in the league.

And the object of my fantasies since she first showed up at training camp.

Unusually, she's in street clothes, having not joined us on the rink for practice—she hasn't missed a team event, not since that first day she was on the payroll.

I tense, expecting her to comment on the shitshow of my performance out there.

But though her eyes catch mine for a moment, she doesn't stop me and tell me I'm a failure and to get my ass out of here (not like our old coach would have done, not like my dad would have done). Instead, she nods, murmurs a soft "Hey" that I feel in my dick, and stops Rome as he steps off the ice.

"Can I borrow you for a second?"

God, her voice.

I fucking love her voice.

I hear it in my dreams sometimes.

My dick twitches, and I ignore my pulse of jealousy as I watch my friend disappear down the hall with her.

There's nothing down that road except disaster.

Same as the disaster barreling toward me if I don't get my shit together and memorize the plays, the changes to the team's system.

That's why I promise to grab a beer with the guys another time and go home instead.

It's why I pull out the tablet.

And it's why I force myself to keep staring at it even when the arrows and Xs and Os keep swimming on the screen.

THREE

Diana

"I TOLD you I was going to stop by the store tomorrow."

I smile at the grumpy tone as I carry the bag of groceries into Ernest's house, bending to kiss him on the cheek. "And *I* told you it's the least I can do after the other night."

Ernest sighs, shakes his head. "That fiancé of yours is going to give you trouble, missy."

"*Ex*-fiancé," I mutter.

"Thank God for that," he says shutting the door behind me and following me down the hall. "But still, trouble."

Unfortunately, he's not wrong.

Jason has been blowing up my phone—to the tune of several hundred calls and texts.

Why is this my life?

Only...*nope.*

I'm not allowing the cheating manchild to drag me down, and I'm not going to let his bullshit infiltrate my life.

Instead, I'm keeping a record of his crazy. I've verified that he doesn't have any legal tenant rights because he wasn't living in my house long enough (and, seriously, thank *fuck* he dragged his heels for so long to make the move and saved me one headache at least). *And* I changed the locks and all the codes on the keypad entry systems.

I'm good.

Work is good. Like usual, it's keeping me busy, but it's also keeping my mind off the fact that Jason...is Jason.

And the fact that—arguably worse—I put up with him for as long as I did.

If I had any girlfriends, I would have told them to dump his ass.

Yet...I stayed and put up with it and—

Now I'm here.

Alone and with a hole inside me when I should be on top of the world.

"How's that team of yours looking?" Ernest asks, thankfully

"The boys are doing great."

We have a few things that need tweaking, a few players that are struggling, but we're six and two, and that's a hell of a start. Of course there are seventy-four games left in the season—not counting playoffs—so we have a long way to go.

But we're getting there with the mood in the locker room—though Pat Franklin is still a blight on the roster.

My biggest problem is figuring out how to mitigate him and Duncan and Kane.

The team is locked into contracts and their attitudes are well-known through the league, so moving them is challenging. Most especially Pat, who's the worst of the bunch and has what basically amounts to a no-trade clause because any of the teams on the list of six he was allowed to name in his contract won't touch him with a ten-foot pole.

Then there's Hudson.

Who isn't a troublesome player by nature—he works hard and hangs with what I mentally consider (even though I know this isn't the right coaching move) the Good Crew.

But he isn't adapting well to my tenure as head coach.

Not that he's disrespectful or misogynistic.

He just...isn't doing well.

And I haven't figured out the correct levers to pull to motivate him.

"Just set 'em there, missy," Ernest says, nodding at the counter and I realize I'm standing there, thinking about the guys...and still holding the groceries. "I'll put them away later."

Right.

Enough.

I'm leaving all of the Jason and work thoughts behind, focusing on the fact that my neighbor is sweet and widowed and saved me from what would have no doubt been an unpleasant altercation.

"Nope," I tell him. "I'll put some of them away now and the rest," I add, raising my volume when he starts to protest, "I'll use to cook you something yummy. And *not* frozen."

Because he survives on frozen TV dinners.

Which are fine—hell, every once in a while I crave a Hot Pocket.

But it's not the same as sitting across the table from someone, having a nice conversation, and eating a home-cooked meal.

"Diana—"

"We're eating together," I say firmly.

"You're not wasting your night with an old man."

"I'm not wasting my night with *any* man," I tell him. "I'm having a nice meal with my friend."

"Missy—"

Giving up on words, I nudge him over to a chair at the worn wooden table and pull out a bottle of grape soda—his favorite. "Sit." I pass over the bottle. "Drink." I turn back to the bags. "And tell me what's happening with your grandkids while I cook." The only topic that can distract a stubborn old man from what he wants.

He scowls.

But only for a moment.

Because, as I mentioned, he loves talking about his grandkids.

I put away the perishables aside from what I'm going to use for the fish and veggies—give the man something healthy and something green. Well...and something tasty.

"Is that rocky road ice cream I see?" he asks, pausing in the description of his kindergarten grandson's first time at show and tell—when he showed and told the class about his collection of crayons.

Yup.

Crayons.

All one hundred and sixty-two of them.

Because he and the class had counted.

My lips twitch—both at the crayon counting and Ernest's laser-eyed focus of the tub of ice cream. "It's vanilla," I say (though I take note of the rocky road thing for later), "and I'm using it for the root beer floats we're having for dessert."

His face lights up.

I smile, go back to chopping veggies and prepping the fish. "Now tell me about what's happening with Donovan."

"Oh you know," he says, leaning back in the chair and crossing one leg over the other, "he's himself—breaking hearts and preparing to take over the world."

"As all three year olds do."

"Exactly."

I set the fish in the pan, the butter sizzling as it begins to cook then season the green beans and toss them in too.

Garlic and butter, salt and pepper and lemon.

Nothing earth-shattering.

Ernest can't handle anything with too much seasoning but that doesn't mean it won't be delicious. It'll just be...Midwest spicy.

Grinning, I flip the fish, stir the green beans, and slice the loaf of freshly baked bread into thick hunks I coat liberally with butter.

By the time I've put a few on both of our plates, it's time to take off the fish and veg, so I load those up too and then carry the food over to Ernest, along with forks, knives, and napkins.

"...we'll meet in San Diego and take the crew to the zoo and wild animal park," he's saying, lifting one of the paper napkins I set on the table and tucking it into the neck of his shirt.

Amused, I bite the inside of my cheek then figure, what the hell, and tuck mine in too.

At least with a makeshift bib, I'll keep my shirt clean.

We chat as we make our way through our food and then, later, the floats, but eventually, Ernest starts flagging. So even though I'm reluctant to end the night and go back to my sad, empty life with the potential of my annoying cheating ex showing up and knocking on my door to harass me, I still finish up the dishes and say goodnight.

Then I walk home.

Go upstairs.

I fill my bathtub with the hottest water I can stand.

As I soak, I pull up that night's hockey highlights on my tablet and focus on gleaning every bit of information I can use for the Eagles.

And I do it at such a volume that I can't hear the doorbell going again and again.

Or the pounding on the door.

FOUR

Hudson

THE CROWD GROANS, and I curse, knowing that I need to get my shit together.

That I *have* to.

But it's the same rejoinder that I've told myself over the last couple of weeks.

Get it together.

Calm down and focus.

Just keep your head down and push on and it will all come together.

Except, spoiler alert, it's *not* coming together.

And every single fuckup continues to stack on top of the previous one so that I'm clenching my stick tighter and I'm getting more and more tense with each play, each practice, each game.

Until...

I do shit like I just did.

Coughing the puck up.

Now the Sierra have a breakaway with Lake Jordan—underwear model, face of a big vodka brand, and all-around pain in the ass—leading the charge.

"Fuck," I hiss, digging in my edges, sprinting forward, giving chase even though I don't have any hope of catching up, not in time to stop that first shot, anyway.

But I don't stop chasing.

I can't—not on this one simple fucking thing I can do: the backcheck.

I tear over the blue line, the red line, the opposite blue line, skating hard into our defensive zone. As expected, I don't make it anywhere near in time to stop the first shot.

Or the second.

But I manage to tie up the trailing forward's stick in time for Rhodes to get back and scoop up the puck, clearing it out enough for me to haul my sorry ass off the ice.

Coach Dee glances at me as I haul myself over the boards, and I'm not surprised in the least when my ice time is significantly reduced for the rest of the game. I'm a fucking liability and even though my fuckup didn't directly lead to a goal—tonight—that doesn't mean I should be back out there putting the team's lead at risk.

Hell, part of me is starting to think that I don't deserve to be back out there at all.

And Christ, how pathetic is it that these thoughts are winding their way through my mind, clinging to my confidence, dragging it down and just generally fucking with my head?

Too goddamned pathetic.

I need to focus.

I need—

"Huddy," Coach Dee calls and I jump, head whipping in her direction.

Her gaze locks on mine and my heart skips a beat at the intensity in her green eyes.

"Ready?"

I hope the fuck so.

But I keep that thought in my head and just nod at her.

She nods back. "With King and Cam, yeah?"

"Yeah."

The whistle trills and we hop on the ice, skate down to the opposite end of the ice, into the offensive zone. Where I should, theoretically, be less of a liability.

Except, that worked so well earlier, didn't it?

"Hey," Cam mutters, pausing in front of me, his eyes full of concern as they search mine. "Easy, yeah? Just do it exactly like we practiced the other day."

Practice.

Christ.

Because that's been going as well as the games.

But I nod instead of saying that.

"Just drive to the net," he murmurs. "King will do the rest."

Great.

Like I'm a fucking baby.

I shove that down, nod again, and watch as he peels off for the face-off dot, King lining up on the far side of the ice.

I find the hashmarks, take my position, and brace myself for the contact that's going to come at puck drop.

The whistle trills.

I clench my teeth together, grinding them tightly against my mouth guard, ignoring the bolt of pain in my jaw as I get ready for the drop.

Before that can happen, the fucker from the other team I'm standing next to slashes me, and I bite back a curse, the sting burning through my hands.

But I ignore that too.

And focus.

King nods at me.

Cam settles his stick on the ice.

And...

The puck drops.

I shove forward, thankful that all my extra time in the weight room of late means I can do at least one thing right—knocking the asshole on the other team to the ice.

That done, I don't stop moving, just keep skating, keep grinding, keep battling my way to the net and parking my ass in front of the goalie. I get shoved and punched, slashed and cross-checked, but I just dig in and don't allow myself to be moved.

At least I have size to my advantage.

And it's something that Cam uses when he wins the puck back to King, who tips it to our defenseman at the blue line and then cuts hard to the corner, drawing the center on the other team with him.

This gives King—and Rhodes, the other D at the line—some space to move, to get into a better position to receive a pass, to draw the other team toward them and free up lanes to the net.

It all happens in a matter of seconds, and because I'm not thinking about it too intensely, not worried about doing anything except keeping my ass out of the crease and in front of the goalie...and not getting beaned in the ass by a shot.

Well, the ass shot would be tolerable if it deflected off me and into the goal.

Or off my ass and to one of my teammates for them to put in.

Either way would work for me.

But that's not what happens.

Cam cuts behind the net, scooping up a hard pass that Rhodes sends from the point, corralling it on the blade of his stick then flicking it over to King who slides in behind me at the back door.

But the puck doesn't make it there.

The goalie gets a piece of it and the puck ricochets up, faster than my eye can track, certainly faster than I can react as it flies toward my face.

"Fuck," I hiss as pain explodes across my cheek, followed quickly by a gush of warm liquid.

Of blood.

It drips onto my jersey, onto my gloves, onto the ice.

Onto...the puck.

I react instinctively, shoving my stick at it and...missing.

Missing so fucking badly that I lose my balance, that the sudden change in direction has me breaking free of the hold the defenseman has on me.

I fall forward, my stick in front of me, and it's pure fucking luck that the blade just barely glances off the puck, sending it skittering, changing its direction, touching it *just enough* that when the goalie lunges to the side, trying to cover it, to get a whistle and stoppage in play...it slips between his legs and crawls, oh so slowly, over the goal line and into the net.

It's not pretty. It's a fucking mess.

But it happens before the play is called dead because of the blood.

And the review on the play calls it a good goal.

So the crowd roars and my teammates—except Pat and Duncan and Kane—give me a chorus of "Fuck yeahs!" and a plethora of fistbumps.

I'm smiling—I make sure of that—as I accept the congratulations, the nods of approval from the coaches.

But I don't really feel that goal, don't really feel the high from scoring, same as I don't really feel the towel the trainer presses against my cheeks or the stitches they give me back in the training suite before I go back out to the game.

Because it was another fuckup.

And I know that I may have bought myself a little more time.

But eventually, the fuckups going to catch up with me.

Eventually, everyone is going to find out.

And eventually...

It's all going to be over.

FIVE

Diana

"DEE, BABY—"

I grind my teeth together and wish—God, do I *wish*—that the morning hadn't brought me to the team's practice facility but the arena.

At least at the arena, there's a security guard and a fenced-in parking lot.

At least at the arena, I don't have to deal with Jason's shit.

Reaching into the back seat, I snag my backpack and straighten.

Unfortunately, that brings me in contact with Jason's body.

Because he's come even closer.

And he's big. He's strong. Not to mention, he smells great.

Something that makes me hate myself a little.

I have a type. I know I do.

But I'm not a slender woman—I'm full of compact strength and want someone big enough and strong enough to hold me without breaking a sweat...or their back.

The smelling good part is just...

Adult humaning.

Something that Jason struggles with in a multitude of other ways.

Like washing his dishes or throwing in a load of laundry or —you know—keeping his fucking hands and lips and dick to himself at my place of work.

But he's got the smelling good thing down pat.

He steadies me, hands wrapping around the tops of my shoulders.

"Don't," I snap, brushing him off.

Yeah, he's big and strong and smells good.

But he also kissed another woman in the back hallways of what amounts to my office while I was working several floors below.

And he did it on camera.

Worse?

The arena wasn't the *only* place he did it.

Something I discovered just this morning.

When a woman showed up on my porch, looking for the bastard.

"Baby," he says, stepping close again, but I shove my backpack between us, halting him with all manner of hockey equipment (gloves and skates—because I have a new stick on order and I hope to God it's come in because I really need to hit something...repeatedly), electronics (laptop and tablet to research, plan, and coordinate with my staff), and office supplies (notepads, pens, sticky notes because there's something about physically writing a to do list and then crossing things off that feels freaking great).

"Who's Becca?" I ask, then take advantage of his blip of shock to close the door, to round the hood of my car and start for the rink.

Alas, I don't have teleportation skills.

Which means my ass is stuck walking into the rink.

And that Jason has the opportunity to use his longer legs to catch up with me.

"Becca is a friend."

I snort, slant a glance up at him. "I thought you haven't been able to make friends?"

Guilt rippling across his face.

And calculation.

Trying to come up with an excuse I'll buy.

"Save it," I tell him as we approach the rink's entrance. "If Becca coming to my house because she's been calling and you haven't been answering your phone isn't bad enough—"

"Like I said, she's a friend."

"Her looking for her bra she left behind—"

He opens his mouth, likely ready to spout more bullshit, but I keep talking.

"—and coincidentally, one that Becca and I found together, underneath my bed—"

His mouth closes so quickly, his teeth click together.

"I *saw* you on camera," I finish.

"Baby, that was just a weird angle, I was trying to get out of the way and—"

"*And* I have the fucking video in my email, Jason. I saw it live and I've watched the tape. You were kissing another woman and touching her—"

My voice breaks and I hate that weakness.

But I do what I always do when I'm hurt.

I hold tight to my anger, blink back my tears of frustration, and I press on.

"So don't try to gaslight me and tell me what I saw—"

"You need to—"

"Same goes for telling me what I *need to* do," I add icily

holding my bag up between us when he comes close again, using it like a shield to stop him from touching me. "This isn't something we can come back from. You broke us. You cheated."

"You're never home," he snaps, shoving my bag away from him. "And you work too damned much."

"And now that gaslighting me isn't working you're going to get angry?" Sighing, I reach for the door to the rink, tug it open. "What's next? Tears? *Hurting* me?" I say, when he takes a step in my direction, his face full of all that scariness from the other day.

Luckily my tone is icy cold and unaffected, despite the blip of fear in my belly.

I'm not alone here.

The guys are within shouting distance, the back office staff probably even closer.

But, God, I don't want to be seen as a woman who needs rescuing.

Hell, I *can't* be seen that way.

Not and remain in charge, not and keep their respect, not and...

Be a coach.

Just a coach.

Luckily, my words have Jason pausing, reconsidering.

"You need to leave me alone," I say. "There's no getting us back. Not today. Not ever. *You* did that—"

"I can fix—"

"No, you can't." I take a breath, strive for patience. "Please, Jason. You know me, so you *know* there's no going back." His expression changes and I think I may be finally getting through to him. "Because if you don't stop this, I'll have to get a restraining order. And then," I add, playing the one card I have left, "I'll have to call your mother and tell her what you did."

Yup. I'll tattle like a little whiny toddler.

But if there's one thing in this world that Jason is afraid of, it's his mother.

So, I'll pull whatever punches I need to.

"You won't—"

I lift my brows, ask quietly, "Want to try me?"

"Why can't we just talk this out?" he pleads. "Find a way forward?"

I sigh, let go of the door, and step back outside.

I don't miss the blip of hope in his eyes, but I don't let myself feel guilty, and I don't soften my resolve as I say, "Because you broke us, and you did it in a way that can't be repaired."

His face falls.

I don't stay around to watch it, to deal with it, to make it *my* problem.

I just go back inside, get my skates on, pick up my new stick from the equipment guys, and head out to the ice, hoping that the team will have gone over the drills I sent, that they'll have focused and prepped, and done their fucking jobs.

Rome and Cam have.

So have King and Rhodes.

Pat and Duncan and Kane are their typical lost causes.

But it's Hudson that hurts.

I've been giving him a lot of time and space to get adjusted to the changes I implemented. I know that it's not easy for everyone to just jump into a new system, especially after the previous coaching staff did such a shitty job of looking after the guys.

It's just...

It's been weeks now.

Months if we're talking about the extra on-ice sessions I held and the preseason games and practices.

Months where he's been not on board.

And...

I'm done.

With men fucking around with things that are important to me.

With them not listening.

With them taking advantage.

I'm just fucking *done.*

Exhaling, I lift my glove, blow my whistle. "That's good on my end, boys," I call, and they start to scatter, some staying on the ice to work on individual skills, but most heading to the locker room to change.

But I don't immediately turn and get the fuck out of here like I want to.

Instead, I deal with the other thing I've been putting off.

"Hudson!"

His gray eyes come to mine.

"My office. Now."

SIX

Hudson

I'M FUCKED, I realize as I sit in the chair in front of Coach's desk and stare up at the tiny spitfire of a woman.

I didn't come directly to her office—or I did, but it was to get the okay to shower and change first. So now it's after taking my time doing that, after lingering in the locker room as the other guys headed out, waiting until the hallways became clear of support staff and players alike.

Until it was just me.

And Coach.

She wouldn't go home, not without speaking to me.

And I kept her waiting.

It was a total dick move, I know, making her stay late because I didn't want to face this shit.

Didn't want to deal with what I knew was coming to me.

A lecture.

Which doesn't sound bad—I get that—especially when it's

given in her lilting voice I can't help but get lost in the melody of.

But it's fucking terrible because it's also the beginning of the end.

Coach's patience is up, I still can't get it together, and...

Better to sit here smelling clean and fresh and not in sweaty ass gear while I face the beginning of my inevitable end.

Dramatic? Yes.

Deserved? Of course.

I just...

Fuck, if I'm not trying.

Fuck, if *nothing* I'm doing is making one bit of difference.

"...and I really need you to take some time to focus on this new system," she's saying, gesturing at her iPad, the screen a mess of Xs, Os, and arrows that swirl, impossible for me to process.

Fuck.

Why can't they just make sense?

Why can't I get my shit together and just do my fucking job?

"I know it's new and it's tough to make these changes," she goes on, voice firm but it's nowhere near the screaming the guys and I endured with the last coaching staff.

That's not Coach Dee's style. Nope, she'll lead by example, with encouragement. Not ignoring the problems or failing to address them—hence my ass currently sitting here listening to this lecture—just doing it in a way that means she's not spending her spare time at work screaming at us.

It'd be easier if she was a bitch about it, easier if she was shouting or off-base or if her coaching was shit.

Instead, she's really quite brilliant. Intuitive, yet not over-planned. Plenty of room for creativity but with a backbone of structure that means we have things to fall back on when shit goes wrong.

She's even folded in some of Cam's plays, something that went a long way toward building trust and camaraderie, and also something our old Coach wouldn't ever have dreamed of doing.

If I could just get it all to stick in my damned head.

"...but focusing and getting this down will make it much easier for us to mobilize your speed and strength and get you on the ice more." She tucks a strand of her hair behind her ear and leans back against the edge of her desk.

Fuck, she's beautiful.

In sweats and an Eagles tee.

Sneakers on her feet and her hair mostly corralled into a ponytail.

Except for that one strand that keeps escaping, keeps slipping forward to dance across her cheek.

She pauses, raking that piece back again.

And I realize I'm staring.

That I'm so caught up in the beauty of her, I haven't processed she's expecting an answer.

She flicks up her brows.

"Got it," I manage to rasp out, even knowing it's fucking hopeless. "I'll go back to the beginning and get it down."

That has her stilling, head tilting to the side, that strand of hair slipping free again. "Is there..." She pauses again, eyes on mine, as though searching, delving into the depths of my soul.

My stomach clenches.

"Do you have any concerns?" she asks quietly.

"Concerns?"

"Anything that's impacting you? Getting in the way of you reviewing things?"

Fucking hell.

What is she getting at?

Suspecting?

Knowing?

"I'm good," I say, gripping the arms of the chair so tightly I swear I hear the wood groan in protest.

Her gaze goes there, lingers, and I force myself to loosen my grip, to relax against the cushion.

Green eyes on mine, holding for a long moment.

Then she nods and pushes off the desk and hell if I don't see—imagine?—a flicker of disappointment in her eyes. But it's there and gone so quickly, I can't be for certain. "Okay, well," she says. "If that changes and you need anything—a new tablet, different resources, just let me know, yeah?"

"Yeah," I say. "Thanks, Coach."

"I'm here for you guys." She wrinkles her nose and fuck if that isn't the mostly adorable thing I've ever seen. "Which sounds cheesy, but I mean it."

I want to kiss the ridges there, smooth them away.

Then kiss her somewhere else.

Kiss her *every*where else.

Before I can do anything insane—like commence with that kissing—she moves to the door, pulling it open so I can see the hallway beyond.

"I'll see you soon," she says in that quiet, sure, melodic voice.

And...

I'm staring again.

Committing every freckle, every eyelash to memory.

Obsessed.

Christ, I'm losing it.

No. I've *lost* it, gone so far down the path of delusion I can't see a way out.

All while my career might be falling apart.

Cool, Huddy. You're doing awesome.

She clears her throat, brow furrowing. "Is everything okay?" she asks quietly.

Because I'm fucking staring again.

Because she all but invited me to leave but I'm still sitting here.

"Sorry," I mutter, shoving to my feet and moving to the door, feeling like a fucking lumbering giant as I get close to her. "Just tired," I add by way of explanation. "I'll be good by next practice though."

Her expression smooths. "Of course," she says. "It's been a long couple of days."

Said like *she's* had a long couple of days too.

And the shadows beneath her eyes support that.

What's happened?

Is it shit with the team? Shit I've contributed to?

Fuck.

I open my mouth—

Her phone buzzes on her desk, and she steps back from the door. "I'll let you get out of here, Huddy."

That does something to me.

No, not *something.*

Her soft voice calling me my nickname wraps invisible fingers around my cock and strokes.

"See ya," I rasp, bobbing my head at her like an idiot as I start to step out into the hall.

Stupid.

So goddamned stupid. Hopeless. Pathetic.

Stupid.

Christ.

I can't do this.

"Huddy?"

Heart leaping, I stop, glance over my shoulder.
She opens her mouth.
But I never do hear her question...
Because that moment, the world starts violently shaking.

SEVEN

Diana

ONE SECOND, I'm thinking that I'm missing something, that there's a piece to the situation with Hudson that doesn't quite add up.

The next...

I'm being tossed violently to the ground.

Pain ricochets through my knees.

The floor's rumbling. No, it's undulating, *rolling* in a way I've never experienced before.

Then it's like everything around me suddenly goes to max volume—the noise so loud it's overwhelming.

And it hurts my ears.

Then my back.

No.

That's not the noise.

It's...the ceiling tiles—they're falling out of the metal frames overhead and crashing down, taking the fluorescent lights with them.

One of which is flying straight for my face.

I cry out, hands coming up to shield myself, but suddenly there's an arm around my middle and I'm being lifted bodily off the floor. The light drops right where I was a bare heartbeat before, shattering and sending tiny shards of glass in a thousand directions.

Little bites of pain on my cheeks, my neck, my arms.

"Move!"

Jerking, I realize that Hudson is the one who's pulled me free of the light's path of collision, the one who's shielding me with his big body, the tiles crashing down onto his back and shoulders without him seeming to notice.

Probably because I'm frozen in place and he's done with it.

He starts crawling, dragging me along with him, shielding me from the debris crashing down around us—

Until we're suddenly beneath something solid, something that doesn't seem to be moving.

Or maybe that's because he's right there next to me.

Grounding me.

Keeping me safe.

That feeling is so right, so intense, so completely over-whelming that despite the world quite literally shaking violently beneath me, I've never felt more like myself.

He jolts and I snap out of my head, realize that while I'm crammed beneath my desk, the biggest, most stable piece of furniture in my office, Hudson isn't.

"Come in," I say, shoving myself farther back, giving him as much space as I'm able.

He hisses out a pained breath, but dutifully slides forward, shoving closer, plastering his body against mine.

I inhale, surrounded by the scent of him, the heat of him, the *strength* of him.

Until he grunts, hurt ricocheting across his features, and I realize that he's still not completely shielded from the debris, not fully beneath the desk. "Fuck. My leg."

I don't think, just clamber on top of him, smacking my head hard against the underside of the desk.

His eyes go wide. "Wh—"

"Get *under* here," I snap.

My head fucking hurts, but I just start tugging at his waist when he doesn't immediately move, bringing him farther beneath the piece of heavy oak furniture, thankful for the first time since I inherited this office that the last asshole who occupied it was on such a fucking power trip that he needed a CEO-my-penis-is-larger-than-yours sized desk so that with me pressed close and straddling Hudson's waist, his legs bent up behind me, we're both covered as the floor bounces and rolls and the earthquake goes on for what seems like an interminable amount of time.

Until...all at once, the world stops shaking.

I wait a beat.

Then another.

Then—

I exhale and start to crawl off him—

"Wait," Hudson says.

It's my turn for my eyes to go wide, for me to begin to ask what's going on.

But I don't get that far.

Because the world starts shaking again and this time it's short, but it's somehow more violent—jerking rather than rolling, threatening to toss me from his lap like I'm riding a bucking bronco.

I cry out when my head hits the underside of the desk again, but Hudson reacts faster than I do—cupping the back of my skull, putting his hand between the hard wood and my head.

Protecting me.

Drawing me down more securely against him.

Until the shaking stops as abruptly as it started.

When it doesn't immediately start up again, I slither off Hudson and out from under the desk.

He hisses out a pained breath.

"Shit," I say. "I'm sorry."

"It's not you." He grunts softly as he pushes himself out from the desk, long legs sending the items that have fallen off the top in all directions. "Sorry," he mutters.

"Not your fault," I whisper, surveying the damage.

Or starting to, anyway because, Huddy grunts again and this time I'm together enough to recognize that it's not just discomfort.

It's *pain*.

I whip back toward him—

"Your leg!"

Shit.

He's bleeding. A lot.

I rush back over to him, dropping to my knees.

"It's fine," he mutters. "Just a scratch."

It's more than a *scratch*. It's soaked through the front of his thigh, coating the denim covering it. Worry eating at me, I search through the mess of pens and pencils, my keyboard and papers, the overturned monitor and chair, and manage to locate my scissors.

"Diana," he says. "*Easy*. I'm fine."

But I just bat his hand away when he reaches for the shears and make short work of cutting through the fabric of his jeans.

He hisses as I part the material, and I don't blame him.

"Just a scratch?" I mutter, setting the scissors aside and eyeing the six-inch long gash. Thankfully, it's not gushing blood, but it certainly isn't showing any sign of stopping bleeding.

"It's fine."

Stubborn man.

I bite back a sigh and stand. "I'll go get a first aid kit, see if I can find one of the trainers or Doc to patch you u...*ah shit!*"

The last is said as I catch sight of the door.

Or rather, where the door used to be.

"What is it?" he asks and I jerk toward him as he staggers up to his feet.

"Hudson!"

He ignores me, gaze going to the door—blocked with debris from the ceiling and walls—and then he curses softly.

But he does it going pale, staggering slightly.

Shit.

I hurry over to him, drawing him back down to the floor close to the desk in case we need to take cover again. "Stay there," I mutter when he tries to get up again.

"I can clear the doorway—"

"You can sit there and let me bind up that leg, Huddy." I fix him in place with a glare. "And if that needs to be an order from me as your coach then it can be."

His brows drag together, but he doesn't argue further.

And I don't know if it's because I pulled the coach card or because he's lost too much blood. Whatever the reason, he stays where I put him. Standing, I kick the debris aside, searching my desk drawers and file cabinet for something that will be helpful in this situation—like, for example, a hidden first aid kit that I've forgotten about.

But the drawers turn up nothing.

And Huddy is looking paler by the second.

Damn.

I kneel back at his side and do the only thing I can think of.

I tug off my shirt.

His mouth drops open.

But I ignore it, ignore that I'm now topless aside from a truly skimpy sports bra (the uncomfortable one I never wear but had to today because I've been avoiding laundry like the plague), and use the scissors to slice my tee into makeshift bandages.

It's not sanitary.

But at least he won't bleed out while I figure out how to get him help.

I layer the strips and wrap them around his thigh, tying them into a knot.

"This wasn't how I expected it to go," he says, words slightly slurred.

Concerned, I press down harder, tie the knot tighter. "How you expected what to go?" I ask, trying to keep him focused... and conscious.

"When I dreamed of you naked," he slurs, eyes going hazy. "This isn't how I expected it to go."

My mouth falls open.

I'm not naked.

Just...almost halfway there.

And, probably more importantly, Hudson has dreamed of me?

Naked or not that's...

Well, I don't know how I feel about that.

And I don't have the chance to formulate a reply.

Because he passes out.

EIGHT

Hudson

SLOWLY, the blackness surrounding me begins to fade.

The first thing I feel is my leg. It's throbbing, a red-hot pain that yanks me out of unconsciousness.

The next thing I'm aware of is my back—stiff and getting jabbed in multiple places, like I'm camping and I've managed to set up my tent on a bunch of rocks.

The final thing that pulls me into reality and has my lids peeling back is the soft voice from next to me.

The soft, melodic voice I've heard in my dreams.

"Come on," Diana is saying, frustration in her tone. "Just fucking work already."

"What's not working?" I ask, my voice barely more than a rasp.

She turns and looks at me, her face barely visible in the room.

I frown, glance around.

"Power's out," she says quietly. "Not sure if the grid is

down or they cut it to prevent fire. But I found a flashlight and I have my computer"—a nod to what's giving her face a soft glow —"I was just trying to get in contact with someone to let them know we're here and need help."

"It's not working?"

A sigh and shake of her head. "Unfortunately not. No cell service. No power. No Wi-Fi. We'll have to wait it out."

"All good," I say lightly, even though I'm not feeling the least bit amused at all. In fact, I'm pretty much feeling like shit. "I've got nowhere to be."

She snorts then turns the laptop in my direction. "Let me check your leg."

"It's fine—"

"Save it, Mr. Stubborn Hockey Player. I had to deal with Unconscious and Bleeding Hockey Player, so you'll deal with me making sure my first aid skills aren't going to be the reason you kick it in my office."

"With that bedside manner? Never," I say dryly.

"Damn straight." I hiss when she peels back the strips of her T-shirt. "Sorry," she murmurs, voice gentling as she tucks the makeshift bandage back in place. "You scared the shit out of me, Huddy."

Guilt ripples through me and I don't think when I say, "Sorry, DeeDee."

Her eyes go wide in the illumination of the laptop's screen and I realize what I called her.

Shit. "I mean, sorry Coach Dee."

She leans back against the desk beside me. "No, that's okay." Turning, she glances over at me, lips curving up at the edges. "It's just been a long time since anyone's called me that."

I lift my brows in question.

"That was my grandma's nickname for me."

"This the same one who also made those killer oatmeal

chocolate chip cookies?" She brought in a huge batch of them for the team after our first practice of the season—likely to bribe us into not hating her after she kicked our ass from one side of the ice to the other.

Her mouth curves. "The same one."

"So, I'm in good company."

"Yeah." A flicker of sadness.

"What?" I ask quietly.

"Nothing," she says. "I just miss her. Miss them."

"Them?"

More sadness, but this time I only see it for a moment before her gaze drops to her lap. "My parents," she says quietly. "They died in a car accident when I was nine."

I tense so violently that pain shoots through my leg again and I have to close my eyes against the wave of nausea before I can speak. "I'm sorry," I rasp.

A long, taut moment. "It was a long time ago."

"Doesn't mean it was easy."

More quiet. Then a soft sigh, "No," she agrees. "It wasn't easy."

"Did your grandma see you coach?"

A shake of her head. "Not professionally. But she knew where I was going already. Bought me my first suit to wear on the bench."

"The one you wore to the first game this season?"

"Yeah." She looks at me, confusion in her green eyes. "How'd you know?"

"It's a little different from your normal style." Something I probably shouldn't have picked up on.

But...obsessed.

"It mostly lives in my closet because I'm too scared to ruin it. But I've worn it the first game of every season with the teams I've coached." Her face softens. "And on her birthday because it's nice to feel close to her."

I wonder what that's like.

To feel close to your parents.

To want to remember them fondly—hell, to *have* fond memories at all.

Yelling and high expectations. Fists and disappointments. And...

Oatmeal chocolate chip cookies and such a belief in what Dee was doing that she invested in a suit she never saw worn.

I'm glad Diana had that.

Even as I tamp down on the jealousy that I didn't.

But that's a familiar feeling—shoving down the envy. I've had years of practice doing it, which is why I'm able to say, "I bet she would love that."

"Yeah," Dee murmurs. "She would. Of course, she would absolutely hate that I pair it with sneakers. Grams had high expectations for accessories."

I chuckle. Then promptly wince.

"Sorry," she says.

"Not your fault."

"It kind of is."

"You make the earth shake?"

"No." She scowls. "But I didn't exactly react quickly. I just stood there and waited for the ceiling to cave in on me."

If it had truly caved in, we would have been fucked.

We're lucky it's just the door blocked and that the desk was here for cover. We're fine. Stuck for however long it will take to dig us out, but safe and sound.

Though, I really would like some pain killers and for my leg to be stitched up.

But seriously, *thank fuck* I showered after practice.

"Was this your first quake?" I ask instead of thinking about the fact that we're trapped, my leg hurts, and who knows how long it will take to get out of here.

She nods. "I...well, I guess I don't really have much of a choice, but I'd really rather not go through that again. You?"

"Ditto on the not going through that again," I say. "But not my first—though the only other quake I've felt barely registered. This was, hopefully, a once in a lifetime experience."

"Yeah." Then, "You got hurt because you helped me."

"No, I got hurt because some idiot clearly installed subpar ceiling tiles and lights."

Her teeth work at her bottom lip. "Well, I'm still sorry. And—"

Something jabs my back, and I shift uncomfortably.

"Your leg?" she asks.

"It's—"

"Don't say fine," she grumbles.

"Okay," I murmur. "It's not *not* fine. It hurts, but I've had worse."

Her nose wrinkles. "I know you have."

My head tilts as I study her. "You do?"

"Three stitches in your cheek that you just got removed."

Oh, yeah.

"And eighteen stitches last season."

I wince. I took a puck off the jaw and that shit *hurt*. But I just shrug as well as I'm able to considering I'm horizontal and my leg's a mess. "Well, that happens."

"And a broken humerus the year before."

Another semi-shrug. "Freak accident. Could finish that play a thousand more times and I'd be fine."

Her gaze fixes me in place. "And a strained groin, a broken ankle, three fake teeth, more stitches on your cheek and your eyebrow *and* glue across the bridge of your nose."

Warmth through my chest, making it just a little bit hard to breathe. "That's hockey," I say through the tightness.

"It sure is."

"How'd you know about all that anyway?"

A pause. A flicker in her eyes I don't understand.

Then *she* shrugs. "Just doing my job."

Right. Her job.

She can recite my injuries from the last five seasons because she's good at her job and does her research and cares about her players.

That's it.

I need to remember that.

I squirm again.

"You're hurting," she murmurs.

"Just some debris behind me—"

Almost before the words are out of my mouth, she's using the light on her phone to find the debris—tiny shards of plastic and glass—then helping me shift so she can check the carpet beneath me.

"Dee—"

"If we're in this for the long haul then I need a place to rest too."

If she'd said anything else, I would have kept protesting, but she's right. Especially since she's in her bra and the scraps of her T-shirt are wrapped around my leg.

God, she's got a great rack.

If she wants to climb on top again, give me a view of those tits bouncing as she take me deep, I'm sure I can find a way to make both of us to feel good.

Christ.

I'm a sick fuck.

But leave it to my dick to still be functional even with a debilitating injury.

"Oh!" she exclaims. "I found it!" She holds up a small black bag and I frown. "Ibuprofen," she explains, unzipping it and pulling out a palm-sized white bottle. "And I think—" A grunt as she shoves her rolling chair back and then yanks at something. "Yes!"

Her backpack is covered in dust, but the water bottle is still tucked into the side pocket.

She grins and retrieves it with a flourish then comes back over to me, shaking a couple pills into her hand and offering them to me.

I take them, start to sit up then freeze, grinding my teeth together.

Fuck.

Maybe I couldn't make us both feel good after all.

"Here," she says softly, slipping an arm beneath my shoulders, gently easing me up enough to swallow the pills down. "Good?"

I nod, carefully lie back down.

Sweating from sitting up six whole inches.

There's a joke there—if only I didn't feel like puking.

"Breathe," she says softly, but I do the opposite when she runs her fingers through my hair, my eyes flying open, my lungs freezing. "Huddy." Her fingers still. "*Breathe.*"

I do, and I do it in a rush.

"Good," she whispers. "That's good. Now again."

I inhale. Exhale. Repeat.

"That's it." Her fingers start up again and fuck, but this might be the best shit of my life—lying next to her, Diana touching me, looking at me, seeing *me.*

But if she keeps this up, I'm going to do something supremely stupid.

"Dee," I rasp.

Her throat works and she leans in, mouth dangerously close.

The scent of her in my nose, the gold flecks amongst the green of her eyes, the lush pillow of her almost naked breasts on my arm.

Christ, I want her.

And fuck, if that yearning doesn't show on my face given how quickly she pulls her hand back.

Like she's been burned.

"Diana—"

She looks away. "We should get some rest," she whispers. "It might take a while to get a signal out."

I want to reach for her.

But her hands are clenched into fists and there are goose bumps on her skin.

She's cold.

So, I do the only thing I can.

I wrestle my shirt off before she can protest.

"Hudson!"

"You're cold."

Her eyes fly to mine, and what I see there doesn't make this shit any easier.

Because it's appreciation for my body.

Even though I can do fuck all about it.

"Put it on," I order.

"You're hurt—"

"And you're a buck twenty with goose bumps all over and your shirt serving as a bandage. Put on the shirt, Coach."

I don't want to remind her off all the barriers between us.

Don't want to do anything except draw her close and find all sorts of creative ways to keep us both warm.

But...she's my boss.

I'm the fuckup on her roster.

Even with all my fantasies, I know this is all we can be.

Thankfully, she doesn't argue further, just pulls on the tee. "Better?"

Her cheeks go a little pink, her teeth press into her bottom lip, and she avoids my eyes when she whispers, "Yeah." A beat. "Thanks."

God, what I wouldn't give to see what's in that gaze of hers.

To hold it close when I go to sleep at night.

But she doesn't look at me, not even as she says, "And...I, uh, should save the battery."

"You're right." Then when she doesn't move, I ask, "Want me to get it?"

A jerk, those eyes flashing to mine for the barest bit of contact. "I got it."

Then she quickly shuts the laptop.

And the room goes pitch black.

NINE

Diana

I'M a strange mix of comfortable and not—wrapped in a spicy male scent, my front warm, my back cold, and my side aches.

Like really aches.

Like I'm lying on a boulder covered with ants that are crawling all over me, biting me.

Wincing, I open my eyes—

To darkness.

No, it's not completely dark—or maybe it's that my eyes have adjusted enough that I can see shadows, can see the outline...

I gasp.

Of a body.

A male body.

Hudson's body.

My front is plastered to his, and I'm half laying over the top of him, my arm resting on his belly, my leg tossed over—thankfully—his uninjured thigh.

And my side hurts, the prickles of pain because I'm lying on the hard, industrial carpet, and it's not exactly a mattress at the Ritz.

It's probably also because though I've cleared up as much of the debris as possible, there are still small pieces embedded into the floor around us.

Not the most comfortable place to sleep.

Then again, I hadn't meant to actually fall sleep.

It was just...

Hudson's scent all around me.

Hudson. Hurt and in pain and...still concerned I was cold.

Hudson. Staring up at me with heat despite his injury, longing and desire that I felt mirrored in my own body, the sudden urge to kiss him nearly overwhelming.

Oh, and insane too.

Because I *just* caught my fiancé cheating. Because I'm almost certain that I haven't fully uncovered all the lies that Jason told in our relationship. Because...

I'm his coach.

Right.

That's the most important thing to remember.

I'm here. I'm finally doing what I've dreamed of.

I can't jeopardize my dreams just because Hudson is big and strong and smells good, can't risk what I've worked my whole life toward just because he's my personal brand of kryptonite.

I can't do that to myself.

Or him.

When I dreamed of you naked. This isn't how I expected it to go.

I shiver.

Then realize that I'm still pressed against Hudson.

When I hadn't meant to sleep at all, when I'd sat in the

darkness and listened to him breathe for far too long, neither of us saying anything for a long, long time.

Until, eventually, his breathing evened out and he fell asleep.

I intended on staying conscious—checking the internet, the cell service, hoping to get us the fuck out of here.

But the only thing I succeeded in doing was draining down the devices' batteries.

Until I forced myself to put them aside and lean back against the desk, trying not to think...and yet my mind far too full of thoughts I didn't want to process.

Jason and what he did.

Grams and how much I miss her.

The fucking earthquake and if the world was going to start shaking again.

Hudson and his leg...and also what had been in his eyes just before he'd started to leave my office before everything went wrong.

There's something I'm missing.

And that *something* is what I turned over and over in my mind as time passed.

As I shifted and stretched out on the floor, trying to relieve the crick in my neck.

But I didn't figure out an answer to what was bothering me, hadn't discovered all the pieces to the puzzle that is Hudson by the time I fell asleep.

And now...

Shit.

I'm pressed to him.

Still pressed to him.

God, I'm such an idiot.

I jerk back and I do it so abruptly that Hudson grunts in discomfort.

"Dee?" he rasps.

"I'm sorry," I say, unable to stop myself from opening the laptop. It has more juice left and with my phone only at five percent, I'd rather drain the computer. "How are you feeling?"

"Fine," he says, and even though the screen isn't exactly casting natural light, it's easy to see that for the lie it is.

I reach out, trail my fingers over his forehead.

Hot.

"You have a fever."

"We'll be out of here soon enough." He grunts as he sits up. "Still no cell service?"

I pick up my phone, press the button on the side.

Then sigh. "No."

"All good," he mutters.

"Are you this optimistic by nature?" I ask. "Because I'll admit I haven't seen this side of you."

He tilts his head, studying me.

"What?" I ask.

"Nothing," he murmurs.

"No, tell me." I lean closer. "Why are you looking at me like that?"

A long blip of quiet. "No," he finally says. "No one has ever considered me optimistic, not even myself."

"What does *that* mean?"

"It means..." He sighs and shakes his head. "This isn't shit you want to hear."

I wave a hand at the blocked door of my office. "I've got nothing but time."

He chuckles dryly, shakes his head. "Seriously using my line on me?"

"It was a good line." I smile, gently touch his shoulder. "And I mean, how bad can it be? I already told you about my orphan status and Grams never getting to see me coach..."

I trail off.

Because his expression—however much I can see of it from the laptop's illumination—tells me that it's bad.

Very bad.

And in all my research of my players...

I don't have a clue what it might be.

His parents are alive. I haven't met them, but I haven't met most of the guys' families. They're adults and even the young players live on their own—or with other guys on the roster. Some of the guys' extended families have come in for team events before the season started, but that was mostly the wives and girlfriends and only a few parental units who happened to live close by or were in town visiting.

Cam's family is a hoot.

And obviously, Jean-Michel is highly involved, both because he's the team's owner and also because his daughters are involved with two players on my roster.

But I don't know anything about Hudson's family.

And that...well, it seems like that may be pertinent information right about now.

"Right," I whisper. "Never mind with that." I turn for my backpack. "You should take some more medicine. I think I have some Tylenol in here. That should help with your fever. And I should check the door—see if I can shift any of the debris—"

His hand covers mine, staying its search of the second pill bottle. "It's okay, Dee. My childhood wasn't pretty, but I'm here getting to do what I do."

That's true, of course.

Loads of guys don't make it this far—in fact, most of them don't.

But there's more.

I can see it in his eyes.

And it has me leaning closer.

"We don't need to talk about it," I say, squeezing his hand. "I was just trying to distract us." My mouth kicks up. "Sometimes my words get ahead of me and I don't think before I speak."

Now *his* mouth curves. "Like when you yelled at the ref the other day?"

"That offsides call was bullshit, and you know it."

His rough chuckle strokes me right between my legs. "It *was* bullshit."

"See?" I say, leaning a little closer, smoothing back a lock of hair that's fallen over his forehead. "I was right to yell."

His eyes go soft. "You're right about a lot of things."

"Oh?" I know it's dumb, but I can't help but run my fingers through his hair.

It's so soft. Like silk.

And surrounded in the scent of him, the strength of his body on display, the gentleness in his expression...

I can't pull back.

Instead, I lean forward.

So close I can see the scar on his jaw, the reddened line on his cheek from those stitches. So close that the flecks of sunshine in his stormy gray eyes glimmer. So close I can feel his rough inhale of air on my lips. So close that—

My phone rings.

TEN

Hudson

"SORRY ABOUT THE WAIT MR. BLACKWOOD," the nurse says as she pulls back the curtain and steps into the cubicle I've cooled my heels in for the last six hours.

A big ass earthquake means that a cut doesn't garner much attention.

Unfortunately, a deep cut paired with a fever garnered enough to get my ass carted here and shoved into a bed next to a boatload of other people with far more serious injuries than mine as I was given IV antibiotics and eventually stitched up. Most of the others have been treated and sent home or triaged and sent upstairs. Meanwhile, I've been stuck behind a curtain until the IV finishes.

"I know you guys are busy," I tell her, lifting my arm so she can scan my wristband. "I'll try to get out of your hair as quickly as possible."

Something that's going to be difficult considering I don't have a ride home and the city's streets are a mess and I don't know the state of my house and I have no clue where Diana ended up after cell service was restored.

But I'll figure it out.

I always do.

Except...that's not true.

I shake my head, trying to jostle the thoughts from my brain.

"No?" Kelly, the nurse, asks, brows flying up.

"I'm sorry," I admit. "I was zoning out."

She pats my hand, checks the flow on the tube pumping shit into my arm then moves to the blanket. "I was just asking if it was okay to check your wound?"

I nod. "Oh, yeah. Of course."

She lifts the edge of the blanket, peels back the gauze to peer at the line of neat stitches. "That's looking better already." She smooths the edge back down, tucks the blanket in place. "Your wife—"

I go stiff.

"—has gotten her cuts cleaned and bound and she's picking up both of your prescriptions from the hospital's pharmacy. They're pretty slammed, so it may be a while. But you're almost home free and as soon as that's done"—a nod at my IV—"you'll be free to head out of here."

That's good news.

Great news.

But I'm still stuck on the whole *wife* thing.

"My wife?" I rasp.

Kelly's typing on the computer, but she pauses and glances over at me, reaching for my hand and squeezing lightly. "Oh, don't worry. Most of the cuts were surface level. Only a few had to be irrigated and closed, and most of those were with glue. But Ms. Diana is a trooper. I swear she barely flinched."

Diana.

My wife.

Fuck, only in my fantasies.

Another squeeze of my hand. "Don't worry," Kelly teases. "I won't tell her that you cried like a baby."

I scowl.

She pulls back and winks. "I'm kidding. You were tough too." A few more taps on the keyboard and then she's pushing in the keyboard. "I'll check back in a bit."

"Thanks."

A moment later, she's bustled out and I'm left alone behind the curtain, acutely aware of how much quieter the department has gotten.

Hopefully, that means the worst is over, that people are getting back to their lives.

Hopefully, that means mine will go back to normal too.

Yet, even as I think that, I know it won't be true for some. There were casualties, injuries that will linger for a lifetime, families affected, people who've been traumatized.

Life will be normal.

And it will be forever changed.

I inhale.

Because I know which side of the gamut I fall on.

Soft breasts pillowed against my chest, the floral scent of Diana's shampoo in my nose, fingertips running through my hair, lips coming oh so close—

Then a phone call.

Then a rescue, a path through the debris blocking us inside cleared in record time.

Then an ambulance ride.

How will I ever go back to normal knowing what Diana feels like in my arms, knowing what she smells like, knowing what she looks like on top of me, even knowing what she sounds like when she sleeps?

I won't.

I know it.

But none of that really matters…

Because life goes on. Finds normal, or a new normal, and—

"Go on in, darlin'!" I hear, and my eyes jerk to the curtain just in time to see it tick back and for Diana to come through, her skin pale, black circles beneath her eyes, a bevy of small bandages on her face, her arms.

And she's still the most beautiful woman I've ever seen.

She's holding two white paper bags and freezes when she sees I'm watching. "You're awake."

"Uh, yeah," I say inanely.

She hesitates, teeth nibbling at the corner of her bottom lip then she seems to take a deep breath, seems to shore herself up, and steps into our private corner of the hospital, allowing the curtain to swish closed behind her.

"You're not hurting any longer?"

"No," I say. "They gave me the good stuff."

"Right." It's a whisper. "I…I got your medicine." She holds up the bag like it's the grand prize of a raffle.

"You didn't have to do that"—she didn't have to do a lot of things—"but thanks," I add before she can protest.

"Um. You're welcome."

Christ, can this be anymore awkward?

"Wife?" I blurt.

Spoiler alert: yes.

Yes, it *can* get more awkward.

By me opening my dumb mouth.

Her cheeks go pink and the bags crinkle under duress from her tightly clenched fists. "It was, um"—her eyes skitter to mine then away—"it was the only way they'd let me stay with you."

"You didn't have—"

She moves to me. "I did."

And there's no embarrassment now, no hesitation.

Just the firm resolve of this beautiful, capable, *stubborn* woman.

"DeeDee," I whisper. "You didn't."

"I *did*," she says more firmly and suddenly exhausted, I give in.

"Fine," I mutter. "You did."

She smiles approvingly then gets down to business. "So drugs are in hand." She holds up the bag. "The nurses say you're almost ready to blow this joint. I followed the ambulance with my car, so as soon as you're discharged, I'll get you home and then we can get back to normal."

Back to normal. Right.

Of course.

Back to me wanting her. Back to me fucking up my life, my career.

Back to me unable to—

"What's the matter?" she murmurs.

My throat is tight. "Nothing," I say. "Just been a long ass day."

Her face softens. "I hear that. I think I'll cancel practice tomorrow and spend the night soaking in my bathtub while watching my favorite trash TV."

A bath.

Diana naked.

Christ, she's trying to kill me.

But I will my dick to not twitch and let the bath comment go, asking instead, "Trash TV?"

Pink cheeks again. God, where else does that blush show up?

"I'll admit," she says. "It's my guilty pleasure to watch reality television and the various train wrecks it spotlights."

"What's your favorite?"

"90 Day Fiancé."

"I've never seen that one." I've never even heard of it.

"Well," she says, "maybe I'll make watching it your homework while you heal up. That way I can properly oversee your indoctrination to the glorious world of all things 90 Day."

"Only if you watch it with me," I blurt.

Danger. Danger.

But, again, I can't fucking stop myself.

Her eyes go wide, and I brace for her to tell me that won't happen.

Only, she doesn't get that far.

Because I hear, "Where's my son?"

Right before my dad bursts through the curtain.

ELEVEN

Diana

YEAH, it took me precisely one glance at the man bellowing for his son for me to know that this wasn't going to be a happy reunion.

And one second beyond that to recognize how much of an asshole the man was.

Demanding that the nurses get the doctor "immediately" and then when she came in, clearly exhausted after dealing with the influx of patients in aftermath of the quake, he demanded to see a "real doctor."

Yup.

Asshole.

Thankfully, I didn't have to step in because Hudson took care of it—kicking his dad out a heartbeat after he'd spouted that bullshit.

Something that was made easier because the IV antibiotics were administered and the discharge instructions were in the computer and Hudson was ready to be sprung from hospital jail.

That didn't mean we—and I do mean *we*—were free of torture, though.

Mostly because Hudson's parents had taken a cab from the airport to the hospital.

So, I was driving all of them home.

"I always knew my parents living an hour plane ride away was annoying, but who knew that not updating my emergency contact information would come back to bite so hard?" he mutters from the seat next to mine.

Not that he needs to keep his volume down.

I have to strain to hear him over the bellowing in the back seat.

Jesus, this is what he grew up with?

His dad bitching about how much the emergency flight up cost. And bitching about having to fly into San Francisco instead of Oakland because flights were grounded on this side of the Bay where the quake was centered and hit hardest. Oh, and bitching about the lack of cabs at the airport whose drivers would take them across the bridge. And don't forget bitching about how long it took for the hospital staff to let him back to Huddy's room—and God, I get that there were visitor limits, but did the parent they let in to see Hudson have to be his dad? His mom—whom I've literally heard speak less than a dozen words—would have been a far superior choice.

Mostly because she's not talking.

But not an ideal one—because she's not doing anything to shut her husband up.

Though, I'm not sure anything will stymie Jim's bitching.

He's bitched about the back seat being uncomfortable and then when I offered to let him drive (because no fucking way would I let him displace his son from the front seat) he bitched about not knowing the way.

And as we've driven, he's bitched about the traffic—worse because of damage from the quake—and he's bitched about stoplights being out and debris on the side of the road and diversions that mean the drive to Hudson's house has taken about five times longer than it should.

He's also bitched about me making him wear his seat belt, the speed I've been driving at, and, oh yeah, he's still bitching about the fact that the back seat of my compact is well... *compact*.

I grind my teeth together, smothering the urge to agree with Hudson about it being a big mistake to not update his emergency contact information—a freaking *huge* one—and flick a glance over at him, attempting to keep my tone neutral. "Almost to your place."

Which also, thankfully, means that we're almost to my place.

Turns out that Hudson and I live within three blocks of each other.

Far too close to where Jim and Betty Blackwood will be staying.

But near enough that the end of the asshole bitching my back seat is in sight.

"Right," Hudson mutters.

But there's misery in his eyes.

And on his face.

Damn, that means the pain is creeping back in.

It took a lot out of him to lift himself from the bed and into the wheelchair, no matter that Kelly, the nurse, and I each grabbed one of his arms to help with some of the load (while Jim bitched).

And it took more to haul himself into the passenger's seat of my car.

And each bounce and jar—and there are a lot of them postquake—deepens the lines around his mouth, his eyes.

Yeah, he needs to be in bed.

Without a bitching dad in earshot.

But I've yet to come up with a plan as how to accomplish that.

"Just up here on the left," Hudson says. "The white house with the oak tree out front."

It's a charming bungalow built in typical California craftsman style—a wide open porch that's dotted with pillars, their bottom halves covered in stone and the top framed with natural wood. That same wood is carried over to the windows, to surround the front door. A path winds its way down several steps that are going to be a bitch for Hudson to traverse.

And a plan begins to form in my head.

An idiotic, dangerous for my heart and mind and *job* plan.

So dumb and perilous that I'm likely to come to regret it.

And yet—

"Christ, will you just pull into the driveway already? I've got to take a piss!"

"Jim!" Betty gasps, adding the thirteenth word to her list for the evening. And then her fourteenth, fifteenth, and sixteenth. "Don't be crass!"

"Is your bedroom on the second floor?" I ask Hudson.

He frowns, eyes coming to mine, confusion in the gray depths. "Um...yes?"

"Right," I mutter.

I turn into the driveway, park, but catch Hudson's arm when he reaches for the door handle. "Wait."

His frown deepens. "What is it?"

"Do you have a code for the garage? Or a hide-a-key?"

Jim shoves open his door. "I have a key. Let's fucking go."

I lift my brows at Hudson, silently questioning his choice on *that* matter.

He sighs softly then shrugs as if to say, "Have you met the man?"

Right. Bitchy McBitchFace likely demanded a key.

"Let me handle this," I murmur.

"I—"

But I take a page out of Jim's book and pop my door, getting out and avoiding Hudson's protests all together.

Betty joins me at the trunk, where I crammed their bags earlier, but I nod to the house. "I've got these, why don't you go inside? I'm sure you've had a long day."

She nods and trails Jim up to the front door, which now stands open.

I grab the bags, slam the trunk, and then pause next to Hudson, who's ignored me and is trying to get out.

"Trust me when I say, you're going to want to stay put."

"Dee—"

I reach out, brush my fingers along his jaw. "Trust me?"

His eyes close, like my touch is the sweetest sort of torture.

Or maybe that's just what *I'm* feeling.

I don't have time to know for sure because he peels open his lids and he nods at me. "I trust you, DeeDee."

A pulse through my middle—heat, need, desire, softness, some fucked-up combination of all them.

Then I'm pulling back and moving into the house.

The lights are blazing, so the electricity is on, and when I test the stove, the gas is working. Good. No curveballs.

Not yet, anyway.

I walk through the ground floor, giving everything a quick scan and probably soaking in far too many details about Hudson.

A tablet has ended up on the floor, print-outs of my drills scattered around to it.

So he is studying tape, trying to learn the drills.

Maybe there's hope for him yet.

Pictures have fallen from the walls and the coat rack is overturned, but there isn't any obvious sign of damage. Lucky for us to have been far enough from the epicenter to have escaped true danger, something that gives me hope for my place, though not for the wine bottle I left on the counter this morning in preparation of my reality TV and bath time that was supposed to happen tonight—

Or *last* night, now, since it's past midnight.

Yup. I'll definitely have glass to clean up and stains to scrub out of my floor.

Along with some time spent mourning over a wasted bottle of merlot.

The toilet flushes—the plumbing works then—and I don't miss that the sink in the bathroom doesn't run before Jim comes out, still buttoning his pants.

Ew.

Ignoring him, I go to the kitchen sink. Turn on the faucet.

Water's working too.

Great. This makes things easier.

So now it's time to implement my plan.

Betty comes into the room, eyes searching, but Jim beats her to the question she so obviously wants to ask by scowling and griping, "Where the fuck is that boy? He never could move his lazy ass."

Rage in my belly.

At Jim.

At Betty for going mute and not standing up for her kid.

But I keep it carefully banked when I toss their bags on the counter and declare, "I'm taking Hudson home."

Betty's eyes go wide. "H-home?"

Jim scowls at me. "What are you talking about, girl?"

Girl? I'm a twenty-eight-year old woman.

God, this man knows no bounds. (And can I just say, I'm *so* over men?)

But I don't let myself get sucked into his whirlwind of bullshit. I just say, "There's your stuff. I'll call you in the morning with an update."

Jim's brows fly up. "An update about what?"

"Hudson." I jerk my head toward the stairs. "He can't navigate to the second floor."

"He—" Jim begins.

I turn and walk toward the front door, tossing over my shoulder, "Bye-bye, now."

Then I march down the driveway, get into my car, and back out, leaving Hudson's parents gaping in the open front door.

"Um," Hudson says as we start down the street. "Want to clue me in DeeDee?"

Dumb.

Dangerous.

And yet, I still keep driving.

And yet, I still say, "I'm taking you home."

He glances back. "That *was* home."

"No"—I slant a glance at him—"to *my* home."

TWELVE

Hudson

I SIGH and stare at the ceiling.

Same as I've been doing for the last few hours.

Ever since Dee helped my heavy ass up and out of her ridiculously tiny car—but then again, *she's* tiny. Or at least, tiny compared to me. Somehow we made it to the house, she got me settled in her guest room, which was, thank fuck, on the first floor.

Part of the argument she gave my parents for bringing me here.

Though, from the sound of it, she didn't really argue at all.

Just made a decision and acted.

Christ.

My dad is going to love that.

Not that I want—or need—them here.

I've managed on my own for a decade now—or longer if I'm taking into account all those afternoons and nights and early mornings on my own in the back yard or the neighborhood outdoor rink or the indoor barn where my team had practices or games.

I don't need my dad in my fucking face, telling me what a pussy I am and to toughen up, all while my mom frets around with nervous energy but doesn't do one goddamned thing to make it better.

So, something else I owe Diana for.

My head pulses, and I rub at the ache, hating that items keep getting scratched onto my mental thank you list for her.

Mostly because I hate that I have no idea how to repay her.

Hate that she clearly took pity on me by bringing me here.

Hate more that she's seen what my parents are like—and clearly has opinions on them.

Who wouldn't?

No one in their right mind.

My dad's not a lovable old codger, and my mom isn't going to bake delicious oatmeal chocolate chip cookies.

They're barely interested in my life.

Except to tell me all the things that I'm doing wrong.

Something I also hate...and something that brings me to *more* things I hate—like lying awake when I should be sleeping, and being slightly nauseous from the pain pill Dee forced me to take but also sort of hungry because the crackers they gave me at the hospital didn't exactly fill me up. And, perhaps worst of all, critically aware that Diana isn't asleep either.

Her soft footsteps sound overhead—her bedroom clearly on the floor above.

I listen to them echo through the ceiling, knowing she's trying to move quietly. They're too precise, too gentle to be anything but.

I still hear them, though. Can follow their sound toward my door, to the hall, down the stairs...

There I lose them, and I think she's probably going to the

kitchen for a midnight snack—something that makes my stomach rumble—or maybe to move around laundry or pour a glass of wine from the bottle she'd rescued earlier. One that had been perched near the edge of the counter in her kitchen when we made our slow way inside. One she'd left me teetering in place to save.

And then had turned back to me with pink in her cheeks. "It's really good wine."

Her blush, the chagrined smile.

Yeah, I'm so totally fucked.

But I just made some joke about not having to clean up glass as she came back to me and we continued on the way to the bedroom I'm currently staring at the ceiling of.

Water and pills.

Then an order to rest.

And I had fallen asleep so quickly that I barely remember the door shutting behind her—maybe it's the drugs' fault, maybe it's my parents bringing their special brand of chaos. Maybe it's just been a really fucking long day.

After a really fucking long series of long ass days.

Whatever the reason, I was out as in *out*.

Until I wasn't.

And now I'm creeping on footsteps I can hear overhead, wondering about what kind of midnight snack Diana prefers and wishing that my phone wasn't lost somewhere in the debris of her office so I could watch some boring ass war documentary and fall back asleep.

Then wake up in the morning feeling good enough to get my ass out of here, send my parents home, and I don't know, since I'm making all sorts of idiotic wishes, fixing my brain so that I can understand Dee's fucking drills.

But wishes don't come true in my world.

Never have. Never—

For fuck's sake.

Because seriously? I need to get my ass off the pity wagon. Oh, boo hoo, the poor professional hockey player has it *so* bad—a long-term contract and a nice house and car, good friends and a great retirement account.

I need to stop bitching and start problem solving.

It's going to be a bit before I can play with this fucking leg, so I'll use the extra time to figure them out, even if I have to hire a professional to help.

There.

Done.

Except, I can't help but think it's never been that easy. No one in school could help me. Not the counselors or teachers or specialists. My doctors were shit and—

Creak!

I shift on the pillows as the door slides open a couple of feet and Dee slips inside.

Fuck, she's even more beautiful in the moonlight, a pair of shorts putting her long, curvy legs on display, a tank telling me—and my dick—that she's not wearing a bra.

"Oh," she says, stopping in the opening. "I didn't know you'd be awake. I just..." She glances down at her feet and I see they're bare.

And seriously, why the fuck have I just developed a foot fetish?

"...wanted to check on you."

I sit up, some perverse part of me loving the way her gaze clings to my naked chest, the small indication of her being attracted to me.

Sick and twisted and so totally bad for the both of us?

Abso-fucking-lutely.

But do I still allow the blanket to pool in my lap, to preen like a fucking peacock under that heated emerald gaze?

Yup. Yup. I sure do.

Dee isn't one to be stymied for long, though. She's smart and capable and recovers quickly. "Since you're up," she says.

Then disappears, leaving me preening in bed...and alone.

For several long minutes.

God, I'm pathetic.

Eventually—thank fuck—she reappears, a bottle and two glasses in one hand and a tray in the other.

"What's that?" I ask, even as my brain processes that there's fruit and cheese and meat and—fuck yes—big ass oatmeal chocolate chip cookies on the tray.

"A bribe." She shrugs and sets it on the bed next to me then turns and puts the wine and glasses on the nightstand.

"A bribe?"

"Uh-huh." She pulls open the drawer, starts rifling through the contents. "Ah-ha!" She holds up the remote. "Because I figure sleep is about as far away for you as it is for me."

She jabs at the buttons, turns on the TV I'd forgotten was there.

"And that has to do with a bribe?"

"Yup." She loads up a streaming service then turns and pours two glasses of wine, passing one over to me before queueing up the show.

And I start to get it.

Christ. Anything but this.

Before I can protest, though, she sinks down next to me and picks up an apple slice. "I'm about to indoctrinate you into the glorious world of the *90 Day Fiancé* franchise."

And she smiles so widely that I can't stop her from hitting play.

Then my stomach rumbles, and I decide to put myself out of my misery by devouring the tray of food.

Then...I sort of like the show?

And I sort of hate myself for it?

Especially when she pauses the second episode before it starts and asks, "What did you think?"

"This *is* really good wine," I hedge.

Laughter in the air. "Good thing the earthquake didn't ruin it, right?" She leans in, picks up a cookie and breaks it in half, passing me the larger chunk before sitting back against the headboard. "You want to know the best part?"

I want to know everything about this woman.

"Yeah," I murmur.

She picks up the bottle of wine and tops me up. "The more of this you drink, the better the show gets."

Then I'm laughing.

And she's pressing play.

And...

She's not wrong.

It does get better the more you drink.

Or maybe it's just that she's beside me.

THIRTEEN

Diana

I'M WARM.

No, I'm hot, almost scorching, sweat having gathered between my breasts, behind my knees, my elbows.

Like I fell asleep on the beach on a blistering summer day and the sun had the audacity to move, to burn my unprotected skin—

Only it's not the shifting grains of sand that are cushioning my body.

It's the surprisingly comfortable mattress in my guest room.

Oh, and Hudson too.

I fell asleep beside him...and then woke up plastered against him.

Again.

The TV is paused on a truly abysmal still of one of my favorite villains, but it barely captures my attention beyond me noticing that it's on the screen, illuminating the room.

Illuminating *him*.

And he's so damned beautiful, lashes resting on the tops of his cheeks, his lips slightly parted, his breaths slow and even and steady.

Peaceful.

Big and strong.

And he smells great—my kryptonite.

Still dangerous.

Still dumb.

Still...unable to keep my distance from him.

The man saved me from being squished by a falling ceiling, was injured in the process...and there was that puzzling look on his face just before the earth started shaking, the pained resignation when he listened to his dad make a fuss. Plus, the heat in his eyes when I took off my shirt, and the whole—

When I dreamed of you naked. This isn't how I expected it to go.

I shiver.

Right. There's that part.

And him watching my show with me, not denigrating it, but listening to me as I ranted...and then making me laugh with his sly sense of humor.

Hudson is funny.

I didn't know that before.

Quiet, yes. Dependable, definitely a yes. Or I would have said it was a definite before the whole issue with learning the plays and tweaks he needs to make to accommodate the new system.

But possessing a wicked sense of humor wouldn't have rated on my list of Hudson attributes.

He's a puzzle—or maybe a multi-faceted pair of dice, every roll bringing a different outcome, revealing a different layer of him.

Maybe that's why I don't move.

Maybe that's why I stay cuddled close, studying his sleeping form—trying to figure out that puzzle, rolling the dice to see what outcome I'll reveal.

Or maybe—

He shifts, sighing softly, and the hand that's resting on the small of my back flexes, drawing me even more flush against him. And maybe that's why I'm not moving—because the blazing weight of his palm soaking into my skin through the thin material of my tank top is intoxicating.

I don't *want* to move.

Even knowing this is a mistake, I stay pressed to him.

It wouldn't do to wake him when he needs to rest, right?

And trying to extricate myself from the big, bulky hockey player's grip might hurt him.

Better to stay in place.

Ah, the lies I live to tell myself. Still...I don't move.

Except to hit the button on the smart remote to turn off the TV, another to turn on the fan and off the lights overhead.

Except...maybe to shift a little closer, to allow my eyes to slide shut, and to let sleep drift up and drag me under again.

I sit up on a gasp, hand clamped to my chest.

Not scorching hot this time—not with the fan in the overhead creating hurricane force winds.

But, rather, in a cold sweat, gaze whipping around, expecting the world to be rolling around me again.

Feeling the reverberations of it in my dreams.

"Hey. Hey!"

I gasp again, eyes shooting to Hudson's.

He pushes up with a pained grunt beside me, cupping my

face in his hands. "Breathe, DeeDee," he says. "It was just an aftershock," he says. "We're fine, just breathe."

"I thought—" I suck in a breath, the reality mixed with my nightmare far too intense.

"I know," he says, drawing me against him. "But it's over. We're good. So for now, just breathe."

I let him hold me, and I do what he orders.

Because I don't have the wherewithal to do anything else at this moment.

"I fucking hate earthquakes," I whisper into his chest long minutes later. Because it takes until then for me to finally speak.

He chuckles softly, smooths his hand over my hair. "For good reason."

"I'm sorry."

He pulls back. "For what?"

"Freaking out and making you hurt your leg again."

"Hey," he says, hand still gently tangling in my hair, "I think earthquakes, especially after yesterday, are a completely legitimate reason for you to freak out."

God, he's nice. And sweet. And holding me so gently. "Thanks for being so cool about everything," I whisper.

He tugs a lock of my hair. "Thanks for rescuing me from the nightmare that's my parents."

"They're not so bad."

He gives me a look that calls me on the complete and total bullshit that statement is. "They're bad," he mutters, "but luckily they'll hang around for a day or two, my dad will tell me all the things I'm doing that don't meet his standards and my mom will flutter nervously about, supposedly outraged but not actually saying anything to call him out, and then they'll go back to living their best retirement lives."

I scrunch up my face. "I'm sorry."

"Again." Another tug of my hair. "Not something you need to apologize for."

He's so resigned and settled in the fact that his parents are douche canoes, has been so casual about the fact that he got hurt for me, so—

When I dreamed of you naked. This isn't how I expected it to go.

Well...*that.*

So while I know I shouldn't have come here in the middle of the night with wine and snacks...

And that I certainly shouldn't have crawled into bed beside him...

And shouldn't have stayed next to him when I woke up a couple of hours ago...

I can't make myself pull away.

Not from the warmth and strength and spice of his body, not from wanting to do something about the sadness clinging to the edges of his eyes, not from the man himself.

I touch his jaw. His skin is prickly with stubble, a soft abrasion against my palm, and suddenly I need Huddy to know he's not alone in the whole shitty people in his life situation. "My fiancé cheated on me during the first game of the season," I blurt.

He stills, big body beyond stiff.

And I tell him the rest of it, give him more details than I gave the only other person in the world—Ernest—who knows about Jason and me breaking up.

"I looked up at the jumbotron to watch the replay," I whisper, "and I saw him making out with a woman who, obviously, wasn't me—"

Eyes flaring, Hudson sucks in a breath.

"So I broke up with him." I close my eyes. "Turns out, it wasn't just that woman. There were more—one who showed up here looking for her bra, maybe a half-dozen more who I've found on social media."

"Asshole," he growls.

"Oh, most certainly," I say, trying to affect light and casual. Jason and I are over and I won't go back to someone who could do this shit to me. But it still hurts, still has all the normal doubts slinking through my head—I'm not good enough, I did something to cause this, should have done something different to prevent it. "But I'm fine," I add, still going for light and casual. "It sucks, especially since we were together for so long. But better to find out now than when we were actually married."

See?

I can be the optimist now, can look on the bright side—even with earthquakes and complicated bed mates and an ex who's a fucking nightmare.

Fingers on my cheek. "Baby."

Heat in my belly, drifting down to dip languid fingers between my thighs.

What was that about complicated bed partners?

"You shouldn't call me that," I say softly.

But I don't shift back, don't pull away from his touch.

Maybe I'm the one who's too fucking complicated.

"I know," he says. "But you need to know—*baby*"—firm gray eyes on mine, holding, making a point, one that has my insides fluttering, those phantom fingers between my legs drifting up, teasing, drawing me closer to madness, and I can't find a fuck to give—"your ex was a fucking idiot."

Then, as I'm absorbing the words, the intensity, those gorgeous eyes and reeling...*falling*...

He leans even closer.

And his lips press to mine.

FOURTEEN

Hudson

THIS IS DUMB.

This is likely to get me traded, especially considering my poor performance of late.

And this is...fucking *incredible*.

The best kiss of my entire life.

There's only the barest moment of hesitation, of shock, her body going still and stiff. But it's a blip, the slightest moment in time, and before I can even think of letting her go, she's parting her lips...and kissing me back.

Her tongue darts into my mouth, tangling with mine, and I chase it back into hers, tasting her, devouring her, committing each and every flavor to memory.

She moans, and it goes straight to my dick.

I was already hard—lying next to her, smelling her, all that temptation within arm's reach...no surprise my dick was ready and raring to go. The stuff of fantasies, having her in my bed, my arms. But having her on my tongue is...

More.

It's a single spark on a pile of tinder, setting me ablaze in an instant.

I roll, the stitches in my leg protesting, but even the burst of pain through my thigh can't extinguish the need blazing through me.

I trail my hand along her side, dragging up her tank top as I move.

"Hudson," she moans, her head dropping back, breaking the kiss, arching into my touch.

"Too much, beautiful?" I ask softly, bending and tracing my tongue over the tattoo on her ribs. It's a flurry of lines, criss-crossing this way and that, forming an image I can't quite see—or maybe one I can't quite process because I'm too focused on what's north of the ink.

The lush swells of her breasts, bouncing slightly as she keeps arching back, as her breaths come in rapid succession.

Christ, she's beautiful.

All that silken skin, her curves, that tat, her—

Tits.

I've succeeded in tugging up her tank, and fuck but her tits are perfect. Tear-shaped and large enough to overflow my palms, pink nipples tightened into taut buds that call out for my mouth.

Giving in to that call, I bend and suckle one deeply.

"Hudson!" she shouts, fingers diving into my hair, holding me against her flesh.

I take her cue and keep doing what I'm doing, but I take note of what has her fingers tightening in the strands of my hair, what has her hips bucking, seeking purchase. My dick, fuck it wants to be buried inside the tight, slick heat of her cunt, wants to give her what her body is so wildly seeking out, but I know I can't let it go that far.

I can make her feel good, though.

Can make her feel fucking *great*.

I yank the tank top over her head, spend my time feasting on her breasts then kissing my way up her throat, along her jaw, and finally back to her lips.

God, her mouth is everything I've ever dreamed of.

Everything I've needed.

Her moans vibrate from her tongue and then along mine, her body writhing, her leg hitching over my waist as she grinds against me.

Red-hot pain along my thigh, but I don't stop kissing her.

I do slide my hand along her side, dragging my fingers over her rib cage, across the dip of her torso meeting her hip, along the soft curve of her belly and the adorable divot of her belly button, and then down down *down* until I reach the waistband of her pajama shorts.

Silky soft, but not nearly as soft as her skin.

She stills when I dip a finger beneath the elastic and I freeze at the sudden stiffness in her body, lifting my head, tearing my lips from hers.

"Too much?" I ask softly.

Her mouth is swollen, the stubble on my cheeks, my jaw having reddened her skin, and I might feel guilty if it wasn't so fucking hot to see my marks on her flesh. "T-too much?" she stammers out, eyes hazy, those swollen lips parted on the question.

I tap my fingers and those pretty green eyes go wide, her pelvis tipping as though trying to coax my hand down.

But she'd gone still at that first touch.

So I need to be sure.

"Baby," I say, "I want to touch you." I tap my fingers again, watch her eyes heat, feel her hips buck. "*Here.*" I slide my hand a little lower, until the tip of one finger is just brushing the slickness of her desire, loving the little gasp she makes, the shiver that trembles through her body when I ask, my voice a rasp, "*Everywhere.*" When she still doesn't reply, I stroke lightly, mouth curving up at the edges. "Is that okay, baby?"

A little furrow appears between her eyebrows, confusion drifting across her face. "Is what okay?"

Grinning, I bend, nip at her bottom lip, catching her gasp with my mouth, tasting her on my tongue.

Only when my lungs protest, do I pull back, kiss my way along her jaw, pausing at her ear. "I want to make you come, sweetheart." I nip at the lobe and she shivers again. "Let me?"

Still.

She's so still.

Then she melts, hand sliding up my back, diving into my hair, holding me close when she says—or maybe orders, "Give me your fingers, honey. Make me feel good." A nip to the corner of my mouth. "And when you're done, I'll return the favor."

Blood arrowing for my dick, making me so fucking hard I could pound nails.

But I don't delay in sliding my hand further into her pajamas, parting the slick folds of her labia.

"Hudson," she moans softly, pelvis tilting as she grinds herself against me.

I explore slowly, noting what has the slick evidence of her desire growing, what has her head pressing more firmly into the pillows, a moan slipping free and filling the air.

But it's when I focus on the bundle of nerves at the apex of her pussy, lightly circling, stroking, that I know I have her.

I know it won't be long.

I know—

This will be far better than any of my fantasies.

FIFTEEN

Diana

I'M CLOSE, so fucking close I can taste the edge of my orgasm.

It's going to be good.

It's going to be great.

It's going to be the best ever, so huge, so big that it may rip me in two, so intense that I'm actually a little scared of the Mack truck of pleasure barreling down on me.

But the brakes are out and the collision is imminent and—

Hudson freezes, his fingers on my clit, but no longer *working* my clit.

And I need them moving again, need the gentle circling, the deliberate stroking.

Because...I'm close.

Because...I'm *close.*

"Hudson," I say, clenching at the strands of his hair, attempting to drag his mouth back to mine.

But he's frozen in place, and my orgasm is hovering in the air, just barely out of reach.

"Please—"

His eyes flash back to mine, but they're no longer twin thunderstorms of need. They're confused and pissed and a little sad.

"What's—?" I begin to ask.

Though, I don't finish.

Because I hear it then.

The voice echoing through the hall—well, at the end of it. Because it's being projected up the stairs.

To where my bedroom is.

"Yoohoo, darling! I wanted to check in on you after the quake," Ernest calls. "I've brought your favorite—" I hear the crinkling of what I know is a brown paper bag. Because it's morning. And I have one favorite morning meal. More crinkling and I'm imagining Ernest shaking the bag like it's a container of kitty treats and he's trying to get the pussies to run out.

Too bad mine is—

I freeze.

Because Ernest and the word *pussies* is about ten steps too far.

And because *my* pussy is exposed, my pajama shorts shoved down to just above my knees, Hudson's fingers between my legs the only thing covering me.

"Diana?" he calls. "Missy, are you all right?"

I hear footsteps coming closer.

Know that he may go upstairs and check my bedroom first, but that sooner or later he's going to make his way down this hallway and—

I'm practically naked.

And Hudson is in bed next to me.

Another crinkle, that bag shaking.

Only this time it sounds much, *much* closer.

As though, he's going to skip the upstairs searching and check the downstairs level first.

Shit. Shit. *Shit—*

Hudson moves faster than me, reaching for the blankets and dragging them up and over me.

And not a second too soon because the second—the freaking *second*—that I clutch them to my chest, Ernest toddles into view.

His gaze is pointing down the hall, toward the door that leads out to the back yard, so it takes him a minute to realize the guest room is occupied.

Then he turns to face us and if I wasn't naked and throbbing and so fucking close to an orgasm that my skin feels like it's on fire and my nerves are aching (not to mention other things), his almost comically shocked expression would have made me laugh.

As it is, I'm too close to the edge to be truly amused.

Hudson grunts softly as he slides out of bed and I watch Ernest's expression change, watch it become somehow even more shocked as Huddy limps to the door—it's better than yesterday but more than I like to see as the woman in bed beside him, and definitely far more than the coach who has him on my roster.

A thought that has cold water dumped over me.

Icy fucking cold water.

In an instant, I'm not turned on.

Hell, in an instant, my orgasm is about a million miles away, a universe away, so fucking far away that I'm not even sure I'll ever have another moment of pleasure in my entire life.

What am I doing?

Like, seriously— What. The fuck. Am I. Doing?

"Missy?"

I jerk, glaze going back to Ernest's.

"Are you okay?"

Okay?

I almost laugh. I'm so far from okay, it's even less funny than having a giant orgasm barreling down on me...and then it missing me by a millimeter.

But Hudson is in cane reach.

And injured because of me already.

If I don't answer in the affirmative—and really, Hudson is only here because of me, literally *because* of me, both in the bedroom and formerly beside me in the actual bed—Ernest is going to start wielding that cane like a weapon.

Huddy doesn't need another injury that I'm the cause of.

So I sit up, nearly losing my hold on the blankets, and all but shout, "Yes!"

Hudson's head jerks in my direction, and I don't miss his wince. Dammit.

I clear my throat. "Yes," I say more calmly. "Ernest this is Hudson, my, uh, friend." Hudson's brows fly up but I see Ernest's hold on his cane tighten so I hurry to add, "Hudson, Ernest is my next-door neighbor."

Ernest scowls even as Hudson's expression smooths out. Then he asks, "We leave the front door open or something?"

Ernest rocks back slightly on his heels, looking slightly chagrined.

"No," I say, still clutching the blankets, but supplying the necessary information. "Ernest has a key."

Hudson's eyes come to mine.

I shrug as well as I'm able to considering I'm basically naked beneath the covers. "He waters the plants when I'm out of town."

"Didn't you have a fiancé to do that?" he asks quietly.

"I think I mentioned already that Jason was an asshole," I

say just as quietly. "He wasn't all that good at remembering to water anything."

"He wasn't all that good at anything," Ernest grumbles then lifts his cane and glares at Hudson. "What about you? Are you as much of a loser as the last one?"

"Ernest!" I exclaim, eyes shooting to Hudson, mouth opening to apologize.

Only...there's something on Hudson's face that slithers through my middle.

It's the same sliver of emotion I saw just before the earth started shaking.

And, just as before, it's there and gone before I can really get a lock on it.

But seriously...what the fuck is that?

"She deserves a lot better than any of us assholes," he mutters, "and certainly better than that asshole of all assholes, Jason."

Ernest had opened his mouth too.

Hudson's words have him clamping it closed.

For my part, mine is hanging open.

"Now, if you'll give us a minute"—Hudson reaches for the door, starting to shut it—"we'll be right out."

Then he doesn't wait for an answer, just closes the wooden panel in Ernest's face.

He turns to face me and I clamp my lips together, trying to figure out what to say. Then my mouth promptly drops open again when he announces, "I should leave, should pretend what just happened between us didn't just happen because it's messy and fucks with both of our jobs and you deserve better... but"—he moves close, tugs the blanket off my body, hand diving back between my legs—"I know I may never get another chance with you, baby. So"—his head drops, words damp puffs of air on my lips—"I'm taking this moment to fulfill a fantasy."

Before I can ask what the fuck he's talking about—and frankly, that's barely a thought because his hand is hot and his fingertips are in the motherland—he drops his head further, taking my mouth in a kiss that steals any thought left in my head.

And *then* his fingers start moving.

And it turns out that my orgasm isn't a million miles away.

The moment his thumb hits my clit, his fingers sliding through my labia, thrusting inside, it's suddenly right there.

A circle.

A press.

Slow and steady thrusts...

"Oh, my God!" I gasp, tearing my lips from Hudson's, my hips jerking as pleasure rockets through me.

It's not gentle, not lapping at my toes and spreading through my body.

It's an inferno, racing over me, reducing me to nothing except cinder and ash.

And it's not short and I don't come down quickly—my descent is leisurely, and when I finally open my eyes, he's leaning over me, his face gentle.

My throat goes tight. "I—"

He cups my cheek, palm warm, eyes unreadable. "Get dressed, DeeDee." A tug of my hair. "I'll be gone before you make it into Ernest's crosshairs."

SIXTEEN

Hudson

TURNS out hobbling home a couple of blocks on a bruised and stitched up thigh...and then dealing with the shitshow that is my parents will tire a guy out.

I calmed them down after I made my way inside, got some food in all three of us—frozen shit that was easy to toss in the oven...and seriously, paying for that meal delivery service was the best thing that I've ever done.

Maybe not the *best* thing, considering where my fingers and mouth had been earlier in the day.

But pretty damned efficient so I didn't have to deal with parents' nonsense.

Food. Beer. Listening to them bitch.

All fucking afternoon.

Before tossing more shit in the oven and doing more dishes and then sending them off to bed so I can pass out on the couch.

No stairs for me, not tonight.

I'm too fucking tired.

Especially after spending long minutes searching for the plastic bag of my belongings from the hospital and then through it until I find my phone. My charger takes longer to track down because my parents have mysteriously relocated it to the laundry room for some reason. I hobble back to the living room, plug in my dead cell, and wait for it to have enough juice so I can book an outrageously expensive flight for them to return home in the morning. Then book them an equally expensive Uber to the airport since I can't drive them.

I do this partly because I know there's nothing for them to do for me here (except make me fucking insane) and partly because I know they want to go back to their own lives.

My dad has his bowling league.

My mom needs to walk with her friends and then hit the garden center to add to the flower-filled back yard of the house I bought them in Southern California a few years ago.

And I need them the fuck out of my hair.

So, I make those arrangements, text them their boarding passes—and get no reply aside from a thumbs up. No surprise there. The false show of concern. The attention grabbing. Then, because they didn't get the reaction they wanted and because they're tired of pretending to be actual parents, they're ready to go right back to their lives.

Which is the best case scenario for me.

I don't have to put up with their shit.

They can keep on living as they like.

Sighing, I settle slowly onto the couch, trying to summon the energy to turn on the TV because I have the—not-so-odd, considering last night—urge to watch 90 Day Fiancé.

But the remote is nearly out of reach and I'm fucking tired.

And I should probably just sleep.

Or if that won't come because my sleep schedule is completely fucked and my leg hurts and the stitches are starting to itch in a way that I know is only going to get worse over the next couple of days then I should study some fucking drills.

Maybe the pain killers I downed on my trek through the house will slow the spinning in my brain enough that they'll stick in my fucking head.

Unlikely considering that nothing has ever made that shit stop.

I still pick up the tablet, spend a good thirty minutes trying to focus.

Newsflash—it's the same old shit. The words move, the arrows shift, the entire screen doesn't make any bit of fucking sense.

Scowling, I toss the tablet aside and lean back on the couch.

And as I do so—Jesus fuck this next thought makes me pathetic and I fucking know it—but Diana didn't come after me.

Not a surprise.

And yet...*damn*, that shit stings.

Grunting, I shove the feeling down. Like I said, not a surprise. She's *Diana*. I'm me. Whatever we had was a product of the moment and now I need to move on, need to accept that we're just...work colleagues or maybe friends at the most.

That's it.

Still, as I reach for the remote I'm thinking that, leg aside, I'm mostly grateful for the hours trapped in that office. Not only did I get that time with Diana (which led to *that* time with Diana), but also because we missed much of the craziness from the aftermath of the city trying to shake itself apart. By the time we left the hospital, many of the rescue efforts and fire suppression work and emergency services were winding down.

People were slowly getting back to normal, something that's continued today.

Yes, it was a big quake, one that caused several casualties and damage throughout the city, including at the practice rink (according to the email operational services sent all of us in the Eagles organization), but most of the buildings in the Bay Area are built to withstand the big one.

So, it's not as bad as it could be.

Which means that life goes on.

They've delayed the next couple of home games in order to conduct some inspections of the arena and are coordinating with several local rinks to find somewhere else for us to practice, considering the ceiling caved in throughout most of that practice facility.

But most of the focus is getting back to business as usual.

We'll be just a blip in the news cycle soon enough, some politician doing something outright fucking crazy or corrupt or a celebrity getting married to take the focus.

Still, the videos and pictures I see as I scroll through social media are intense.

The shaking, the fires, the cracks in the roads and the hillsides sliding down, glass cracking in high rises, street signs falling down, tree limbs landing on cars, power lines down—fucking intense and I'm aware of exactly how lucky we are that the fatalities were so low.

And that Diana and I were okay aside from the bumps, bruises, and cuts.

I wonder if she's sleeping right now or if the nightmares are going to wake her up again.

"Fuck," I mutter, pushing that aside and jabbing at the remote.

And turning on the damned show she introduced me to.

I know I'm going to watch the whole fucking thing, know I'm going to devour that small piece of her then clutch it close.

And I do exactly that as I finally fall asleep.

And as I dream of her all fucking night.

THE NEXT AFTERNOON, I've gotten my parents to the Uber and out of my hair (and actually all the way back to their house, considering the flight is so short), and I'm trying to figure out what the fuck to do with myself.

There's no hockey.

I worked out my upper body.

I texted the guys, checking in and making sure everyone was good.

I tried to study the fucking drills to no avail.

And now I'm hobbling around my house, feeling unsettled.

"Christ," I mutter, limping toward the fridge, thinking that getting drunk sounds like a fucking plan.

Only I don't get that far.

Because there's a knock at the door, and when I hobble my ass down the hall to answer it, my heart leaps.

Because through the side pane of glass, I see it's Diana.

Hope, full and rampant, tears through me.

She came.

She fucking *came*.

I whip the door open, lips parting...

But my words immediately stopper up.

Because Diana's there, but she's not alone.

Standing behind her is...Jean-Michel.

Owner of the Oakland Eagles.

As in, the boss of all the bosses in the organization.

I think of slick heat and soft moans, plump lips and lush breasts. I think of quiet words and sad revelations and—

One look at Dee's face tells me she's thinking of them too.

And not in a good way.

Fuck.

I'm so totally getting traded.

SEVENTEEN

Diana

MY HEART IS in my throat until I see Hudson's form materialize in the hallway, slowly moving to the door.

I know the minute he realizes it's me because he pauses for a heartbeat.

Then starts moving faster.

And so does my pulse, picking up its pace until it's thrumming through my veins so intensely that it's hard to hear the lock being disengaged, the handle being twisted as the door is pulled inward.

My stomach does a funny little dip before worry takes over.

There are dark circles beneath his eyes and sweat on his forehead.

"You're pushing it," I mutter, stepping forward and slipping by him, totally forgetting that Jean-Michel, that the man who holds my job, my future, my *dreams* in the palm of his hand is on the step behind me until he catches the door as I swing it shut before it can fully close.

I jerk slightly at the noise, glance over my shoulder, murmuring, "Sorry."

He just smiles and jerks his chin forward, silently telling me to precede.

An uncomfortable feeling settles between my shoulder blades, but I push it down and keep moving into Hudson's house, knowing that I'm likely revealing too much when I make my way into the kitchen and over to the fridge without hesitation.

"Have you eaten?" I ask, pulling the door open and searching the contents...which, frankly, are pretty dire—and that's coming from me.

I've spent most of my time since the move DoorDashing, stopping at In-N-Out on the way home from the rink, or eating dry cereal right out of the box.

Only on my rare days off do I cook—and that's only if I had the energy.

Or if Ernest needs a homecooked meal.

And God knows, Jason wasn't exactly meal planning and serving up a three-course feast for me the moment I walked through the door after work.

Jason—

Ugh.

I don't want to think about the jerk, but since the quake he's been blowing up my phone double time (and I didn't even know it was possible to have *more* missed calls and messages from him, but the man's really putting in the effort to drive me batshit insane).

He's "worried" about me.

Wanting to come back home so he can make sure I'm okay.

Attempting to weasel his way back into my good graces.

That's not going to happen.

Especially since I had a taste of what a real man can do—

saving me from falling ceilings—and what a real man can do between the sheets...or rather, between my legs.

That orgasm...

I shiver.

"No, I haven't eaten yet today," Hudson says and I jump, jerked from my thoughts as I spin to face him. "But I have some premade meals in the freezer—do you...um...do you want me to heat something up for you guys?"

"No!" I reply quickly.

Too quickly.

So quickly that Hudson's brows fly up and when my gaze jerks to the side, I see Jean-Michel wearing a similar expression.

"I just mean...we're here to check in on you," I manage to push out, only half sounding like my lungs are being compressed by an elephant. "You don't have to feed us."

"Right," he murmurs, slowly lifting his arm and reaching behind me to close the fridge door.

"Oh. Uh, sorry," I whisper. "I should have—"

His fingers trail down the outside of my arm, on the side the Jean-Michel can't see. "All good." A soft whisper.

"Are your parents still here?" I ask, even though I suppose I know the answer to that already, considering that my ears aren't being assaulted by Jim's bitching.

"No," he says, gentle eyes holding mine as his mouth hitches up, and fuck if I don't feel that smile like phantom fingers stroking me between my thighs. "I put them in an Uber to the airport this morning."

"That's why it's so quiet," I say lightly.

"Well until the next time they decide to storm into my life." He shifts, wincing and I reach out to steady him.

"You should sit down."

One big shoulder lifts and drops. "I'm fine."

"But—"

He tugs at my ponytail. "I'm fine, DeeDee. I promise."

I wrinkle my nose because he's obviously hurting, but before I can argue with him further, Jean-Michel clears his throat.

Jean-Michel.

Yup, I forgot my boss was here.

Again.

Holy hell, I need to get my shit together.

Hudson's eyes slide from mine and he glances over at the powerful businessman and team owner. When he looks back at me, our gazes connecting for only a short blip, I watch the warmth from his expression disappear, as though he's carefully tucked it away, before he steps away to lean against the island. "What can I do for you guys?"

Do?

For me?

And just like that, my mind goes to all the wrong places.

And just like *that*...I can't think of a single appropriate thing to say.

Thankfully Jean-Michel steps in to save the day, though he does it with a look in my direction, a look that has the hairs on my nape prickling, a look that tells me he sees far too fucking much.

"We wanted to check in," Jean-Michel says. "Make sure you're feeling okay and arrange some time with Doc to take a look at your leg."

"I..." Hudson glances at me. "Okay."

"You saw the email from operations?" he asks.

Hudson looks back. "Yeah."

"Good. The schedule will be a little off for a bit, but we'll be back on track soon. And if your leg is up for it and Doc clears it, we'd like you to travel with the team on the road trip."

"Okay."

Jean-Michel glances over to me, something in his bright blue eyes I can't read.

Or maybe don't *want* to read.

Then he looks at Hudson. "Well, that's everything on my list." He flicks his stare down to his watch. "I'll leave you two to discuss the details."

My mouth drops open.

This wasn't the plan when Jean-Michel showed up on my doorstep to check in on me. We were supposed to look in on Hudson, make sure he knew how thankful we were for the whole *saving* me thing (and maybe also for the whole giving me the best orgasm of my life thing, though Jean-Michel didn't know that part) then discuss logistics for the next couple of weeks.

But before I can formulate any of that, my boss tosses me a long, unreadable look, tosses a goodbye over his shoulder, and walks right out of Hudson's front door.

EIGHTEEN

Hudson

HER FACE WOULD BE comical if—

Hell, who am I kidding?

It *is* comical.

And beautiful.

Then the soft *click* of the front door closing jars us both out of our stunned silence.

Diana reacts first. "I'm sorry," she whispers.

My brows flick up. "About what?"

Pink on her cheeks, her eyes sliding away.

"My leg?" I say, pushing off the island and moving toward her, the stitches barely pulling now. Or maybe it's that I'm feeling nothing even close to pain. Not now that she's in my house, my *empty* house. "You've already apologized for that."

Teeth pressing into her bottom lip. "I know. I just—" A breath, and I watch her shake herself, try to focus.

Yeah, I don't want that.

I like her befuddled.

I step closer...then closer still, not stopping until my socked feet are brushing the tops of her shoes. "You just what?"

"Jean-Michel and I showed up on your porch without warning."

I shrug. "It's not the first time one of the guys from the team has randomly shown up on my doorstep." I tuck a strand of hair behind her ear. "Did he call and make arrangements? Or just appear on yours too?" Taking advantage of our closeness, I lean in, inhale the scent of her. "You smell like apples."

"It's my shampoo—" She blushes. "Wait, what?"

I don't bring up the whole my sniffing her thing, just shift a little closer so that the foot separating us turns into just a few inches. "Did Jean-Michel randomly show up on your porch or did he call and give you a warning first?"

A beat, her eyes warm and liquid on mine, her mouth curving. "He just showed."

I give in to the urge to stroke her skin, running my knuckles along her jaw. "See?"

She blinks and fuck, she's so damned cute it takes my breath away. "See what?"

I grin. "That I don't give a fuck if you show up on my porch unannounced, DeeDee. Any time you get the urge, any day of the week, any hour of the night. You show up and I'll open up the door to you."

Her inhale is so sharp, I'm shocked that she doesn't choke.

Then I watch her deliberately try to pull herself together.

I fucking hate that.

So much so I'm not going to let that happen.

"Yesterday—" she begins.

Yeah, no. Not letting her taint the memory of what she gave me yesterday. No fucking way.

"Don't," I say, stepping closer. "Don't do that."

"Do what?" she whispers.

"Don't ruin what you gave me yesterday with bullshit about it not meaning anything or being a mistake," I murmur, now trailing my knuckles over her cheek.

Her eyes close, shutting me out of the deep green depths, cutting me off from the tumult of feelings inside her, and when they reopen, my gut twists.

Befuddled is gone.

Regret is in full force.

"Huddy," she whispers. "We shouldn't..."

"Maybe not," I agree, and even though I try to hold the next words in, they're torn right out of me, "but it was still the most beautiful fucking gift that anyone's ever given me."

She sucks in another breath.

And I brace.

Expecting—no, *knowing*—that this is the moment she cuts ties and walks right the fuck out of my house.

I'm the fuck-up on her roster.

She's the coach who's trying to put us in the best position to win a Cup.

I'm just another loser of a man in her sphere.

She's the most beautiful woman on the planet.

I'm—

"Dammit," she whispers.

And I don't finish my thought because she's suddenly leaping up, launching herself into my arms.

There's a bolt of pain down my leg, but it's there and gone in a heartbeat.

Mostly because I'm grabbing her so she doesn't fall, and her legs are going around my waist, and suddenly my hands are full of the woman I've wanted for months, the woman who lives in my fantasies, the woman who didn't see me...until now.

Because she's plunging her hands into my hair and she's dragging my head down and—

Her lips are pressing to mine.

I groan, mouth opening, tongue sliding out.

She's right there with me, meeting me stroke for stroke, moan vibrating along my tongue. Tits pressed to my chest, legs tightening, bringing that sweet pussy of hers firmly against my stomach.

There are too many fucking layers between us.

But I can still feel the heat of her, still remember the slick evidence of her desire, the way my name tumbled off her tongue when she came apart.

Spinning, I bring her over to the island, feeling something pull in my thigh, something warm start dripping down my leg. I'm not feeling any pain, though—or not anywhere aside from my dick. That's rock-hard and pressing against my pants, desperate to be inside the tight, wet clasp of her pussy.

"Hudson," she groans when I set her on the edge of the counter and reach for the hem of her shirt.

I freeze.

"We shouldn't," she whispers.

"I know," I whisper back.

But she doesn't stop me when I drag her shirt up and over her head, doesn't stop me when I bend and kiss her again, long and deep and wet...and filled with every bit of longing I've built up over the last months.

In fact, she meets me there.

Meets me stroke for stroke with her tongue, tightens her fingers in my hair, rocks her hips against mine.

Fucking perfect.

Fucking hot.

Fucking *dangerous*.

Because she's sliding her hand down my front, diving her hand beneath the waistband of my sweats, and the elastic means she has far too easy access...

Far too easy because my control is dangerously thin.

Which means that access, the way she slips her hand into my underwear and wraps her hands around my dick, stroking without hesitation and doing it tight and fast—

It's...well, *fucking dangerous.*

So, I snake my hand down, wrap my fingers around her wrist and tug it free.

"Hudson," she says, her lungs working fast, sending those tits of hers I love bouncing in the confines of her bra.

"Now *that's* a fucking great view," I mutter.

"Wh—?"

I don't waste words...or time. I just bury my face there, flicking out my tongue, tasting the lush globes, running my nose along the curves, plumped up by the tight fabric of her sports bra. She shivers...then gasps when I yank the material down, her breasts popping free.

"That's a better one," I groan then bend a little further, capturing one nipple between my lips.

"Hudson!"

Fuck, but I love it when she cries out my name.

I roll my tongue over the hardened bud, stroke my hand down her belly, flick open the button of her jeans.

No hesitation this time, she lifts her hips, helps me shimmy them down those lush thighs.

I get them past her calves, off one foot, but can't be bothered to pull them off the other.

"Where the fuck are your panties, sweetheart?"

Pink cheeks. Teeth pressing into her bottom lip. But when she tries to close her legs, I stop her with a palm on each thigh.

"No, DeeDee"—I nip at that lip, freeing it—"you have such a pretty pussy, it would be a shame to cover it up."

Her throat works.

That pink darkens to red.

"Now," I murmur, kissing my way along her jaw, pausing at her ear, the words glazing her lobe and making her shiver, "tell me why that cunt I like so much is bare."

Another shiver.

But this time it's paired with a buck of her hips, as though she's seeking out my fingers.

And who am I to deny her anything?

I slide my hands up, trace my thumbs along the creases of her thighs. "Well?"

"J-Jean-Michel surprised me when I was just getting out of the shower." A shudder when I slide in a little further, trailing one finger along the seam of her. "I-I didn't have time."

NINETEEN

Diana

I'M SLOWLY LOSING my mind.

I'm so fucking turned on I can't even process what I'm doing, what I'm thinking, what words are tumbling off my lips.

And all the while, Hudson is close, his fingers stroking along my labia.

Teasing and yeah, it feels great—those roughened fingertips trailing over me, light and making me ache for more.

But it's making me *ache for more*.

And he wants to have a conversation.

About my *pretty pussy*.

I shiver again, the memory of his raspy words hot as hell.

Almost as hot as what he's doing with his mouth...slowly dragging it down my throat, along my collarbones, down, down, *down*.

He makes a long pitstop at my breasts, using his free hand to palm one and leaning in to take my nipple into his mouth, using tongue and teeth and lips to drive me slowly insane.

And all the while, his fingers are slowly moving, trailing through me, getting me so damned wet that I'm probably creating a flash flood risk here in his kitchen.

"Hudson," I moan, my head dropping back, my eyes unseeing.

Because all of my focus is on what I'm *feeling*.

What he's creating in me.

It's good.

No. It's *great*.

And look, I'm not a girlie with a high sex drive. I don't need to be fucked six ways to Sunday, don't need to have multiple orgasms or hit three different positions on my way over the edge. Hell, more often than not in my past experiences, I was happy to content myself with just enjoying the process.

Because it was...nice.

But it wasn't *explosive*, not like what I'm feeling now, what I felt yesterday—a gathering deep inside me that threatens to explode, to eviscerate me, to turn me into an empty shell of a woman. Nope. It was nice, so *nice* that even one orgasm was a pleasant surprise.

That wasn't what happened yesterday.

Absolutely not. I imploded like a damned rocket ship on a collision course with an asteroid.

And...I already feel it closing in on me again.

He's not inside yet—fingers *or* cock—and there's no tongue action—at least not between my legs because my breasts are seeing *plenty* of action from his mouth—but it's already here.

And there's no stopping it.

"Hud—"

"Shh," he murmurs, "just let it come baby."

It's going to come. And it's going to be huge. And it's kind of terrifying, how big it feels like it will be.

"I—"

He circles my clit. "I'm here. I've got you." A nip to my flesh. "Just let go."

I remember the world shaking and falling apart and his big body protecting me. I remember the quiet confidences we shared while we were trapped. I remember him putting himself —even injured—between me and Ernest before he knew my neighbor wasn't a threat. I remember his knuckles brushing along my arm in silent reassurance when I left the fridge open.

Big things.

And small things.

And yet, the important things.

Because I haven't ever have that with a man.

Truthfully, I hadn't had that since Grams.

"Sweetheart"—another brush of my clit—"I want to watch you come apart for me."

The memories slide away. The moment crystalizes back into fingers and tongue, sensation and need and pleasure, *oh so much* pleasure.

Then it detonates, exploding through me so intensely that I cry out and arch so far back on the counter I distantly feel my hair brushing along the granite as wave after wave of bliss pulses through me.

I come to with my back flat on the cool counter and Hudson's big, warm palms still on my thighs, keeping them spread for his gaze.

And he's watching me, trailing those fingers through me again before lifting his hand, tongue flicking out to taste the evidence of my desire.

I shiver when he sucks the tip of one finger.

His eyes hit mine and before I can react, he's lifting me off the counter, carrying me through to the other room.

My jeans are still hanging off one foot as he settles me on the couch.

He bends and drags them off then snags a blanket that's draped over the back of the sofa, tucking it around me.

It's so unexpectedly sweet that my lungs compress and I find I can't speak for a few seconds.

I only unstick when he sinks down next to me, his big body pressed to mine, his arms coming around me, his hand smoothing up and down my naked back.

And that's it.

That's. It.

He doesn't allow that hand to drift south, doesn't slip between my legs, doesn't get naked and thrust deep.

He just holds me.

Warms me.

Oh, no. I'm so totally fucked.

I think the certainty of that is why I react the way I do—or maybe it's *part* of the reason I react the way I do. Because the other half of my next actions are because even with that glorious orgasm he just gave me...I'm empty.

And I think the only person who can fill me up is Hudson.

I shift, allowing the blanket to drop from my body, but as I do it, I roll, drawing him over the top of me.

"You can be my blanket," I say, reaching for the hem of his shirt while simultaneously pushing at the waistband of his sweats...and not really succeeding in getting either of them off, so I add, just to make it very clear what I want, "My *naked* blanket."

Sparks of lightning in those gorgeous gray eyes.

But I don't miss the hesitation either. "DeeDee, you don't have—"

I give up on the shirt and focus on his sweats. Mostly because while I want to spend some quality time with his naked torso and all the muscles I glimpsed there in our time together in my office, and while he was working hard in the team's gym, the lower half is what is going to bring us both the most pleasure.

He groans when I get my hand under the waistband, then again when I grip his cock tight.

And fuck if I'm not already close again—wet and aching, the tendrils of an orgasm in my belly.

Just from touching him.

Just from watching his head drop forward, the cords of his neck standing out in sharp relief as he thrusts into my hand, his eyes scorching as they burn into mine.

Beautiful.

He's beautiful.

"I want you inside me," I whisper and just saying the words out loud ramps me higher. "I need you, honey," I say when it looks as though he may protest. "Please."

A long, taut moment.

I tighten my grip, say again. "Please, Hudson," I all but beg. "Make us both feel good."

Shuddering, he grinds his teeth together, expression unfathomable.

Then he...rears back and his shirt disappears.

Or maybe it's tossed across the room.

Or maybe I just don't care.

Because he's reaching for a bag on the coffee table—the bag of his belongings from the hospital. I frown, but only for a second because then he's pulling out his wallet, opening it, and extracting a condom from inside.

Oh, thank fuck.

Relief pours through me...but only for a second.

Because then he's rolled the condom down the hard length of his cock and he's nudging my legs further apart, notching himself at my entrance and thrusting in and—

"Oh, my God," I whisper, head falling back again.

"Too much?" he grunts.

There's a burn and stretch because he's proportional—thick and long and *so damned hard.*

"DeeDee?" he rasps when I don't answer.

Can't answer.

I'm too busy reveling in the fact that I'm currently being so thoroughly possessed by this man I can barely breathe.

But when his face clouds and he starts to pull back, I react faster than I think possible, grabbing his hips, stopping him.

"You're big," I say, stretching up to press my lips to his. "That's good." My mouth hitches up. "Just a little over-whelming."

There's a blip of silence.

Then he's grinning. "You can handle it."

"I—"

"Hang on, sweetheart," he says, stealing my breath as he draws out and then strokes back in—doing it hard and deep. "You're about to have the best fucking ride of your life."

And then I have no choice but to do exactly that—to wrap my legs around his middle, to cling to his shoulders, to meet each and every thrust that he delivers with perfectly brutal intensity.

Fast. Deep. Hard.

I moan.

I hold tight.

And I take everything this man dishes out as he delivers on that promise of a great fucking ride.

Especially since he gives me another orgasm along the way.

TWENTY

Hudson

I'M LIMP, barely having had enough presence of mind to roll my heavy ass to the side so I don't crush Dee and my lungs are working like I've just chased down some asshole on a breakaway.

But I just had an orgasm that threatened to split me in two.

And Diana's in my arms.

And...fuck, but I never expected to ever get this.

"You good?" I manage to ask when my voice starts working again.

"Mmm," she moans softly, stretching her arms over her head, arching her back, putting her tits on display for me.

It takes just that much for me to be hard again.

Something she feels pressing against her hip, if her eyes going wide are any indication.

"Already?" she asks, the word a shocked sigh.

I shrug. "You're beautiful."

She stares at me, as though trying to process that. Then her expression softens and she murmurs, "The fantasies."

My stomach clenches. "What?"

"In my office, you said"—a flicker of heat in her gaze—"that you'd had fantasies about me."

I had?

Jesus fucking Christ.

I close my eyes, stifling my groan.

Her hand lifts and she runs her fingers through my hair. My eyes fly open, my heart squeezing tight. "After you saved me from the ceiling collapsing, just when you were about to pass out"—apology in her eyes—"you said you'd had fantasies about me."

Fuck. Kill me now.

"I don't remember that part," I mutter.

"Is it..." Something creeping into her expression that I don't like. Because it reminds me of the hurt that had clung to the emerald depths of her eyes when she told me about her dirtbag of an ex. "Did you not mean it? Or"—teeth pressing into her bottom lip—"maybe I misheard?"

Giving me an out.

"Sweetheart"—I smooth my hand down her spine—"we're naked and cuddled up on my couch after you just gave me the best sex of my life." I tangle my fingers in the ends of her long brown hair. "What do you think?"

She's quiet for a long moment.

Then her face goes soft and she strokes a hand over my jaw, running her fingertips through the stubble there. "I think *you* were the one giving me the best sex of my life."

My dick get harder.

Something she also feels because her lips curve and she gives my jaw another stroke. And seriously, if she likes my beard that's grown in over the last couple of days this much then I will definitely be keeping it.

Anything that gets her to keep touching me.

Anything that keeps her interested.

Anything that means I'll get a little more time with her.

Because maybe then I'll figure out a way to keep her.

"And just goes to say," she murmurs, hand sliding from my jaw down to my chest, "that you're not actually naked—*oh my God!*" She jerks back so quickly she nearly topples off the couch.

I lurch forward and catch her before she cracks her head against the coffee table, but I'm not fast enough to stop my papers and tablet, the beer I'd opened earlier and the TV remotes from scattering in all directions.

"Shit," I mutter, tucking her next to me as I sit up and reaching for the bottle that's tipped over, spilling beer onto my hardwood.

"No!" she exclaims, hands coming to my chest and pushing me back.

"What the fuck, sweetheart?" I ask, gently dislodging her and reaching for the bottle again.

"No," she repeats, shoving me back once more, but because she pairs it with, "Your leg!" I still, my gaze going down to my thigh.

I curse softly.

What a fucking mess.

She jumps to her feet and the way she seems at a loss for a second, her gaze going from side to side, hands flapping, clearly at a loss as to what to do is cute.

But I'm bleeding.

Damn, I'd felt the pull of pain, the warmth of blood dripping down my leg.

I'd just been too distracted by other things—namely the fact that DeeDee is the subject of every single one of my fantasies—to realize that it soaked through my sweats.

Sweats, thankfully, that I didn't fully take off before I fucked her.

Because I really like my couch and I don't want to spend the next who knows how long scrubbing blood out of the cushions.

Even as I think that—and then think that I need to *stop* thinking and start getting my shit together to say, stymie the blood and clean up the beer—Diana stops flapping her arms around and goes into Coach Mode.

A.K.A. take no prisoners and get shit done mode.

She pushes my shoulder back. "Sit. Stay." Then she rushes from the room, heading for the kitchen.

Since that's where the paper towels are, I content myself with righting the bottle then picking up the papers, the tablet, and am reaching for the remote closest to me when she bustles back in fully clothed.

"Damn," I say under my breath, wondering if I can talk her into doctoring me naked.

Considering the intensity of her scowl when she spots me having moved, I don't think this is likely.

Even *if* her glowering at me like that is fucking adorable.

I suppose it also means that she likely won't appreciate me kissing it off her face.

"Here," she mutters, handing me a wad of paper towels. "Put pressure on your leg."

I do as she says and don't hide the fact that I'm watching her ass as she bends down and wipes up the beer.

"I hurt you again," she whispers. "I shouldn't have jumped into your arms."

Reaching forward, I snake an arm around her middle and haul her back to me.

"Ack!" she squeaks. "Careful."

"I'm fine, DeeDee." I kiss the hinge of her jaw. "And I promise you that you jumping into my arms was the best thing that's happened to me today." I smile at her, love that her face goes soft. "And in case it's not obvious, I wasn't feeling anything close to pain."

That soft only lasts a second.

Because the guilt charges back in.

"Nope," I interrupt when she opens her mouth, no doubt to apologize again. "I'll put some pressure on my leg. We'll get something to eat. And then it will all be good. I promise," I add when she begins to protest in earnest.

"But I need to call Doc," she whispers.

"I'm fine, sweetheart."

"I still need to call him."

"No phone calls." I tug her ponytail. "Because I'm *fine.*"

She surprises me by leaning in and slanting her mouth over mine.

"Fine or not," she says after she's kissed me long and deep and wet, leaving us both panting for air and me hard as a rock again (seriously, who's worried about the bleeding on my thigh when all of my blood is in my dick). "You're my player, and I need you back in commission ASAP. And," she adds before I can think about how that stings, to just be a player, and to remember that I'm also one that's become a problem because I can't get the new system down, "you're also a man who I care about, a man who I hurt again and I need to do something to get rid of all this guilt that's eating me up inside"—gentle fingers on my jaw, running through the strands of my beard—"so just shut up and quit bitching already."

The gentle fingers.

The soft tone.

The fact that I want to get rid of all her guilt...

No surprise it takes me a second to actually process her final words.

And by then, she's already reached into her pocket and pulled out her phone.

"Hey, Doc," she says into the microphone, "I need a favor."

And now *I'm* the one who's scowling.

TWENTY-ONE

Diana

"SHIT," Hudson mutters, muscle in his jaw flexing, eyes deliberately avoiding what Doc is doing to his thigh.

Meanwhile, I'm riveted.

Because those big, strong legs are clad in nothing aside from a tight pair of boxer briefs.

That have ridden up.

And are lovingly cupping a part of his body I've now become intimately familiar with.

Just the thought of all that power and strength (and, it has to be said, girth) has me shivering—

He hisses out a breath.

"Sorry," Doc says, his gaze thankfully focused on what he's doing.

And...I'm a dick.

Thinking about, well, about *Hudson's* dick while he's in pain.

Again.

Because of me.

Again.

I here, just sweeping into his life and creating chaos—fucking up his game with my new system, calling him into my office because I was pissed at Jason when our talk could have waited so we both didn't end up trapped there, not reacting quickly enough and getting him injured...and then reinjured because I ignored all my reservations and jumped, literally, his bones.

So yeah. I'm seriously a dick.

And a half.

He hisses again, but it's softer this time, and when I glance back at him, his gray eyes are on mine.

Seeing far too much.

"I'll go make something to eat," I blurt. "Doc, you hungry?"

"Nah, Dee. I'm meeting up with some friends after we're done here."

More things to be guilty for.

Pulling Doc in on his day off.

Just add it to the pile already sitting heavy on my shoulders.

"Right." I start to turn away, but a hand on mine stalls my movement.

"Don't," Hudson says quietly.

I slant my eyes at Doc, who's still working on Huddy's leg but hasn't missed the whole hand-on-hand action and is now doing that working while blatantly observing us.

Damn.

This shit will hit the back office.

And then the gossip will sail right into to the locker room.

And how the fuck am I supposed to look at the guys, to *lead* the guys when I'm boning one of the players?

"Don't," Hudson says again, even softer.

But I know he's seen that too.

Know he knows that whatever this is between us is a bomb ready to explode and fuck up both our lives.

I scowl.

His fingers lace through mine then squeeze lightly.

A silent *"Don't,"* this time.

My scowl deepens, then he hisses again, a bead of sweat forming on his temple.

More guilt adding itself to the pile on my shoulders.

Maybe that's why I don't pull my hand away.

Maybe that's why I hold on a little tighter.

Or maybe...it's that I just don't want to let go.

Of him.

Of this fantasy.

Of—

Hudson grunts.

"Sorry," Doc says. "But that should be the last one."

I wipe the bead of sweat off Huddy's temple, smothering the urge to lift my thumb to my mouth, to taste the salt and spice of him. Instead, I ask, "Is it supposed to hurt this much?"

"It is when dumb fucks decide they don't want pain injections."

My mouth falls open and I turn to Hudson. "Are you seriously that stubborn or just a fucking idiot?"

Doc snorts.

I glare at him. "You should have given him an injection anyway."

Doc lifts his gloved hands in surrender, surgical clamp thingie in one hand, a wicked looking needle in the other. "I've dealt with stubborn ass hockey players enough to know to pick my battles carefully"—a pointed look—"plus, I'm done."

I shift my glare to Hudson. "You ripped your stitches!"

"Only two of them."

"Two too many. You bled so much you soaked through your sweats."

A shrug. "I've bled more."

Doc snorts again as he bandages Hudson's leg.

"You've bled *more*?" I ask archly.

"You're the one who's memorized my injury list." A beat. "What do you think?"

I resist the urge to throttle him. Just barely. "I think that you've likely delayed yourself from playing for at least a few more days—" Now I slant an arch *look* at Doc.

Who wisely agrees.

"Coach is right," Doc says, peeling off his gloves. "The injury isn't serious, but it needs time to heal. So listen to reason, keep your ass on the couch for the next ten days—"

"Ten!" Hudson exclaims.

"Ten," Doc repeats. "Lucky it's early in the season and you won't miss too much, but you will if you push it again and I have to pull rank."

Hudson glares at Doc.

Then at me.

Then he closes his eyes.

Which, I have to admit, is an effective way to end a conversation.

Though, he doesn't let go of my hand and when I try to slide mine free, his hold tightens.

I sigh. Men.

Then I tug again, adding, "I'm going to walk Doc out."

His lids peel back and his gray eyes are full of emotions I can't read.

But he loosens his grip, allowing me to pull my fingers from his. Instantly, I miss the warmth, the strength, the...connection.

Shaking myself, I step back from the couch and follow Doc into the hallway.

His eyes are dancing and he opens his mouth.

"Don't start—"

He bumps my shoulder with his. "FYI, I know I'm biased because I work with the team, but I like Hudson a lot better than Jason."

"You only met Jason once."

"That was enough," he says dryly.

And I suppose it was.

"We broke up."

"I noticed." I frown and he flicks his gaze down at my naked ring finger. "I'm observant, Dee." Then his face gentles. "Are you okay?"

I shrug. "Turns out Jason is a cheating jerk."

"Asshole." Said with such intensity that I smile.

"Thanks for that."

"Just calling them as I see them." He reaches for the front door, twists the handle then looks back to grin at me, voice dropping. "Also, if you're thinking about testing the limits of the stitches again, give it at least twenty-four hours, yeah?"

"I—"

But I don't get more than that one syllable of what would be a false denial of my involvement in Hudson's stitches and/or testing their strength because he opens the door, steps outside, and shuts it behind him.

All before I can get another word out.

All before I can so much as *think* of another word to even say.

Men.

Sighing, I just flick the lock and walk back into the living room...

Where Hudson isn't.

"What the fuck?" I grind out, whipping around, searching for a six-foot-two, two-hundred-fifteen pound hockey player who's suddenly disappeared into a puff of smoke.

After tearing his stitches.

After Doc told him to spend the next ten days on the fucking *couch*.

"Hudson?"

No answer.

"Hudson!"

I sweep into the kitchen, full of piss and vinegar and ready to give the big, stubborn hockey player a piece of my mind.

Then I hear it.

The sound of a toilet flushing, followed by a sink turning on.

A door opens, and Hudson limps out, mouth curving up on one side. "You rang?"

"You're supposed to be resting," I say, even though I know it's ridiculous because it's not like he was standing here in the kitchen, dancing a jig. He was using the bathroom.

"Don't be grumpy, DeeDee," he says, smiling as he tugs my ponytail, not looking at all like the man who was in pain earlier as Doc stitched him up without pain relief. "Now, do you want Chinese or Mexican for dinner?"

TWENTY-TWO

Hudson

TURNS out that Diana loves Mexican food, so I got to show her one of my favorite places.

Well, by *show* I mean I ordered delivery and we both ate our body weight in chips and salsa and chicken and potato enchiladas with green chili sauce and rice.

"This may be the best food I've ever had," she says through a bite of enchilada.

I shove another chip into my mouth and nod in agreement. "Muriel's is the absolute best," I say. "I eat there far too often."

"I can see why." Her mouth quirks up after she chews and swallows. "And I can also foresee many a delivery order in my future."

Eventually, our plates are empty and the chips are eaten and we settle back onto the couch—because she demanded that I make the order, and eat, while sitting my ass down on the cushions—and quiet descends.

This isn't the quiet of shoveling food in our mouths because it's delicious and we're starving.

This isn't the easy silence of eating and watching a Breakers game on my TV.

This is...

Dinner is over and the game is on intermission and I'm fine and...

She's still here.

She could go.

I'm good.

But she's here, and I don't know how to proceed—or even if we *should* proceed. Was this a one-off? Or are we...doing this?

And, if so, what is *this*?

Player and coach time?

Definitely not.

Friends with benefits?

Sort of. But also...no.

Yeah, we've done the sex and we're hanging out, eating together, watching a game on TV.

But it's not just that.

She's here in my house. On my couch. We're spending time together. We're eating together. Again. We're talking (well, except for right now). We're fucking explosive in bed. She held my goddamned hand while I was in the hospital, while Doc stitched me up, stepped in to create a barrier between me and my parents and brought me to her house to keep me safe.

That's not nothing.

It's *something*.

Something that means something.

And great, now I sound like an idiotic life coach on social media.

The point is...

Fuck it.

I'm going to do this—take what she's giving me. The time, the space, the touching, the eating together, the talking (and also, the silence). I'm going take it all, and if I can manage it, I'm going to figure out how to keep her.

Forever.

I just...need to figure out what I should say next.

Especially since the silence has now grown to epic proportions.

I mentally groan then open my mouth, not sure what I'm going to say, just certain that at some point I'm going to have to say *something*, idiotic life coach vibes or not.

But I don't get the chance—or maybe it's more like I'm saved by the bell, er, phone so I don't *have* to.

Dee's cell rings.

And instead of answering it, she freezes.

Right.

I don't like that. Not at fucking all.

"What's wrong?"

She shakes herself. I watch her literally shake off whatever had stopped her from immediately reaching for her phone. Then she flashes a smile at me, snags her cell off the table, tossing a blatant lie across the cushions of the couch when she says, "Nothing's wrong," as she looks at the screen.

And hits the button on the side to silence the call.

"Nothing's wrong," I reply dryly. "Except that you're screening your calls?"

A flippant toss of her hair. "Don't we all do that? The robo-calling has been out of control lately."

She's not wrong.

But a robo-call doesn't explain the expression—worry mixed with annoyance—that came on her face before the afore-mentioned screening.

So, I push it. "Want to give me the truth, DeeDee?"

"No," she mutters. "I want to enjoy my belly full of delicious Mexican food then watch the last period of the Breakers game before I go home and pass out, because we've had a reprieve for a few days but the Gold are letting us use their practice facility starting tomorrow and that means I have work to do—it means we *all* have work to do," she adds pointedly, eyes flicking to the tablet and stack of papers on the table.

"You're right," I say and watch relief seep into her frame, her shoulders relaxing, her expression smoothing out. "You're also full of shit."

That relief disappears in a flash, her jaw tightening, her eyes flashing with annoyance.

"If you want to talk about being full of shit," she says. "Why is it that you've clearly been studying the drills"—another nod at the well-worn papers, the tablet next to them—"and yet when you get out on the ice, it's like you've never been on a rink before?"

I grind my teeth together and look away.

"Exactly," she murmurs.

"I'm going to get it down," I mutter. "I just—"

Fuck.

"You just what?"

"I'm going to get another beer." I push up from the couch.

And manage to stay on my feet for all of two seconds before she's grabbing my arm and hauling me back down. "If you really want another beer," she says, "I'll get it. But considering that yours is still full and you're using grabbing another one as a diversion tactic then I think you can just sit there, drink it, and tell me what's really going on."

"Nothing—"

"Not nothing."

Okay seriously.

How had I lost control of this conversation so fucking quickly?

One second, I'm trying to sort out why she's acting so cagey.

The next, she wants me to spill my guts about something I have absolutely no intention of sharing.

Something I make clear by clenching my jaw and looking away from those gorgeous green eyes of hers.

The silence stretches between us—long and taut and intense.

Then she sighs, shakes her head...and reaches for the tablet. "All right," she says. "Then let's go over this together." I stiffen, start to get up, but I barely move an inch before she's leaning against my side, her hand with the tablet moving in front of me, her arm pressing into my abdomen.

Keeping me in place.

And I can't even enjoy the plush pillowing of her tits against my torso because this is literally my worst fucking nightmare.

"Now," she says, tapping the screen to wake it up. "What's your passcode?"

"Wh-what?" I rasp.

"Your passcode, Huddy." A flick of her eyes to mine. "Give it to me."

"4-2-5-9," I recite robotically, dread growing as she types the numbers in and the tablet unlocks.

"Right," she says, navigating to the team's app, sounding positively gleeful. Because she loves this shit. Because she works hard. Because this is part of the legacy she wants to build. "I think it's probably easiest if we start at the beginning, figure out the disconnect and then we'll be right as rain."

We'll.

Right.

She'll be right as rain.

I'll be fucked.

"I'm tired," I say. "We should do this another time."

"It won't take long." She starts tapping at the screen, pulling up a page with all those fucking X's and O's.

And just like before they start moving.

And just like before they don't make even the slightest bit of sense.

And just like before I *know* I need to get the fuck out of here.

"I can't do this right now," I mutter, looking away from the tablet. "I'm too—"

"Just look," she says, tracing a pattern that dissolves into a jumble of disjointed lines and letters. It swirls and moves, switches places just when I think I've pinned it, disappearing and reappearing at the least opportune times. "If we shift a player here"—a tap—"instead of here then it's basically what you're used to except with a bit more flexibility and freedom. You see?"

I grit my teeth together and nod, temple throbbing as I try to get that to stick. "Yeah," I rasp.

"And so if then someone goes here—"

More throbbing. More jumbling of arrows and letters.

"—we'll free up some space here, yeah?"

"Yeah," I lie, frustration and fear eating me up inside.

"So where should this player"—another tap—"go?"

I still.

She shifts, glancing up at me expectantly.

Fuck.

"Here?" I rasp, picking a spot at random since I don't have a fucking clue.

Because my fucking brain is broken.

Her pause in response tells me enough.

That was wrong.

And her disappointment is palpable.

"No," she says after a moment. "If they go *here* then where should *you* go?"

Spoken louder and slower than before. As though I just heard her wrong.

"I don't think—"

She sighs. "Just try?"

Shame bubbles up, mixing with the frustration and with... anger.

Because why am I like this?

But I still lift a finger and point.

Her sigh this time is displeased and razor sharp and—

Something snaps inside me.

TWENTY-THREE

Diana

ONE MOMENT, I'm tapping the screen of the tablet and trying to keep the frustration out of my tone—

The next he's on his feet.

I lurch forward, reaching to tug him back down next to me. "Your leg—"

"Fuck my leg!" he snaps, jerking out of range and shoving a hand through his hair so hard that I worry he'll rip the locks from his scalp. "It's my fucking brain that doesn't work!"

And then he's storming out of the room, his limp barely evident in his quick, furious strides.

I'm torn between shock and annoyance.

Then settle on annoyance.

Because that man better not tear those fucking stitches—I'll never hear the end of it from Doc...and also, maybe I don't want to see him bleeding again.

Something that has my annoyance fading.

And transforming into concern.

Because his reaction isn't like Huddy. Not at all.

"Dammit," I whisper, shoving up to standing and following the wake of his anger out into the back yard.

He's pacing on the porch, one hand clenched in his hair, the other fisted at his side.

Terrorizing those poor sutures.

"You need to cool off and sit down," I order.

His head snaps up and the cold look in his eyes has me bracing.

Here it is.

The part where they turn mean.

It's always there in men, bubbling under the surface, waiting for the most opportune time to explode out and wound me.

I clutch at my armor, knowing that no matter how protected I am, this man is going to have a unique ability to wound me—so much so that I should probably turn and walk the hell out of this house.

Right fucking now.

But something else has me rooted in place.

Almost *hoping* this man will do it. That he'll hurt me so irrevocably I won't have all these complicated feelings, and I'll be able to put him back into the box in my mind for a player on my roster (and *only* a player on my roster) and then everything will go back to normal.

Except, that's not what happens.

Instead of lashing out, he releases his hair, drops his hand to his side, and when his words come they're not sharp, not designed to wound.

They're even.

Almost...pleading.

What the fuck?

"You should go home," he says. "If you leave now you won't

miss the start of the third period." Because we live just blocks apart and the walk won't take me long. "That way we can both get some rest."

Seriously. What the actual fuck?

I shift closer to this man...inside *and* out.

It's dangerous, more complicated, but I can't find it in me to care.

Because his tone isn't sharp, isn't mean.

Because my armor isn't needed.

Because...there's real fear in his eyes.

And because I fucking hate that.

"I promise to not give up on you," I say and take another step toward him when he jerks, gray eyes locking with mine, proving to me that I'm not wrong. There's fear inside of him—a fuck ton of it. "We can work through whatever mental block you have and with a little patience..."

My words trail off because I have the distinct notion that I've said completely the wrong thing.

Now both of his hands are clenched into fists.

And I'm back to clutching at armor, to bracing, to wishing, to hoping but knowing that's going to come back to bite me.

He shakes his head sharply.

Then exhales.

"Patience won't do a fucking thing, DeeDee." A beat. "And it sure as fuck won't fix me. Just go home, yeah?" With that, he turns and moves deeper into the back yard, not stopping until he's by a huge oak tree. There he rests a palm on its trunk and his shoulders slump, his chin dropping toward his chest.

It's my fucking brain that doesn't work!

Patience won't fix him.

The meeting in my office and that look in his eyes—no, I realize now, the *shame* in the stormy gray depths.

I hadn't recognized the emotion for what it was.

Because it was so damned far from anything I was possibly expecting. It wouldn't have even been on my top one hundred list of reasons why Hudson wasn't getting with the program.

I thought...late nights getting drunk with the boys or wild times with women or too much time on the golf course—

I didn't think this.

Whatever *this* is.

And maybe I'm weak, maybe I'm just a smidgen of a coward...

But I seriously consider turning on my heel and leaving, walking right out of the house and pretending that I haven't glimpsed whatever it is that I just glimpsed, and making it home in time to watch the final period of the Breakers game.

I need a man—especially one who brings complications to every level of my life—like I need a hole in my head.

I just moved to a new city.

Started a new job.

Broke up with my fiancé.

I'm not equipped for this.

Only even as my weight shifts and I start to turn, I find that I can't actually make myself rotate.

Instead, my feet carry me across the porch and down the steps and...across the lawn.

And I don't stop until I make it over to Hudson.

Carefully, I lay my hand on the small of his back.

He jumps but doesn't move away, and that gives me the courage to keep pushing forward. I flatten my palm, slide it with me as I shift around him, ducking under his arm and putting myself between him and the trunk of the tree.

He doesn't move.

If anything, he's gone impossibly still.

"Will you..." I nibble the inside of my cheek. "Will you talk to me?"

His eyes close and a curl of disappointment winds through me when he doesn't speak, when the silence seems to stretch for an impossibly long time.

"Hudson?" I whisper.

Still nothing.

Damn.

I smooth my hand up his chest, wrapping it around the side of his neck and rising on tiptoe. My front is pressed fully to his, my lips at his ear when I murmur, "Please, honey?"

He shudders, his free hand dropping to my hip, clenching so tightly it's riding that line between pleasure and pain.

But I know he's not trying to hurt me.

I know he's hanging on, and just barely.

And maybe it's mercenary, maybe it's a dick move.

But I know now's the time to push for answers.

So I do.

"Will you tell me?"

A long moment of quiet and then he shudders again, the hand at my hip shifting, sliding around my waist and drawing me to him, clutching me to him, holding me so tightly I'm not sure I can breathe.

Or maybe it's because of what he says next.

"I've tried, DeeDee," he whispers and the agony in his words slices me deep. "I've spent hours with the packet you put together, with the drills, with the videos and explanations and..." He buries his head in my throat.

"And what, baby?" I press.

"And I can't get it to stick in my head. Words are hard but symbols and numbers are harder. They're always moving or changing and every time I sit down thinking this is the time I'm going to get it to make sense, to put all the pieces together, I swear, it's like my brain is fucking with me. One second, a circle will look like a circle and the next it's a fucking X or an arrow or it's floating on the page and I don't know if it's my eyes or my mind or if where it's at is where it's supposed to be or if my brain has shifted it and made it seem like a different shape." He sucks in a breath as I process that, as *my* mind struggles to comprehend and put the pieces together. "I was never all that good in school, but I could usually fake my way through it, do well enough to pass or work it so my teachers passed me anyway. And then I went straight into the league after I graduated so I didn't have to worry about college. But this..." Another shuddering exhale. "It's like the harder I try, the worse it gets... until I'm seeing nothing except a jumble of lines a-and—"

His voice cracks.

I hold him tighter.

"I'm broken," he rasps. "My brain is so fucked that I know —fucking *know*—that I'll never get the system down, so—" He pulls back and the agony on his face slices right through me. "So you might as well get me off the roster now before I fuck things up further."

I rack my brain for how to handle this.

But there's nothing in my coach's handbook for the best course of action on how to handle a player who thinks I should drop him off my roster because he's trying so hard enough he's tormenting himself over failing.

So...I have to follow my instincts.

I draw him back to me, hold him close and tight for a long, long time.

Until he's no longer trembling.

"In school," I whisper, "did they ever diagnose you with anything?"

He lifts his head. "No. Why?"

I cup his jaw and say, "Because I think I know *exactly* who to call."

TWENTY-FOUR

Hudson

"I THINK *I know exactly who to call.*"

That's what she said.

And that's what she did—stepping away from me, pulling out her phone, and then making that call.

Then two more.

And now, less than an hour later, I have an enemy hockey player on my back porch, along with his pretty, shy wife, Kailey.

Connor Smith is a veteran defenseman in the league and was recently traded to the Grizzlies.

Which means he's local.

And the Eagles have to play against his big, old, but still remarkably agile for a man nearing retirement's ass eight times this season.

I much prefer him on the opposite coast with the Breakers, only having to deal with him on the ice twice throughout the year.

"Your back yard is the shit!" he says—or really, yells, because based on the ten minutes he's been in my house, the man seems to only have one volume and that's yelling. The worthiness of my back yard declared (loudly), he reclines in his —*my*—chair, the wood creaking dangerously beneath his big ass body.

I'm no slouch in the muscle department, but my chairs definitely don't protest that much when I drop into them.

Clearly I have some more work to do in the weight room.

Especially since we have a game coming up against the Grizzlies.

Which I may or may not be cleared to play in.

Fuck.

This shit sucks.

Grumpy, but knowing it's less to do with my injury and more to do with the reason that Smitty is here, I turn my focus out at the grass, the mature trees, the flowering bushes broken up by a meandering path that leads to a gazebo that houses my hot tub.

I hate that he's here.

Not because I don't like him—I don't know him well but from what I've heard through the league's gossip pipeline, he's a nice guy who's devoted to his team and wife. Something that's supported by the fact that he's here, that he's in my house, having dropped everything because Dee made a call.

I just...hate that he's here.

That he *has* to be here.

I hate that Diana called in some favors from her previous coaching positions—assisting the Breakers and before that having positions on the support staff with the Grizzlies, the Gold, and the Rush. She's worked hard to get where she is.

And now she's pulling strings for me because my brain doesn't work right.

Fuck.

I clench my beer bottle.

"That a hot tub?" Smitty asks (still loudly).

"Yup," I mutter.

"Damn," he says and glances at his wife. "We need to get one of those." Back to me. "You put some good shit together back here."

"Thanks," I say, even though I had not one thing to do with the design of the yard or picking out the hot tub. It came this way when I bought it, along with the gardener in charge of upkeep. I just cut a check once a month.

I don't tell Smitty that though.

I just scowl at my beer then lift it to my lips, taking a long sip, hoping the alcohol will soften the sharp edges of my shame.

I want to think that maybe this will help.

But I'm fucking scared to be hopeful when I've had so many years of *nothing* helping.

Of knowing I'm no good, that I'm broken.

That I'm dumb.

So while there's a small sliver of hope this will be different, the rest of me is...

Resigned.

Knowing this will be the same fucking shit.

And now it won't only be me who's disappointed. DeeDee—

"Beer's good shit," Smitty says (spoiler, it's loud), lifting his beer and holding it out, the bottom angled toward me.

Waiting for me to tap my bottle against his.

To cheers this fucked-up meeting of minds.

Christ.

My temple throbs.

But Dee is sitting on the other side of the table, her expression a mix of worry and hope, and when she nods encouragingly at me, I know I have to try to make this work.

I have to try.

"It's good," I agree, acknowledging the cheers, the *clink* of our bottles soft amongst the sounds of early evening—wind rustling, birds chirping, the occasional car driving by. And I'm not lying. The beer is from a local brewery near Jean-Michel's winery, Oak Ridge Vineyards, and we—King, Rome, West, Rhodes, Cam, and I—are all obsessed. It's more than good. It's fucking delicious.

But I don't taste it tonight, not in the least.

Because my stomach is in knots.

Silence falls, but it doesn't last—hell, it doesn't stand a chance, not with Smitty here.

"Heard you guys saw some action in the quake."

I pause, set my beer on the table. "It's not like it was war. It was twenty-something seconds of shaking and a couple of hours of chilling."

"Because you were trapped in an office at the team's practice facility," he says dryly, emphasizing the *trapped*.

I shrug. "Plenty of people had it worse."

"That why you have stitches on your leg and Coach Dee just gave you pain killers and antibiotics to take?"

I scowl. "I'll be good in ten days."

Smitty laughs and it's so loud it makes the rest of us jump—well, not Kailey, but she's clearly used to the man's crazy since she just pats her husband's leg and glances at Diana, saying pointedly, "Would you mind helping me take some pics of those flowers in the back planter bed? My friend Lexi would love them."

She doesn't need help taking the pictures.

She's trying to give us—Smitty and me—space to talk.

I smile despite myself—Kailey is quiet and shy, but apparently capable of handling hockey players (grumpy or not)—and some of the tension leaves my gut when Smitty's face goes soft and he catches her hand, squeezing it before she disappears deep into the yard with Dee.

"Plant scouting?" I ask dryly even as I don't doubt that Lexi —the woman who's married to the Breakers' GM, Luc Masterson—would love to get pictures of my flowers.

The yearly plant challenge the Breakers compete in was something she dreamed up and it's famous in the league's circles. Everyone on the roster receives a plant during the beginning of the season, and the player who keeps it alive the longest wins a prize.

Us hockey players are all competitive fucks, so it's no surprise the battle is intense for whatever mysterious prize the winner receives.

But seriously, thank God we're not stuck doing that shit on the Eagles.

I'd much rather climb a thousand steps covered in glass barefoot than be responsible for caring for a plant for an entire season.

Though I guess I do—the climbing steps (minus the barefoot and glass parts)—with Rome before every game and practice.

So, I guess we all have our things.

And maybe that's why when Smitty agrees, "yup," then immediately changes the subject to why Dee called him here tonight, I don't bristle, don't let my pride take over and push him away.

"You know I'm dyslexic?" he says.

"Yeah," I tell him. "You started that charity, right?"

A nod. "The reason I brought it up is because Dee says—"

"I'm not dyslexic," I tell him. "I was tested as a kid, and the specialists said I wasn't."

"I'm not claiming to be an expert." He leans back in the chair, propping his feet up on the railing. "But testing and interventions have come a long way since we were kids."

"I don't doubt you're right. But..." I sigh. "The letters don't reverse on me like that."

"They move?" he asks. "Dance their fucking asses across the page?"

My heart thumps hard and I glance over at him and nod. "Yeah."

"What about their shapes? They get cut off or change, like you never know if it's a B or a D?"

Every cell in my body freezes. "Yeah," I rasp.

"Or sometimes everything on the page jumbles? Like the words and symbols have all compressed on top of one another into one giant letter blob?"

My mouth drops open. "How'd you—?"

He sets his beer on the table, leans toward me, voice quiet for the first time. "I've lived it."

I inhale, hating the hope welling up, but knowing I need to ask. "Are you—?"

"Cured?" He shakes his head.

The hope inside me implodes.

And fuck, that hurts.

"But," he says and hope comes back in a nearly as painful rush, "there are all these fonts that help and programs and specialists. There are resources and research out there that we didn't have as kids. And after working with them, I can do what I never thought I could—I can pick up a book and read something. And I can *enjoy* it."

My throat tightens.

Because I can read, of course I can.

But it's never been enjoyable.

Fucking never.

A struggle, yes. A battle with my own brain just to get some basic comprehension, absolutely.

But to just enjoy it?

That's never been something I even considered remotely possible.

"Smitty," I whisper and fuck if my voice isn't tight, if my eyes don't sting.

"I know," he whispers back, and the gleam in his brown eyes tells me he does. "You want that?"

I nod. "Yeah."

"It'll take work."

"I'm not afraid of hard work."

"Yeah, with that one at the helm"—his mouth turns up into a dry smile as he jerks his chin at Dee—"I know you aren't."

"She's not work." I turn, glare at him. "She's a fucking gift, and I don't care what fancy shit you can bring to the table to help me sort out my brain, I will knock your ass out if you talk about her like that again."

Smitty's expression is full of thunderclouds.

Then the storm clears and he smiles a big, toothy grin.

"You'll do, Blackwood. You'll just do."

TWENTY-FIVE

Diana

KAILEY IS SWEET.

And thoughtful.

And definitely has a high emotional IQ.

She did take pics of the plants, but it was the perfectly timed gesture to get us away from the boys...because just a couple of minutes later Smitty and Huddy were talking.

Actually talking.

Not a clipped-out couple of words from Hudson as I sat on the sidelines, wanting to interject—desperate to, really, in order to make the conversation go more smoothly—but knowing I already overstepped.

And that I did it huge.

So...sitting there like an idiot, dying a slow death at the discomfort of the stilted conversation.

Then Kailey saved the day by pulling me away to look at plants.

She didn't do it by playing coy either—we all knew what she was doing. Roping me into giving the boys privacy to talk, but she did it in such an effortless way that I kind of want to find a way to make her part of the Eagles organization.

Her sneaky, quiet strength could be an asset.

Though, I think, as I glance up at Hudson and Smitty, where they're now talking beside a huge SUV that can fit the oversized hockey player properly, I think she's probably already been claimed by the Grizzlies.

And the Breakers.

Too bad our paths didn't overlap when I worked there.

I could have snagged her early and had her all to myself.

Now I'll have to contend with being hockey rivals.

Ugh.

She glances up at me, lips curving at the edges. "That's an intense expression."

"I'm thinking I wish we met when I was still working for the Breakers."

"Why's that?" she asks, brows drawing together.

"Then I could have poached you and gotten you to come work with me at the Eagles."

Her mouth twitches. "I work with lots of teams."

"I don't mean just your program"—Kailey works with the scouting divisions of several NHL teams because she's excellent at coordinating data and making it go as far as possible—"I mean your instincts," I say, leaning back against one of the pillars on Hudson's front porch. "I was at a loss," I whisper, slanting another gaze at the guys. "I knew I should say something but I froze. You didn't. You took care of him, and you did it in a way that was gentle." I shake my head. "I couldn't have done that."

I just don't have that in me.

"You're sweet to say that, but—"

"But nothing," I say firmly, jerking my chin at the guys. "You helped them connect. You've helped *him*."

She touches my arm. "And you wouldn't have had me here *to* help if you hadn't had the foresight—or courage—to make those calls."

"Kailey," I warn.

Her mouth quirks. "Diana," she warns back. Then leans in, voice dropping. "Want to hear a fun fact? One I think you are—or are *going* to become—intimately familiar with?"

Amusement in my belly. "What's that?"

"In order to deal with a stubborn hockey player, you have to be a little ballsy."

I snort.

"Okay," she corrects. "Or a *lot* ballsy."

"I think you forgot to add stubborn to the list."

She winks. "That too."

We both look at each other...

Then bust up laughing.

"Did we just become friends?" I ask when we've regained control.

"Better that than hockey enemies." A wink.

"If I can coax you into working for the Eagles, we wouldn't be enemies."

"No Eagles."

But it's not Kailey speaking.

It's Smitty.

Hudson chuckles softly, wrapping an arm around my middle and drawing me back against his chest. The warmth of him, the *strength* of him, the gentle possessiveness with which he holds me...it's my perfect blend of kryptonite.

"What was so funny?" he asks, his words brushing against my ear.

I grin up at him. "Stubborn hockey players."

Smitty glances at Huddy's arm around my middle then up at me, and I don't miss the look of approval rippling across his face. And I definitely can't miss his booming smart ass remark—

"I guess my matchmaking prowess isn't needed on the Eagles."

"That's real disappointment in his tone," Kailey stage whispers.

"It is!" He throws up his hands. "I'm a killer matchmaker. Those Breakers boys never saw me coming, and maybe Aiden doesn't need my help, considering he's found himself a good one in Luna, but there are a metric ton of single dudes on the Grizzlies who need my help!"

My lips twitch but when I glance up at Hudson, I see that being upright for an extended period of time along with having walked from the back yard are taking their toll.

"We should get you inside," I murmur.

Kailey's picked up on Hudson fading too. "Yeah, we should let you two call it a night," she says, looping her arm through Smitty's and smiling up at her husband. "So let's save espousing on your matchmaking skills until the next time we get together." She pats his arm then guides him back down the steps, pausing on the walkway and glancing back over her shoulder. "And there will be a next time."

Not a question.

A statement.

"Who's the stubborn one now?" I tease.

She winks again, and then they take off toward the SUV.

Huddy and I watch them get in, Smitty grumbling loudly about there being some unknown matchmaker who specializes in helping hockey players find love who lives up in Tahoe and is "intruding on my territory!"

I snort because that's ridiculous.

"What is it?" Hudson asks.

"A matchmaker." I roll my eyes. "You guys don't need matchmaking help—you get enough women as it is."

"*I* don't," he says.

I deliberately point my gaze down at his arm, still snaked around my waist. "You don't?"

He laughs and it's beautiful. Then he presses his lips to my jaw. "I didn't until you," he whispers. "Or I don't remember any other women anyway."

I giggle despite myself. "Such a handsome liar," I accuse lightly, turning in the circle of his arm and swatting him across the chest.

"Rude," he says, brushing his nose along mine.

"Nope." I pop the p. "The truth isn't rude."

He grins, and fuck, but his smile hits me deeply. Mostly because I know there's no chance at keeping my distance. Not when he put himself between me and the collapsing ceiling, not when he showed me who he is, not when he shared something so deeply personal and painful with me—

He gently runs his fingers through the ends of my hair.

And not when he does things like that.

Soft touches, gentle touches, holding me close like I'm precious.

It's dumb. It could be career-ending.

But I know, without a doubt, that I need to see where this goes. "I thought you might be mad," I whisper.

His expression goes even softer. "For what, baby?"

"For overstepping," I say. "For telling Smitty and bringing him here and—"

He presses a finger to my lips, cutting off the flow of words. "Don't you understand?" he whispers.

"Understand what?" I ask against his finger.

"Don't you understand that you brought me a gift? One I never thought I'd have?"

"But what if..." I nibble on the inside of my cheek.

"What if what, DeeDee?"

I exhale softly. "What if it doesn't help?"

Gentle gray eyes. "If it doesn't help, I'm no worse off. But" —he tucks a strand of my hair behind my ear—"I think it's going to help, sweetheart. I *feel* it. The way Smitty was talking, the things he was saying...it's like the pieces are finally coming together, finally making sense. I might—" He breaks off then exhales quietly. "I might be able to have a different life, and just having the chance to try for that?" His gaze holds mine. "I'm so thankful you helped me get there."

The flurry of emotions in his eyes are so intense that my heart spasms.

I wrap my arms around him, hug him tightly. "I'm glad you're not mad."

He smooths a hand down my back. "Never."

I keep hugging him but I can't resist lightening the mood, can't resist saying, "Because you're being so sweet, I'm not going to hold that lie against you."

He weaves his hand in my hair again, this time tugging my head back. "What are you talking about?"

"I'm definitely going to make you mad, Huddy."

He's still. Then he grins. "Let's go inside."

And he doesn't delay, drawing me into the house, slamming and locking the door, pinning me back against the wooden panel.

His lips find mine, his hand drags my shirt up, pressing against the bare skin of my back.

And sweet baby Jesus, the man can kiss.

It's hot. It's wet. It's deep and has plenty of tongue—so

much tongue that I almost forget what I promised myself earlier.

So much that it takes every bit of control I possess in order to catch his hand when he slips his fingertips beneath the waistband of my sweats, to pull them free. "No," I say.

"Right," he mutters. "The window on the door." He starts to tug me down the hall. "Bedroom."

The bedroom sounds perfect.

It's exactly where I want to spend the next six hours.

Only...he's limping.

His leg.

The fucking stitches.

I dig in my feet, draw him to a halt—not an easy proposition when he doesn't want to be halted. "No," I say again, tugging firmly, getting him to stop, to look at me. "Your leg."

"It's fine."

Those gray eyes blazing with need.

Calling to the same need boiling through my veins.

It would be so easy to give in.

But...I can't hurt him again.

"No, honey," I say when he moves again. "I *can't*."

He stills.

"Not until your leg is healed," I whisper. "Please don't make me the one responsible for hurting you—"

"It would be my decision—"

"Please, Hudson."

He holds my eyes for a long moment.

Then he sighs. "Okay, sweetheart."

"Okay?" I expected more fight.

Expected him to push, to demand.

Instead...he gives.

And I...

Fall.

Which is probably why when he asks, "But do something for me?" I reply with, "Anything."

And when he says, "Sleep—*just sleep*—next to me tonight?" all I can do is nod my head.

And help him up the stairs to his bedroom.

TWENTY-SIX

Hudson

I HAVEN'T BEEN this horny since I was a teenager.

No.

That's a fucking lie.

I've spent more time with a hard-on over the last five days than I ever did as a teenager.

One night sleeping next to Dee, holding her close but abiding by that soft "please" to wait to take things further—and without the side of bloodshed—was the most exquisite form of torture.

But I couldn't push her, not only because she asked me to stop, but also because fucking up the stitches on my leg would further hurt my recovery. And maybe also because she asked so sweetly...and also because...we needed to slow the fuck down.

The previous few days were intense.

The quake, being trapped together, the hospital, that scene with my parents (who no surprise to me, have only called once since I put them in the car and haven't bothered to reply to most of my update texts aside from the occasional thumbs up), Ernest walking in on us, Jean-Michel on my doorstep, and the best fucking sex of my life...that *had* ended with a side of blood-shed. Add in sharing—oh, no big deal—only my deepest, most shameful secret, her bringing in Smitty, and then my actually talking with Smitty and agreeing to meet with his team of specialists...

Not to mention the fact that she finally sees me.

Actually fucking *sees* me.

So yeah, we'd needed to slow down.

I needed to slow down.

So we did.

That night, we made our way up to bed, Dee borrowed an unopened toothbrush then changed into of my tees—and seeing her in my shirt had me right back in hard-on zone. Something I'd ignored—then continued to ignore as she climbed into my bed next to me, I put the Breakers game on TV, and...

We talked.

About hockey and the team, about her Grams and how she got into coaching.

About stupid shit, like the contestants from *Love Island* (another reality show she's obsessed with) and important shit, like favorite foods and restaurants, colors and places to visit.

A horizontal date that didn't end up with us getting naked.

But was somehow even better than that because it ended when she fell asleep in my arms.

It was...the single best night of my life.

Yet somehow the next few days are even better.

My leg doesn't ache as much—something that's helped by the fact that I don't tear any additional stitches. And DeeDee isn't avoiding me. In fact, she goes to her house, packs a bag to stay over and hangs out and works while I take some Zoom meetings with Smitty's specialists.

I need to go see them in person—and several appointments are currently on the books—but for the first time in my life... okay, well, the *second* since the talk with Smitty made me feel the same way, I don't feel broken.

There are other people whose brains work like mine.

In fact, I'm so *not* alone that nothing I tell the specialists seems to take them by surprise.

Which is both a relief and infuriating. Why have I spent so damned long thinking I'm defective? Why have I let people, let my parents, convince me of that fact?

And why have I wasted so much time hiding from the fucking truth, from getting help?

It makes me want to punch something.

Or really, it makes me want to fuck someone...so long as that someone is Dee.

Unfortunately, I made her a promise.

Lucky for me that promise doesn't stop me from kissing her or touching her or getting both of us naked. It's just that when things start to get really good, she stops us.

Which means *I* stop us.

The day after our horizontal date, the team has practice. I have a check-in with Doc, some evaluations on my brain shit (what Smitty calls it and frankly, it's an apt description), and then Dee comes back over to my place with a huge pizza and a six-pack of beer.

And while we watch hockey, drink beers, and down the slices of pepperoni, black olive, and spicy honey pizza, I have a hard-on. One that certainly doesn't go away once all that devouring of food and drink turns into devouring Dee.

Or *wanting* to.

Because as much as I'm desperate to have every part of her again, she's set a boundary. I won't blow past that.

I'm not that kind of man.

So when kissing becomes heavy petting and heavy petting means my fingers are drifting down her naked skin and heading straight for that slick, wet cunt, I hit the brakes, get us dressed, and walk her to her car—because she needs to fly out with the team early the next morning.

I scowl as she drives off, missing her already.

Because I'm obsessed.

And I can't even summon a single damn about my ongoing obsession.

Especially since DeeDee FaceTimes me when she gets home and lets me watch her get ready for bed. And then Face-Times me again after the game where we partake in some seriously hot FaceTime foreplay.

More hard-ons.

Along with a side of blue balls.

I'm so going to fuck her in the nightgown she wore, a nightgown she calls "cute." I don't know who in their right mind can think the slinky silky short-as-fuck nightie is merely "cute," but I'm going to disabuse her of that notion at the first opportunity.

And now, as I drive to her place, thinking about that slinky, silky, short nightie, another five days of abstinence feels like a goddamned eternity.

The team has the day off tomorrow and I'm talking my way into her bed, even if it's just to sleep again.

I need her next to me.

I need to feel her, smell her, kiss her.

Touch her.

I pull into her driveway, turn off my car, then reach into the back seat and snag my overnight bag.

Wishful thinking? Maybe.

But I *am* planning on talking my way into her bed.

I pop the door and climb out, careful to not put too much weight on my leg.

Then I make my way up the path leading to her porch.

Before I get there, the overhead light flicks on and the door is drawn inward.

And suddenly, the sexy, sweet, smart-as-a-whip woman is in the opening, leaning back against the frame, arms crossed, a sinful smile on her lips.

One that widens when her gaze drifts down, presumably to the bag I'm holding tightly in one hand. "What's that?"

I lean down and kiss her.

It's been two days since I've seen her, two days since I've tasted her.

So, I don't waste any time.

I taste that smile...and then her moan as she pushes off the frame and presses herself against me, wraps her arms around my shoulders. I want to scoop her up, to carry her inside.

But...

My fucking leg.

So, I have to content myself with hauling her close and walking us into the house, doing it not lifting my mouth, not pulling away.

Lush curves.

Soft lips.

Moans vibrating along my tongue and down my throat and—

Yup.

I'm hard again.

Something I know Dee feels when she arches against me, her pelvis brushing mine, and she stills. Her head lifts, lips curving, words silky smooth as she asks, "And what's *that* I feel?"

"Smart ass," I mutter, slamming and locking the door.

"No," she says, leaning to the side, gaze sliding down to *my* ass. "That's you. You're smart." A beat. "And because hockey players have the best asses."

"Um."

She rises on tiptoe, her front pressed to mine. "The *best*." Then she drops back to her heels, and smile deepening, she snags my bag from my hand.

"The freaking best."

And then she turns for the kitchen.

And I follow her.

Because I would—or maybe I already have—follow her into hell and back.

TWENTY-SEVEN

Diana

"I DIDN'T KNOW you could cook," I say softly, moving into the kitchen, the delicious smells of whatever is in the pan he's stirring on the stove filling the air.

He glances over his shoulder, mouth curving, and when I get close, he wraps his arm around my middle, drawing me against his side. "It's less cooking and more...throwing shit in a pan and hoping for the best," he says, lips pressed to my temple.

"Liar," I say, shifting closer and snagging one of the carefully trimmed green beans I watched him cut while I was on the phone and pop it into my mouth, instantly moaning at the explosion of flavor.

"Not a liar," he says, lightly swatting my hand with the spoon. "You saw my fridge, remember?"

I pause, thinking of the prepackaged meals he'd bought from a local chef I know a lot of the guys use for their food prep needs. "A bad cook doesn't have perfectly diced bacon in his veggies."

"It's pancetta," he says, using the spoon to scoop up one of the crispy cubes of deliciousness.

"And case in point for your chef skills." I part my lips, he feeds me the piece, and I moan again. God, that's delicious. "Also," I say, "just because you're busy and take advantage of Evelyn's business, doesn't mean you can't cook."

"How'd you know that I use Evelyn?"

"Do I need to remind you that I saw your fridge...and your freezer?"

His lips twitch and he kisses the top of my head. "Okay, fine. I use Evie."

Evie. A blip of jealousy sneaks through me, taking me by surprise.

When was the last time I was jealous over a man?

I stay pressed against Huddy's side as I contemplate that... and come up short. I don't recall another instance of jealousy.

And I'm so lost in that thought, I miss him noticing my stillness, only distantly hear him ask, "DeeDee? What is it?"

"I'm jealous," I blab like an idiot. "I'm jealous of Evelyn, even though I've met her and she's really nice and, yeah, she's shy and it's hard to get her to talk sometimes, but I really *like* her. "I just—" I pull out of his hold, eyes wide, hands fussing with my ponytail, so completely out of sorts that I don't even know how to go on.

"What?" he asks.

"*How* am I jealous? I'm never jealous."

He doesn't move for a long moment.

Then he reaches forward and turns off the stove.

The look in his eyes has me skittering back a step.

"Hudson—"

"You're jealous."

A statement. Not a question.

I can't read what's in his eyes, and my stomach clenches. "I know you wouldn't start anything with me if you were seeing someone else," I blather. "And I'm not saying this is a logical feeling or anything. I just..."

"You're jealous."

Still a statement.

But I suddenly realize it's actually a *triumphant* statement.

"I—"

He sets the spoon down and stalks toward me. "Fuck, DeeDee," he murmurs, banding his arms around my middle and yanking me close. "Do you know how often I wanted to punch something when someone mentioned your asshole of an ex-fiancé?"

Mutely, I shake my head.

"A-fucking-*lot*." His mouth curves. "Pretty much anytime anyone mentioned the prick."

"I—"

But there my words go, flitting away again, making it impossible for me to concentrate.

Partly because he's close.

Mostly because he's bending, slanting his mouth over mine, and...

God, I want him.

So much that I've dreamed of him.

So much that I was getting ready to go over to his place because two days without him was too many days.

So much that—

"I had a sex dream about you last night," I blurt when he lets me up for air.

More blurting.

Heaven help me.

His eyes go wide...and then somehow even hotter. "How firm are you on the No Sex boundary?"

"I—" My heart's pounding. My head's spinning. Because

all I can think, all I can remember is Hudson's big strong body, his hot skin, his hands trailing over my flesh, his cock so thick and deep and—

"Sweetheart," he rasps, nudging me back, back, *back.*

Until the backs of my legs hit something soft and I realize he's herded me to the guest bedroom.

"What?" I ask when he bends, his face in mine.

"The No Sex Boundary?" he asks, tugging off his shirt. "Is it still firm?"

No. It's hard. Really fucking hard.

Or wait...that's his cock tenting the material of his sweats.

"No fair," I whisper as he tosses his shirt aside.

"Am I fucking you, baby?" he asks, his hands dropping to my shoulders.

Yes. *No.*

There was a reason I said we couldn't.

It's a struggle to grasp onto the why with need burning through my nerves, with him so close. "Y-your leg!" I say, feeling like cheering when I pull that out of thin air.

He shoves and my cheer turns into a gasp of surprise.

Then another when he reaches forward and all but tears off my clothes. One moment, I'm fully dressed.

The next?

Naked as a jaybird.

Only, I'm not feeling shy. Instead, I'm about to explode, a moan tumbling from my lips as he puts a knee on the mattress and climbs on top of me.

But he doesn't stay there.

He shifts to his back, grabbing my thighs...

And coaxing me up.

And *up.*

And did I say *up?*

"What are you—?" I choke out when he has me straddling the top of his chest.

"Don't need to worry about my leg if you're up here, sweetheart."

I sputter, but I don't get any words out.

Mostly because he gives me another tug and I fall forward, hands gripping the top of the headboard...and my vagina is on his face.

His face.

Oh, my God. I'm sitting on his face.

I've read about this—a *lot*.

But I've never done it...and I'm not even sure how to begin *doing* it.

Luckily, he doesn't seem to have any of the same reservations. His big, warm, slightly roughened palms settle on my ass and—

"Oh, fuck!" I cry.

Because his mouth is on me. His tongue is *in* me.

"Don't be shy, baby," he says, nipping in the inside of my thigh. "Ride my face."

I shudder, all the breath rushing out of me. "What if I smother you?"

His smile—good God, his *smile* has me practically coming right there and then, and his words send a shiver through me. "Then I'd die a happy man."

"Hudson—"

Another tug and I'm flush against him, his lips and tongue working me, his hands on my ass encouraging me to do as he commanded.

To ride his face.

I start off shy, hesitant.

Then he growls, "Fuck, you taste good," and finds a sweet spot with his tongue.

I jerk...and find that the stubble on his jaw dragging along my sensitive flesh spirals me even higher and I stop thinking, lose the hesitancy, and start moving faster.

Harder.

"That's it, sweetheart," he encourages, speaking against my slick folds, his words vibrating through my nerves, sending me closer to the edge, so close that I'm peeking over, preparing to jump off that cliff into the pool of release below.

"Oh, God," I whisper, feeling it now.

Just. Right. *There.*

"You are so fucking beautiful," he rasps, and I gasp again. But I don't stop moving.

Neither does he.

He works me faster, my hips grinding against him, seeking out that edge, the pleasure that's just out of reach.

And then he does something with his tongue.

My release explodes through me and I'm only distantly aware that there's not a single ounce of hesitation in my body.

I'm riding his face with abandon, clinging to the bevy of sensations—his tongue and lips, his hands encouraging me to move faster, his stubble that's created the most delicious friction, his words vibrating through me in little buzzes of bliss.

My orgasm seems to go on forever, wringing every last bit of pleasure out of me.

And it might as well be hours later before I emerge from that deep, deep pool, finding him lying next to me, his gray eyes full of storm clouds, his expression the most beautiful thing I've ever seen.

"You," I begin.

His hand is stroking nonsensical patterns on my belly. "Later."

"But—"

He pushes out of bed, grabs his shirt and my underwear.

Then makes short work of putting them on me. "Right now," he says, extending a hand and tugging me up to my feet. "It's time to eat."

I blush, my pussy clenching at the memory of exactly how good he is at eating.

"*Food*," he clarifies. A wink. "And maybe you again later."

I shiver.

Then I allow him to draw me out of the guest room and into the kitchen.

And later, after the delicious meal, we both get to eat again.

TWENTY-EIGHT

Hudson

I WAKE—NO surprise—with a hard dick.

But that's because I'm sleeping in Diana's bed and she's wearing that "cute" nightie.

She's kicked her side of the blankets off because I'm quote "a blistering inferno" who makes her overheated, but I don't mind.

Mostly because no blankets means I have a great view.

The silky material has ridden up, exposing the lush curve of her ass.

But that's mostly my doing. I'm trailing my fingers along her thigh, committing skin as silky as her nightgown to memory.

The only thing better would be if we were both naked.

But since I was able to turn No Sex into Oral Sex is Okay last night—*twice*—I didn't say a word when she tossed me my underwear and slipped into the closet to tug on her nightie.

Part of that was because she gave me the blow job of all blow jobs.

The rest was me yanking at the reins and reminding myself *slow*.

So, underwear, nightgown, and sleep.

And now...I slide my hand further up.

More tiptoeing right up to the edge of the No Sex boundary.

And maybe taking a teeny tiny step over it.

Just a small one.

Just an eensy, weensy, teeny tiny—

I'm distracted from the idiotic musings of my mind (and my clearly limited ability to come up with synonyms for small) by a pounding on the front door.

Not the ill-timed knock of Dee's elderly neighbor (since Ernest has a key), with whom she apparently has plans with today.

But *pounding*.

I freeze, body tense, but the noise doesn't cut off.

If anything, it intensifies.

"What the fuck?" I whisper, rolling in bed and reaching for my sweats that are crumpled on the floor. I do this quickly, yanking them and hissing out a breath when the material catches on one of the stitches.

But even as I'm doing it quickly, the noise is intensifying.

DeeDee shifts on the bed, rolling to her other side and stretching, and normally I'd love to stay and watch the gorgeous show of that sexy nightie shifting over her curves, over every luscious part of her I want to stroke and lick and *fuck*, but the pounding hasn't ceased.

And now she's lifting a sleepy head. "Wh—?"

"Stay here," I order and turn for the hall, not moving as quickly as I want—because fucking *stitches*—but still doing it with urgency.

Because I'm going to murder whoever the fuck is on the other side.

"Huddy?" I hear as I move down the stairs, but I don't stop.

Partly because I don't want to argue with her.

Mostly because I've reached the end of the hall, stormed past the kitchen and family room, and my hand is on the doorknob.

I twist, yank it open.

And glare at the fucker who's standing there, arm raised, hand clenched into a fist.

"Who the fuck are you?" he snaps, eyes flashing as he glares down at me.

"I could ask you the same question," I say cooly, shifting to the side when he looks like he's going to try to shove past me.

"What are you doing in my fiancée's house?" he growls, stepping forward and literally bumping his chest against mine.

Seriously?

This is Jason?

Even if I didn't know he was a complete and total asshole, one look at the fucker's face would have confirmed it.

He's objectively good-looking—I'm secure enough in myself to admit that much—but, pounding on *my* woman's door aside, I can tell he's a prick.

Hair that looks like he spent an hour getting every strand right, jeans so tight I'm surprised he made it up the steps to actually start pounding on the front door, a button down that's open to almost his navel...something that shows a pathetically little amount of chest hair.

"I mean," I mutter, smirking at the fucker, "if you're going to try and show it off, Lothario, you should decide if you're in or out on the chest hair." He sputters but I'm more in tune with the slightly hysterical laughter I hear behind me. "It's patchy... and just not a good look," I explain, slamming and locking the door on his face then turning to see that Dee has made her way downstairs, looking deliciously rumpled and sleep-mussed. "Go back to bed, sweetheart," I tell her. "I'll handle this asshole."

The pounding starts up again.

She sighs.

And I really don't like that fucking sigh.

I like her next words even less.

"Jason is being...difficult."

Snaking an arm around her waist, I draw her flush against me. Her eyes go wide then melt, same as her body, and I like that.

I like it a lot.

So much so I'm tempted to ignore the pounding and go back upstairs and push the No Sex boundary just a smidge further.

But...

Difficult.

Yeah, I need to get to the bottom of that.

Instead of the bedroom, I shepherd her into the kitchen. "Talk to me," I order.

"Bossy," she mutters, trying to pull away.

"Talk to me, DeeDee," I say, keeping her close and adding more firmness to my words. I'm uncertain if this will make her dig her heels in further or if she'll open up, but I hope she has enough trust in me to share.

"He wasn't happy when we broke up," she says, gaze darting toward the hall.

"*How* not happy?"

She nibbles at her bottom lip.

"Tell me," I press.

Her green eyes hit mine.

And I don't miss the fear in them.

"He hurt you?" I ask, temper beginning to boil.

A quick shake of her head has my stomach unclenching. Then her next words have it tightening again and doing it even more intensely. "He just scared me," she whispers, a sliver of shame in her tone.

"No," I say and she blinks in confusion. I cup both of her cheeks in my palms. "No," I repeat. "You don't feel shame because someone bigger than you, someone stronger than you, someone who should know fucking better than to *ever* put you in a position where you felt uncomfortable—"

"I didn't tell him I was—"

"You shouldn't have to." I brush my lips over her forehead. "Life can be shitty and uncomfortable and sometimes bad stuff happens, but your partner, your *fiancé* is supposed to share that load, supposed to know if you're scared or hurting and if that's the case, they should be doing everything—fucking *everything*— in their power to make it better."

"Hudson," she whispers.

"No one scares you," I whisper back. "No one hurts you." I draw her closer, settling my forehead on hers. "As long as you let me be here, I'll make sure you're safe."

"Hudson," she says again, her voice soft, her eyes gentle, her body melting against mine.

Despite the knocking.

Despite all the things that could pull us apart.

She's in my arms.

And when I say quietly, "Now do me a favor and go upstairs, so I can get rid of this asshole before Ernest gets involved."

"Last night you weren't too happy about me having plans with Ernest today."

"I wasn't," I admit. "Because I wanted you all to myself." I tug a lock of her hair. "But I'll take Ernest over that asshole, especially if we can hit up Molly's."

She smiles, runs her fingers through my beard. "He usually does treat me to Molly's—"

I grin.

"—but it's payment."

My grin fades. "For what?"

"What today's payment will be? Or what past payments were?"

My temper starts spiking again—payment? What the actual fuck? I thought he was a nice old man who—

She kisses my jaw. "Weeding," she says. "Today it'll be payment for me weeding his planter beds."

I relax, but only slightly. "And before?"

Her mouth hitches up as she drops back onto her feet and steps out of my arms. "Before was weeding too." I resist the urge to tug her back when she tosses a sexy smile my way before walking toward the hall. "Ernest has lots and *lots* of planter beds that need weeding."

I watch the sway of her ass as she moves.

Then I think about how much I hate gardening.

Then I smile...

And head outside to shove her asshole of an ex-fiancé into his car.

I watch as he drives away, hoping he'll actually listen and won't come back.

But not entirely convinced.

Then I head into the house and get ready for some...

Weeding.

Christ.

TWENTY-NINE

Diana

"YOU MISSED ONE," Ernest tells Huddy as he totters over, his cane held tightly in one hand.

Ernest is tired today.

I can tell it by his stride, no matter how hard he tries to hide it.

I'm kind of an expert in knowing when the men in my life are hiding things—

I freeze, my stomach knotting.

Okay, so maybe I'm not an expert at knowing when men are hiding things in general.

But I'm good at ferreting out injuries.

I'm also good at knowing when it's no use to try to get stubborn men to sit down and relax.

Case in point, Hudson sitting in the planter bed, surrounded by the remains of dead plants.

And Ernest nearly toppling as he tries to get the one Hudson missed.

Huddy lurches forward, righting him before he can face plant.

Which is pretty much the moment my temper snaps.

"Enough," I growl, jumping to my feet and brushing my hands on my shorts then marching over to the pair of stubborn males. I take Ernest's arm, guide him gently (but firmly) over to the chair I sat his ass in not fifteen minutes before. "Stay," I order then go back to Huddy.

He's looking up at me.

Smiling.

It's a great smile.

But even though it makes my brain go a little fuzzy and the space between my legs a little soft and warm (and slick) I don't let it distract me.

Much anyway.

"And you—*ack!*"

I don't get my demand out—and truly, I'm not sure what demand I would have made considering that I'm semi-distracted by his gorgeous smile—because he wraps his fingers around my wrist and tugs.

I grunt as I land in his lap.

Then promptly realize what kind of idiocy this man just pulled. "Your leg!"

"Hush," he mutters.

"But—"

"Look down, DeeDee."

I do...and am promptly distracted by all the yumminess that is Hudson, yumminess that is further augmented by the fact that he's a little dirty, a little sweaty, and that the man seriously grimes up good.

"What am I looking at?" I manage to push out, feigning innocence even though I'm looking.

Seriously *looking*.

His lips twitch and he draws me a little closer, warm palm landing on my cheek and turning my head to the side so he can murmur in my ear. "And now," he says quietly, notes of heat laced through his tone, "I'm desperate to know precisely how dirty a thought it was that just slid through your mind."

"I—"

A nip to my earlobe. "But considering we have a senior citizen chaperone"—my gaze jerks to the side, having completely forgotten in the last thirty seconds that Ernest is sitting in the chair across from us, and I see that he's watching us unabashedly—"I'm not going to do what I *really*"—he pairs this with a slight push of his hips, reminding me of how nice it felt to have him between mine—"want to in order to see that lush mouth tell me the secrets in that big, juicy brain of yours."

"Hudson," I begin.

"I really love the way you say my name." Another nip.

I shiver.

"But I wanted you to notice that you're sitting on my uninjured leg."

"Oh," I whisper, looking down and see that, indeed, my ass is currently on his uninjured leg. "Right," I say when his brows flick up.

"Fuck, you're adorable," he mutters and before I can say that I'm *not* adorable, that I'm a kickass professional hockey coach who takes no prisoners while winning a metric ton of hockey games, he leans in and kisses me.

I think he meant it to be a simple brush of his lips, just a taste considering we're in the front yard of Ernest's house with the aforementioned senior citizen chaperone.

But as seems to often happen with Hudson, that soft brush of his mouth becomes *more*.

His tongue slides into my mouth and his hand plunges into

my hair, and suddenly I'm plastered against a big, strong hockey player's chest while he kisses me senseless.

So senseless that I moan into his mouth and crawl closer and—

A tap to my back but I'm too invested in Hudson's hand on my spine, pressing me closer to him, on his soft groan of pleasure coasting along my tongue, on the slight sting on my scalp as he tugs my head back and makes love to my mouth, on—

Another tap, this time harder.

Hard enough to jerk me out of my stupor.

"Missy," I hear.

Ernest.

Christ, our senior citizen chaperone.

Something Huddy seems to remember at the same time I do because he groans again—and this time it isn't in pleasure.

It's in dismay—or whatever the big, strong hockey player equivalent is for dismay.

But he pulls back, resting his forehead on mine, both of our breaths coming in rapid succession, his hands still in my hair and on my back, respectively.

Another poke on my side and I realize it's Ernest's cane. Or rather, it's Ernest poking me *with* his cane.

Sighing, I manage to lift my head and look up at him. "Yes?" I ask archly.

Hudson chuckles and I level a scowl at him.

Something that seems to have absolutely no effect on him.

He just smiles at me.

"Stop playing kissy face and grab that weed," Ernest says, using his cane to jab at the offending dandelion.

Smothering a sigh, I reach over, rip out the weed.

"Good." He starts tottering away. "Now wash up. It's time for dinner."

I look away from my neighbor who never misses a moment

to make things interesting, and I do it because Hudson murmurs, "Dinner?"

I understand the question.

The sun is high in the sky.

It's barely four-thirty.

"Aren't you the one who mentioned the whole senior citizen thing?" I giggle. "This is prime early bird dinner time."

"I'm not even hungry," he says. "We ate those sandwiches from Molly's like three hours ago."

He's not wrong.

Then again, Ernest didn't eat those Molly's sammies. Likely, he ate lunch before we even made it over to his place.

Maybe even before we woke up.

I smile.

"God, you're beautiful."

My heart thuds hard against my rib cage, but before I can reply, he shifts me off his lap, nudging me to the side and carefully climbing to his feet.

"Come on, beautiful," he murmurs, extending his hand, helping me up.

"Huddy?" I ask as we walk toward Ernest's front door.

"Yeah, baby?" he says, wrapping an arm around my waist and drawing me into his side.

"I think you'd better find a way to *get* hungry."

He laughs and I love the sound so much, I commit it to memory, know that I would do just about anything to hear it again.

Then we're at the door and pushing through, listening to Ernest yell at us to "get a move on!"

We grin at each other.

"Hurry up, buckaroo," I order, reaching for the door handle.

"Buckaroo?" He teases, but starts down the hall.

Shaking my head, I start to close the door.

Then stop, my gaze catching on something across the road.

But before I can tease out what has the hairs on the back of my neck prickling, Ernest shouts at me from the kitchen again.

"I'm coming!" I call over my shoulder.

Then look back.

Nothing.

There's absolutely nothing there.

"Losing it," I mutter as I close the door.

And I know it's not just my vision that's playing tricks.

It's my heart...and the fact that it may be lost to Hudson forever.

THIRTY

Hudson

"HOW'S IT HANGING, Sir Limps a Lot?" King shouts down the hall a few days later.

I roll my eyes and sigh. Then turn to the man at my side, the one who's given me light clearance (this being permission to hit the gym and work my upper body). "Thanks, Doc."

He's grinning and shaking his head, but when his eyes lock with mine, they're serious. "Don't overdo it."

I wonder if he considers having Dee sit on my face over-doing it.

But that's a thought I keep to myself.

Mostly because King is striding down the hall toward us.

"I'll catch you later," Doc says, clapping a hand on my shoulder.

I barely have time to thank him before King is on me. "You going to hang out after practice?" he asks, drawing me toward the weight room.

"Don't you have women to get home to?" I mutter.

I don't want to get dragged into a night out with the boys, not when I'm planning on talking my way into DeeDee's bed... or convincing her to spend the night in mine.

"Girl's night in Vegas." He scowls and shoves a hand in his pocket then pulls out his cell and shows me the screen.

My lips twitch when I see Rory, Chrissy, Tiff, Attie, and Belle all cuddled up in a girl pose.

And all of them—except for Chrissy, who's pregnant—are clearly inebriated, smiling wide, drinks in hand, outfits totally and completely *Vegas*.

"Jean-Michel know his girls"—and I mean the plural, since Tiff is his fiancée, Chrissy and Rory his daughters, and Attie and Belle are newly claimed by the grumpy, protective team owner—"are dressed like that and drunk off their asses?"

"Considering he's been watching Quinn"—Belle's son—"while they enjoy the impromptu girls weekend to watch a nineties boy band?" King's mouth twitches. "Yes, I think he's aware."

My brows flick up.

And I'm seriously glad that Diana is busy with the team.

I don't have to worry about her panties landing on stage at a boy band concert.

"And you?" I say as he shoves his phone back into his pocket and we hit the weight room. "How do you feel about your girl drunk—" I pause and decide to leave out the part about skimpy Vegas clothes, not wanting to poke the bear. King, when triggered, can be a fucking monster. "And drooling over millennial pop stars?"

"I think," he says, mouth curving, "that I'm happy Jean-Michel's in charge of the details for the Girl's Trip."

My brows flick up in question.

"They have a bodyguard, a chauffeur, and his private jet is fueled up and ready to bring them home as soon as the concert's done." He grins. "My girl gets to have her night with her friends and she'll be home—and hopefully still drunk—so I can enjoy *her*." One big shoulder lifts, drops. "It's win-win."

I consider this as he heads over to start his work out.

Then realize he's right.

At the same time I'm wondering how soon I can arrange a Girl's Trip or Night for DeeDee.

Normal sex with her almost killed me—and I don't mean the leg wound.

Drunk sex would blow my fucking mind.

Grinning, I move to the mat and start warming up, going through a series of stretches and mobility exercises that have my pulse speeding and sweat breaking out on my forehead. It makes no fucking sense why *stretches* are so goddamned hard, but they are, and considering I can't get my cardio in the way I want it (with Dee, with both of us naked, and with me inside, pounding deep) it feels good to get my heart rate up.

"Christ," I hear as I'm lying flat out on the mat, lungs working far too hard.

I glance over, see that Rhodes has collapsed next to me.

"Long workout?" I ask.

"Long *night*," he mutters. "Hell, who am I kidding?" He rubs his palms over his face and groans. "It's been a long four years."

Rhodes has been a single dad to his daughter Chloe for those *long* four years, ever since his wife passed.

Chloe is five, fucking cute as hell...and is a total spitfire who has Rhodes wrapped around her pinky finger.

"What happened last night?" I ask, knowing it could be anything from Chloe deciding that his bedroom needed to be decorated (and thus took it upon herself to slap an entire book's worth of glittery stickers on Rhodes's walls) or a slumber party of multiple kindergarten aged girls (which coalesced into them giving Rhodes a makeover).

Something he begrudgingly shared with the team the last time we got him drunk.

Something that doesn't happen very often because even though he has a nanny who takes care of Chloe while he's on the road or at practice, Rhodes is a very involved dad and rarely goes out with us.

Not that I'm Mr. Social.

But I'm damn glad I went with the guys that night.

Because Rhodes got drunk enough to share that he had photographic evidence taken by his nanny.

And then King got into his phone.

And so we all got to enjoy the show of our grumpy as fuck teammate wearing bright blue sparkly eye shadow, red lipstick, and blush with tiny, glittery butterfly clips in his hair.

If I'd been interested in anyone else aside from Dee, I would have kissed Rhodes's nanny—it was that good of a photo cache.

He groans again, mutters, "I took her to a birthday party."

"That doesn't sound so bad," I say, pushing up and starting my stretches again.

"Its theme was pink."

I chuckle. "Just pink?"

"Yup. Just an explosion of pink in every corner of the house, all shades from pastel to so fucking bright I was blinded." He sits up too. "Chloe loved it, decided that when we got home, we needed to paint her room. But was it a pastel color that I could maybe deal with?"

I bite the inside of my cheek so I don't burst out laughing. "I'm guessing," I manage to say somewhat neutrally, "that's a no."

"No, of course it's a fucking *no*." He scowls. "She chose the brightest, most assaulting to the eyes pink there was in the paint store." That scowl deepens. "And worse, she found a color that has fucking *glitter* in it."

Now I lose my battle and start busting up.

And I know I'm not the only one—laughter rings out all around us as the rest of the guys lose it.

"Laugh it up assholes," he grumbles. "Because it gets worse."

"How can it possibly get worse?" Rome asks.

"Just wait until your daughter is here," he says. "And you'll know."

King makes a go on gesture, and I'm right there with him—I need to know how its gets worse.

"Chloe decided my room needed a matching wall."

There's a moment of silence.

And then...

More laughter.

And chirping.

And plans to plant all sorts of pink, glittery ideas into Chloe's mind.

Fuck, I love these guys (and I love it more that Pat, Duncan, and Kane aren't here to kill the vibe).

I spend the next hour working out and then the hour after that, trying some of the techniques I learned at my first appointment with Smitty's brain-fixing crew, and for the first time in forever, I didn't end my time studying wanting to launch the tablet and papers against the wall.

I end it, not having learned it all, but having learned *something*.

And that means the day has been great.

What's better?

Dee is finally home.

And so I have an idea how to make it even greater.

THIRTY-ONE

Diana

FRUSTRATED AND FEELING MORE than a little harried, I'm turning the corner, focusing on annoying hockey players and my temporary office and the mountain of paperwork that awaits me when an arm wraps around my waist and drags me to a halt.

Panic hits hard...

For one heartbeat.

Then I recognize the hold, the scent, the man who's stopping me from dealing with the scouting reports and trade offers and supply requests and video coach reports and—

Well, from *all* of that.

"Come with me," Huddy says, lips brushing my ear as he forms the words and making me shiver.

That shudder has him drawing me closer as he guides me down a hallway and then another, the noise in our temporary space at the Gold's practice facility fading with each turn.

"Where—"

His lips come to my ear again. "Shh."

Immediately, my back goes up and I open my mouth, but I don't get the chance to tell him that shushing me is going to end with murder—or copious ladder drills when he's back in skating shape— because he tugs again and suddenly I'm in a shadowy alcove near the Zamboni.

Thoughts of the killer sprinting drill, one that's far *far* below any professional player's abilities disappears as his body presses close.

Big. Strong. Hot. *Mine.*

I shiver again, and his lips curve up.

Cocky.

And I can't even fault him for it.

He's hot, my body burns for him, and each and every moment I spend has me falling deeper for him.

Likely the smart thing to do would be to distance myself.

But, as it's been from the moment his body shielded mine in my office, I'm not going to be smart.

I'm letting the current drag me under...and maybe it's fucking stupid, but I'm enjoying each and every moment of the ride.

His hand settles on the side of my neck, fingers squeezing lightly. "How was your day, DeeDee baby?"

That's a new one.

I've heard Dee and DeeDee and sweetheart and honey and baby and now...DeeDee baby.

My mouth curves up. "Long. Hockey guys are a bunch of whiners—"

"Seriously?" he asks dryly.

"Always crying about their time in the weight room and the extra drills I assign." I shake my head, smothering a smile because aside from Pat, Kane, and Duncan, all the guys on the roster have an intense work ethic that I admire. "Oh, no Coach, don't make me add more weight to my squats." Another shake. "Like I have any control over what the strength team says. I *do* over the drills, but I swear, any more bitching about them and I'll snap! I expend a lot of effort putting them together in order to help you guys."

The last has frustration creeping in.

Because I just had a talk with Pat that makes me want to do my head in.

"I know, sweetheart," Huddy says, hand flexing, forehead coming to rest against mine. "We're a bunch of assholes."

"That's what *I* said." I toss up my hands. "And then there are the interview requests." My nose wrinkles. "I get that I'm the new coach and I'm a woman, but God, there are only so many times I can take being asked about my plans for the season and what I'm going to do to make sure we're a contender for the Cup."

He chuckles. "It does get old answering the same shit." He slides his hand up, cups my jaw. "You going to start turning some down?"

"No," I grumble. "After the PR crises of the last few seasons, I'm doing everything I can to keep us in good press."

His thumb brushes over my lips. "My poor baby." But his tone is far from sympathetic.

I scowl. Then come up with a rather brilliant idea, if I do say so myself.

"And actually," I say. "I shared the story of you saving me, and it was a big hit." His face pales but I keep going. "Numerous outlets want statements and ESPN wants to do a feature." Wide eyes, mouth opening and closing, excuses already forming on the edges of his expression. "Since you're on the Injured Reserve and not playing, I told them you were free to—*ack!*"

He lifts me, still pinning me against the wall, but doing it a couple of feet higher now...and with the added bonus of my legs being wrapped around his waist.

And yeah, that's nice.

Really nice.

"You're lying," he growls, mouth at my ear again.

"N-no—" I say, trying desperately to stay focused. A nearly impossible task considering my current position and the fact that I haven't seen him for a few days, since the team was out of town and he stayed home to recover and take some appointments with the therapists from Smithie's team. "You're giving the interviews," I attempt to order, even though it sounds incredibly breathy.

He lifts his head, mouth quirking, eyes dancing. "You beautiful liar," he says softly.

"I—"

But he doesn't give me the chance to continue that deception.

His lips hit mine and he's kissing me, and it's even better than normal in this position, all heat and tongue, strength and rough-edged need. He tastes like fruit punch Gatorade and smells like spice and the way he rocks his hips, aligning his pelvis—and the hard length of his erection—against mine has a moan rumbling up the back of my throat, my hands diving into his hair, my desperate desire to devour this man beyond intense.

So intense that I snake a hand down between us, shove my fingers beneath the waistband of his sweats—

"Oh shit! Sorry!"

I freeze, the interruption hitting me like ice water.

Hudson goes still then exhales sharply and glares over his shoulder. "Go the fuck away," he growls.

"Right," King says. "I'll just..."

"*Go,*" Hudson says, still growling.

"Right," King says again and this time he pairs it with disappearing.

"Fuck." I push at his chest and Hudson sets me back down on my feet. "I'm sorry," he whispers. "I wasn't thinking. I'll make sure he doesn't say—"

I should be horrified.

I should be *terrified*.

Instead, I do the only thing I can.

I laugh.

It's absurd. I just got caught making out with one of my players in the hallway of the rink by another player on my roster.

It's straight out of a romcom or a romance novel.

Next step, I guess I'm supposed to freak out and push Huddy away, shut down what we're building and put us both through hell.

I just...

I don't have that in me.

This isn't ideal—but nothing about this season has been.

"I—" I inhale and exhale, trying to control myself, to temper my laughter. But it keeps coming. "This s-season started off with me catching my fiancé cheating on me and I only found out because I saw him on th-the Jumbotron! And th-then—" I suck in a breath, eyes catching on movement behind him, but I'm too focused on what I need to tell him to worry about King being nosy and potentially spreading gossip. "*Then* there was the fucking earthquake and us getting trapped and—" I shake my head, laughter fading. Because the next part isn't funny—not at all. "And then...you got hurt."

"Baby," he whispers, his expression so gentle I know I'll never forget it. Not ever.

"Then we had those hours together and you shared that

stuff and Ernest and Jason and—" I sigh. "Maybe I should use this as a sign from the universe to stop what we're doing—"

His expression becomes thunderous. "You're not—"

"No," I say quietly. "I'm not. I like you, Hudson. A lot. Too much considering how new this is and complicated it could prove to be. But...none of that changes how I feel, so—"

"DeeDee?"

I freeze, realize belatedly that I'm rambling. "Yeah?" I whisper.

"I like you too." He touches my cheek. "A whole fucking lot."

Suddenly, my lungs go tight. "Really?"

"Me mooning over you and telling you about my fantasies didn't already prove that?"

Suddenly, I can breathe again. "I suppose that's true enough."

He tugs at my ponytail. "And since we have this whole liking each other thing happening—"

I snort.

"—should we talk to HR about..." He trails off and I don't miss his eyes darkening, a hint of indecision, of worry that I may want to hide this, hide—

"Us?" I whisper.

A nod, but he almost immediately backtracks. "I get it if you don't want to go public, sweetheart. I get it. I know things are complicated and—"

I press a finger to his lips, take the opportunity to enact my own, "Shh."

His mouth curves.

"I'm not hiding this," I whisper. "Because I know *exactly* who we should talk to."

THIRTY-TWO

Hudson

THE NEXT DAY, I move through the rink, mind on my plans for that evening.

Plans for Diana.

Plans for us.

I like you, Hudson. A lot.

Fuck if those words don't make me feel like a superhero.

So much so I've been replaying them through my mind on repeat since I left her yesterday.

I like you, Hudson. A lot.

Yeah, damn those words feel good.

Almost as good as her being willing to give us a chance, to not shut it down just because our relationship is complicated.

And maybe I should be a good person and step back, should take this mess with me so it doesn't add complications to her life...

But I'm not that good.

I'm not willing to give her up.

Not when she got off work late last night and came to my house, not giving a blip of protest when I drew her up to my bedroom, tugged one of my tees over her head and held her close as she fell into a deep, exhausted sleep.

Not when I had to get up early to go to an appointment this morning and she met me in the kitchen before I left, snuggling up against me, murmuring, "Good morning."

Not when I'm going to make sure she knows exactly what it all means to me.

I like you, Hudson. A lot.

Yeah, well the feeling's mutual.

My leg pinches slightly as I walk but I'm in too good of a mood to let it bother me. Mostly because of all that Diana has given me, but also because...two more days and the stitches will come out.

Two more days and I can get out on the ice and crush some fuckers.

Two more days and I can do to Diana exactly what I've been fantasizing about.

Without the side of blood.

Because, seriously, this No Sex shit for my own good is complete and total bullshit. Okay, well it's been fun doing all the No Sex things, but it's less fun my dick is acting like it belongs to a teenager again.

For Christ's sake, I jerked off twice this morning and I was still halfway to hard when I walked into the rink.

Then, of course, I spotted Dee and I went completely hard.

Then harder still thinking about how I wanted to touch her and kiss her and—

I like you, Hudson. A lot.

Remembering her face when she said that.

I glare down at my dick.

Which is fucking hard again.

Jesus.

I need to—

"Ow!" I snap, rubbing at my shoulder as the punch which came out of nowhere—and a fucking hard one at that—stays me in my tracks. "What the fuck?" I say, turning and glaring at the gaggle of my teammates blocking my path.

They glare right back, completely unaffected by my terse question.

"She's fucking engaged, dumb fuck!" King hisses, breaking the standoff and punching me again.

"Ow!" I growl. "Stop it."

"And our fucking coach," Rome grinds out stepping closer, his eyes flaring with warning as he socks me right in the same spot.

Jesus Christ.

"Stop," I snap, shoving him away.

West winds up and hits me too. "She doesn't need to give Pat and his assholes any more fodder for their bullshit."

"Fuck," I grind out. "Stop."

"Are you trying to make her job harder?" Cam says coolly, and my quiet, even-tempered teammate seems abnormally close to the edge. No, he's crossed it, seeing as he's punching me too.

Fuck.

I rub at my now aching shoulder and narrow my eyes at all of them.

But Rhodes hasn't taken his turn.

Though, even as I'm thinking that, he steps close and does exactly that—socking me hard enough on my sore shoulder to make me suck in a breath and wince.

Goddamn, why are these men so good at punching?

And yeah, I know the answer to that—it's the same reason I

can *take* the punches, the same reason I have to grit my teeth together and bite back the urge to sock them back.

No knockdown, drag out fights at the rink.

And anyway, Rhodes is already talking, his words clipped out and striking deep. "She already has to deal with Pat and his merry band of assholes. Are you seriously going to give the internet more fodder to fuck with her?" He lifts his arm like he's going to hit me again.

"Don't," I growl, catching his hand and shoving him back.

His eyes spark with fury.

And even though their words slice at me—though thanks to DeeDee maybe not as much as they might have in the past—I know they're pissed because they like Diana, because they're concerned for her.

So I can't be pissed.

Or not *that* pissed anyway.

"You guys aren't wrong," I mutter, staying King when he tries to punch me again. "I know it isn't ideal. She's our coach, and social media will eat this shit up."

Cam's fury deepens. Rome's head looks like it's going to explode. A muscle in West's cheek flexes. And Rhodes' scowl should be in the fucking dictionary under the listing...well, scowl.

Still, I ignore all of that rage and focus.

"She's not engaged anymore, assholes," I mutter. "Her ex cheated on her, and she dumped him. And I was going to keep my distance because it's fucking messy and I didn't want to make things harder for her—"

"Apparently that shit didn't last long," King says, rolling his eyes.

"No," I admit. "All of that went by the wayside when the ceiling in her office collapsed and we ended up trapped together for half a fucking day."

Thankfully, that shuts them up.

But because they're my friends—and only because of that—I don't just take that victory and get the fuck out of here, go back to planning my evening with Dee. Instead, I brace myself and...give them the rest of it.

"I know she and I are asking for trouble. I know it probably doesn't make sense to you guys. But this isn't a just quick fuck, and it's not only scratching an itch." I inhale. Exhale. "I love her."

Five pairs of brows lift. In disbelief.

"You don't get it," I mutter. "I would do anything for her—retiring, asking for a trade, paperwork, fucking interviews, anything that will keep her and her dream safe, anything that means the heat and pressure is on me and not her."

"We get it," Rome says quietly.

"Yeah," King agrees.

Cam nods.

West murmurs, "I hear that."

And Rhodes...well, Rhodes' expression is pained. Because he lost the woman he loved, and I'm not sure that wound will ever fully heal.

I exhale, some of the tension leaving my body.

Some, but not *all*.

Because I don't love the expression on Rome's face.

And his words have all my plans for the night disappearing into a puff of smoke.

"You're both coming to Chrissy's event tonight."

I frown. "What event?"

"For her charity," he says. "Jean-Michel will be there. You can talk to him, put some precautions in place and get ahead of any fallout." He holds my eyes, as though daring me to put my money where my earlier statement was.

And because it's not a bad idea (even though I hate that my plans are now fucked), I nod. "We'll be there."

"You guys coming too?" Rome asks.

King nods. "You know Rory wouldn't miss it."

"Same for Attie," Cam says.

"Quinn's been wanting a cat," West murmurs with a shrug. "We're already planning on going."

We all look at Rhodes.

Who lifts his hands in surrender. "No," he mutters. "Absolutely not. I need a cat in my life like I need a hole in my—"

"Daddy!"

Chloe beelines down the hall, colliding into his legs.

And the big man goes soft. "What's up, pumpkin?"

"Chrissy says I can go with her tonight and pet kitties!"

Rhodes sighs and tilts his head back, eyes on the ceiling, mouthing, "Fuck my life."

He knows like we all know that it's not going to stop with petting.

He knows a kitten is going home with him and Chloe and that litter box duty is in his future.

Along with feather toys, nighttime feline antics, and ill-timed hairballs.

And yet, we all already know what his answer is going to be, even before he says it out loud.

I still bite back laughter, though, when he drops his chin, expression pained, and says,

"Yeah, baby, we can go to Chrissy's event."

THIRTY-THREE

Diana

"I'M NOT sure this is the smartest idea," I murmur as Hudson leads me through the doors of Chrissy Dawson nee Dubois's adoption center.

The space is lit up and full of people.

People from the team, people I don't know.

People who might talk.

People who might *judge*.

People, I think as I spot Jean-Michel, who may fire my ass.

I was going to talk to him tomorrow.

I had a whole plan.

But then I went home and Huddy showed up on my doorstep and the next thing I knew, he was talking me into attending tonight.

"It's for the pussies," he says and considering my mind was on exactly how the man had convinced me to give up my free evening—and how quickly he got his mouth on mine and his fingers in my pants and my body shuddering with pleasure to do that convincing—it takes me a minute to process his words.

Then I do.

And I choke. "For wh-what?"

He grins and tugs me into his side, lips coming to my ear in that way I love so fucking much. Brushing my skin, making me shiver, my body melting against his. "For the pussies," he teases, nipping lightly at the spot behind my ear. "We have to make sure they all go to good homes."

I push at his chest, pulling my head out of reach, and narrow my eyes at him. "You think you're funny?"

His lips twitch. "Well...yeah. But also"—he tilts his head as I spot the duo coming in through the doors behind us—"I know that you'd want to be here to witness that."

It shouldn't be hilarious.

But it is.

And a mix of adorable and sweet and...lots and *lots* of pink.

Like the shirt big, strong, and scowly Rhodes is sporting as he walks into the adoption center beside his daughter, her hand wrapped tightly in his.

I choke again, but this time it's on laughter. "Do I want to know?"

"Do you need to know anything except that Chloe wants a cat and Rhodes would do anything for his daughter?" he asks softly.

My throat goes tight and my eyes sting.

Because I lost that with my parents.

Because I had that with Grams.

And because Huddy didn't have that with his mom *or* dad.

I feel my body stiffen.

"Fuck," he says, wrapping his hand around my wrist and drawing me away from the doors, from the wall of plate glass windows that lead to the adoption floor, not stopping until we're in a quiet corridor that leads to nothing except a door marked with a little sign proclaiming Staff Only.

"What is it?" I ask.

"You tell me," he counters.

I frown. "I'm fine." And I am. I always am. I always find a way through.

Always find a way to move forward.

"DeeDee baby," he murmurs. "Don't lie to me about shit that has pain slicing across your face and your body going stiff against me."

Exhaling, I debate on what to tell him.

And on how likely he is to drop this because we have a relationship to make public and a boss to talk to and...

Right.

One look at his face tells me how *unlikely* him dropping this is.

So, I give. Partly. "There are people here who might talk or judge—"

He studies me for a long time then sighs and tucks a strand of hair behind my ear. "Yes," he says, "and you were worried about that before we came, but you didn't get stiff, sweetheart, didn't have pain flashing across your face then. So"—he steps a little closer—"tell me what's changed."

I close my eyes.

His hand settles on the side of my neck, squeezes lightly. "Was it seeing Rhodes with Chloe?" he asks gently. "Did that remind you of—"

"Yes," I whisper.

He stills. "But that's not all."

A statement. Not a question.

And it takes me by surprise.

So I go stiff again.

Dammit.

"Tell me, baby," he orders, but he does it soft and he does it gentle and...

I give.

"You didn't have that," I whisper. "Not with your parents the way they are." His expression...God, it *hurts,* but I find I can't stop talking, not now. "I had that with mine until I lost them. And I had it with Grams and y-you—" My lungs hitch but I push through and it's anger that's fueling my rise in volume. "*You* didn't. Your mom and dad showed up that night of the quake like they were trying to earn the Parent of the Year award, but did nothing but make it harder for you to get the care you needed, create chaos, make you feel worse than you were already feeling, and then they were happy to sail back home the next day like"—I clap my hands together, toss them out to the side, jazz hands style—"job well done. My work here is complete and so we'll just go right back to our life of gardening and book club and bitching about everything and everyone and—"

"Baby," he says, face gentle.

"No!" I snap. "They could have lost you. Their *son.* And instead of clueing in about how fucking precious a gift you are, they came in, made an appearance, and then fucking left."

"Sweetheart—"

"And that's after *not* helping you when you were a kid and making you feel like you were broken and—" My voice cracks but I push on. "They were horrible to you and they still don't get it and they haven't even checked in aside from a fucking thumbs up to your texts a-and—"

Oh God.

My voice cracks again, and my eyes are burning like motherfuckers.

And I still can't stop.

"And I really like you," I blabber. "A lot."

"I know, DeeDee," he says gently.

"And what we're building is beautiful and the best I've ever had and it's also a mess and it's dangerous and even though I talked a big talk at the rink about putting my head down and pushing through to find a way to make us work, I'm still worried. What I feel for you eclipses everything I felt for Jason, by a nuclear mile, and we're *new*." My voice cracks. "And what if you hurt me?"

His fingers tighten, mouth opening again.

But I'm on too much of a roll to stop.

"You could hurt me so much more than Jason did, and that asshole cheated on me." A beat. "With multiple women. And he never picked up his socks or made a meal or did the dishes if I cooked. You're wonderful, and you've taken care of me more in a few weeks than anyone has since Grams died."

His eyes go soft.

"And I like that. So much."

"I like it too."

The soft words slow my rant, at least a little bit, and my next words involve less shouting and more...talking. "And because of all that, I'm falling for you and those feelings might mean we both lose our jobs—"

"Well, that last part—at least—I can reassure you about."

THIRTY-FOUR

Hudson

WE JUMP and I whip my head around, seeing that our private chat in the hallway has become not private.

Very *not* private.

Standing in the mouth of it is Jean-Michel.

And behind him, tucked slightly behind him—where he can keep her safe—is his fiancée, Tiff.

Behind them are Chrissy and Rome, King and Rory, Cam and Attie, and West and Belle.

Right.

Very, *very* not private.

I grind my teeth together and glare at them. "Do you mind?"

"No," King drawls, earning him a smack from Rory.

"We definitely don't mind," Cam says on a smirk and Attie shakes her head.

"I actually have a few questions—*ow!*" West shuts up when Belle elbows him in the ribs.

Rome opens his mouth as I'm seriously considering how many years I might get for committing murder in front of an FBI agent.

Considering Attie likes the guys, probably a lot.

Before Rome can let loose whatever snark he's got stored up, Chrissy speaks, her tone gentle but firm as she loops her arm through Rome's. "We're giving them privacy." A beat. "Now."

Thankfully, that prompts the group to go—except Jean-Michel and Tiff—and they do it expediently.

Mostly because no one can argue with her.

Not because she's Jean-Michel's daughter, not even because she's pregnant.

But because she's nice and went through hell and doesn't often pull rank.

"Come on, honey," Tiff says quietly to Jean-Michel when the rest have gone, tugging at his arm.

He rotates to face her and leans close, cupping her jaw with his free hand and pressing his lips to her forehead. "I'll be right behind you."

"But—"

"*Right* behind you," he says quietly.

Their gazes connect.

And then Tiff smiles and nods, dropping her hand to her side. "Okay," she replies just as quietly before she slips away.

Jean-Michel watches her go then turns back to us, staying where he is for a long moment, studying us with unfathomable eyes.

"It's not like you think," Dee blurts, stepping out from between me and the wall, positioning herself in front of me.

Protecting me.

Yeah, no.

That's not going to happen.

I slip an arm around her middle, tug her back into my side at the same time that Jean-Michel's brows fly up. "What do *you* think I think?"

She pulls at my arm, and when I don't release her, shoots an annoyed look in my direction, but doesn't comment on my hold. Instead, she focuses on Jean-Michel. "Hudson and I are not just a quick fling—"

"I got that from what you were shouting down the hall," he says dryly.

DeeDee's cheeks go pink, but her chin lifts. "Right, well, I just—"

Jean-Michel moves closer, eyes connecting with mine for a long moment before he turns to her. "Do you know why I hired you?"

"Auclair—" She begins, naming the former head coach of the Eagles.

"No," he says and the word's sharp enough to stop anything else she might have said. "The reason I hired you has absolutely nothing to do with that asshole."

Her hand clenches into the waistband of my jeans and I draw her a little closer.

"I hired you because you're smart as fuck, hardworking, come with impeccable references, and you care about the guys." His mouth twitches. "Now did I expect you to fall for one"—his smile grows—"even one as great as Huddy here?"

I snort.

He goes on like I haven't made a sound. "No, of course I didn't. And I wouldn't have wanted you to deal with the comments that are going to be coming your way or the trolls or the dickheads who think they get to have an opinion about who you love"—she jerks slightly but doesn't interrupt (a good thing because Jean-Michel doesn't stop talking)—"but I have no fucking room to talk either."

"You don't?" she asks.

"My daughter is married to our captain, is having his baby. My adopted daughter is engaged to the team's leading scorer. I'm about to marry a woman who's twenty years my junior and has deep ties to one of our biggest competitors in the division." He shrugs. "So, I *really* have no room to talk to you guys about appropriate or inappropriate relationships."

"Oh," she whispers, relaxing against me.

"The bottom line is that the heart is a strange and complicated thing and—*fuck me*—but half the time it seems to make decisions that are as bewildering as possible and our brains are stuck just following behind." A shake of his head. "And I'm guessing it's the same for you two—your hearts led and next thing you knew..." He juts his chin toward our bodies, pressed tightly together. "And next thing you knew, you were *there.*"

I look down, see the *there* he's referring to.

God, I love that she can be in my arms, love how she feels pressed close against me, love that when she glances up at me and I smooth her hair back, her green eyes darken to emerald and her expression grows soft.

For me.

Mine.

And that thought has me forgetting, for a moment anyway, that we have an audience. I lean down, settle my forehead against hers. "My heart led me to you the first time I saw you kick ass on the ice," I murmur.

Lush lips curve and she reaches up, touches my cheek, fingertips running through the bristles of my beard. "Thank God that earthquake clued me in to how special you were, huh?"

"Worth every stitch," I say dryly.

A throat clearing has me stilling. Then lifting my head, struggling to smooth out my frown.

Something I think that Jean-Michel clocks, considering his smirk.

"Take your time," he says. "And tomorrow we'll sort out some ways to make this all appear above board to any of the idiots who think they have the right to comment."

"Above board?" DeeDee asks.

Jean-Michel nods. "Like having one of the assistant coaches overseeing Huddy's playing time so we can avoid talk of favoritism."

"Oh," she murmurs. "That's a good idea."

He grins, lifts and drops one shoulder. "You would have thought of it eventually." Then he turns to leave our not-so-private hallway.

I tighten my hand on Dee's hip, mouth opening to speak.

But I don't get the words out because Jean-Michel says, "Oh, guys?"

We glance over at him.

"Don't forget to stop and enjoy these moments."

Dee relaxes against me, leaning more heavily into my side.

"And make sure you hold them close for the inevitable shit storm that's no doubt heading your way."

"I—"

He nods his head once at us. "Hold them tight," he semi-repeats.

Then he's gone.

And any hint of relaxation has left her body.

I bite back a sigh.

Then I see about holding the moments tight.

THIRTY-FIVE

Diana

AFTER THE CHAT with Jean-Michel—one that both settled me and left me completely unnerved—we took his advice and created a moment to hold close.

Hudson's kissing ability is seriously unparalleled.

But after voices came close and we were nearly caught like naughty teenagers for the second time in a half hour, we venture out of the corridor...

And into heaven.

Because it turns out that one of the best ways to stop thinking about unnerving conversations filled with warnings and tacit approval and my entire social circle—including several men I'm supposed to effectively coach—witnessing me pinned to the wall by one of their teammates while loudly baring my soul is...playing with kitties.

Huddy wasn't wrong earlier.

It's really all for the pussies.

Snorting to myself—because apparently I have a twelve-year-old's sense of humor—I settle in, my back resting against the wall, my lap full of passed-out kittens, and survey the room.

We had snacks and drinks in the front, cat-free, room while one of Chrissy's employees with the rescue talked to us about the work they were doing and their current needs and how the event that night would work (it was part socialization for the cats, part to build word of mouth contacts for the rescue's needs, and part adoption night to pair up the resident cats and kittens with their forever families).

Once the spiel was complete, and it has to be said, many a checkbook was brought out by the hockey players in attendance (and myself), the fun started.

And though Huddy and I had Jean-Michel's approval and blessing, such as it was, I was still edgy.

Guys from my team were there—and had seen us.

Their girlfriends and wives and freaking soulmates were there.

The public was there.

Potentially judgy eyes all around.

But...the judgment didn't come.

Instead, the guys introduced me to their women—those I hadn't met officially, anyway, Belle and Tiff. We chatted, along with Rory and Attie, and though Chrissy was running around and overseeing all manner of detail, big and small, she stopped and chatted with us too.

And the women's expressions never turned from pleasant and kind and open toward catty or bitchy or judgmental.

So, even though I spent a lot of that first hour jumpy as hell, searching every sentence and interaction for the smallest hint of derision, eventually—and after two glasses of champagne—I managed to finally calm down enough to enjoy myself.

Which was when Hudson peeled off and left me to my conversations with the girls.

I noted that—the fact he didn't join the male posse holding court in the senior cat room—until I was comfortable, and fell a little deeper.

God, he's such a good guy.

The worry in my belly further unknotted, I went from calming down and enjoying myself to having a great freaking night.

Quinn—Belle and West's son—picked out his cat. Or rather, *she* picked *him*.

The moment he came in and sat down, the sweet little girl jumped in his lap and made herself at home. There was never a doubt that she was going home with the family she'd claimed, and before long, paperwork was filled out, an adoption fee was paid, and the now family of four were walking out the door with a cat name Mossy (for the green in her eyes).

Rhodes—sporting a bright pink shirt that was absolutely not his color—was a different story.

Mostly because Chloe is a bundle of energy who has her daddy wrapped around her adorable little finger.

Rhodes...well, Rhodes didn't end up with *one* cat.

He ended up with two sisters who were just old enough to go home with them that night and whose antics had entertained all the guests this evening as they sprinted through the kitten room, climbed up on furniture, launched themselves at ceiling fans, and just generally created chaos.

Heaven help him.

The man is now completely totally outnumbered.

And that's a ratio only made worse by the fact that his nanny, Finley—or Finn, for short—is a gorgeous brunette with striking hazel eyes.

She breezed into the rescue, a pair of bright pink cat carriers in her hands and helped Chrissy corral the kittens.

Apparently, she volunteers for the rescue in her free time,

and the effective way she caught chaos and carefully ensconced it—times two—into the carriers, definitely spoke to her cat handling skills.

Really, it was so impressive that I considered asking her to break down her wrangling abilities and give me pointers.

They would seriously come in handy when it comes to *wrangling* stubborn hockey players.

I'm thinking that and smiling as I watch Finn, Rhodes, and Chloe exit the building, those pink carriers in Rhodes's hands, held carefully at his sides. He keeps the door open with his back as Chloe and Finn walk out behind him, their fingers laced, completely focused on each other as they share some secrets that Rhodes obviously isn't privy to and—

My breath catches.

Because, oh Lord, the look in Rhodes's eyes as Finn moves by him...

It's like how Hudson looks at me.

And Rome at Chrissy. And King at Rory. And Belle at West. And Jean-Michel at Tiff.

Like he would lay the world at her feet, if she only asked.

"Sweetheart."

Blinking and looking away from the acutely beautiful and incredibly painful expression on Rhodes's face, I glance up at Hudson.

He's staring down at me, exactly as I imagined.

Like he's fallen as deep for me as I've fallen for him.

"I think I'm getting a cat," I say softly, gently scooping up the sweet little cat who did some claiming of her own tonight. Even in the dog—cat?—pile, she's never strayed far from my arms.

His lips twitch. "Considering our surroundings, it's an inevitability."

"You think Chrissy will keep her for me until I can arrange for supplies and a pet sitter for Lola?"

That gorgeous smile of his grows. "I think Chrissy probably has a list of pet sitters and plenty of supplies she can give you."

I cuddle Lola close as I find my feet, her little mew of displeasure at my moving adorable as all get out. "Then I guess I need to see a woman about some adoption paperwork."

I do just that.

And barely a half hour later, I'm walking out with a bag of supplies, Lola protesting quietly about her current confinement in a pink carrier that matches the ones Rhodes carried out earlier, thinking that over the years, and just like anyone else in this world, I've had a lot of good and a lot of bad...

But that the brand of good that's my life currently may be the best I've ever had.

Even with the apparent shitstorm heading my way.

THIRTY-SIX

Hudson

I ROLL MY SHOULDERS, body still sore from hitting the weight room after nearly a week's rest, then snag a towel from the hook and knot it around my waist.

We're at Dee's tonight, and I can't lie.

I like being here, but I like it more when she's at my house. In my bed. Wearing those nighties or my shirts to sleep in.

Usually without any underwear.

Though maybe I can talk her out of hers tonight again.

When I stride through into the bedroom, I realize that's unlikely.

She's sprawled in her bed, Lola on her chest, and both kitten and woman look relaxed and content.

"Did you want to watch something on TV?" she asks absently, her head slowly swiveling in my direction. "We can put a game on or..."

Her voice trails off and her eyes go wide.

Then she sits up abruptly, disturbing Lola. The feline gives a disgruntled meow then jumps off the bed and pads out into the hall, a disdainful look in those pretty green eyes.

For all of Lola's activities, Diana hasn't moved.

"DeeDee baby?" I ask, stepping toward her.

She puts her hand up. "Freeze."

Frowning, I still, and not able to discern the look on her face, and my stomach starts to twist. "Are you okay?"

Fuck, has something happened already?

Has someone posted shit or has Jean-Michel changed his mind or is Jason back and being the asshole he is?

Except her response is just, "Mmm-hmm."

And that doesn't scream worried, like I would imagine imminent shitshows would. Or concerns about job security. Or asshole exes.

I lose patience with holding still and step toward her. "What is it, sweetheart?"

"I—" She pushes off the mattress, but since she doesn't run screaming from the room, I figure the fact that she *again* doesn't tell me what's wrong is less important than say...

The fact that she's walking toward me.

"You're wearing a towel."

I blink, glance down. "Um, yeah. Usually people use towels after they shower, honey."

Her lips twitch and she slowly lifts her hand, settling it on my chest. "I've never seen you in just a towel."

My dick stirs.

Who am I kidding?

That statement paired with her fingers dragging down my pecs, over my abs has me hard as a rock.

And forgetting about shitstorms.

Her leaning forward and flicking out her tongue, tasting me—

Well, that has my control splintering.

"Baby," I warn, my hands dropping to her waist. But do I push her away?

Fuck no.

I draw her closer and keep warning, "You're playing with fire."

"Remember how"—she lifts on tiptoe, her lips coming to my ear, her words soft and sultry—"my No Sex boundaries don't extend to blow jobs?" She drops down onto her knees, gaze locking with mine. Then she deliberately slides her hand farther south.

Control?

What control?

I should probably be the staid and moral hero, stop her from doing this, find a way to take care of her instead.

But even as I'm warring with that, her fingers are working and—

The towel drops away.

"God, I love your dick," she whispers, wrapping her hand around me and pumping hard once, twice, *three* times.

"Fuck," I mutter, already dangerously close to the edge.

But I fight that back. Because I want her to take me in her mouth, to suck me deep. I want to feel her moans on my dick when I fuck her face.

"I thought you were going to blow me," I rasp when she doesn't stop stroking.

Her lips—plump, pink, and parted, though not around my dick—curve. "I thought you might offer to get me off first," she says, one shoulder lifting and falling in a delicate shrug. "You know, be a gentleman."

"I'll get you off later," I promise, mostly because she's kneeling in front of me.

She laughs, the sound brushing over the head of my cock. "No gentleman tonight?"

"You don't want a gentleman between your legs, baby."

More laughter. Another grin.

She leans in and whispers, "You're right."

Then she leans forward the last couple of inches and—

"*Fuck!*" I growl, hand settling on her hair, clenching at the silken locks. I want to pump my hips, to push myself deeper than she's taking me, but I hold off, let her choose the pace, the depth.

And it's no hardship to have that warm, slick mouth around me, the silky, firm strokes of her tongue on the underside of my shaft, the tight clench of her hand joining the party. She's playing. Going slow. Driving me fucking insane.

Then more so when she pulls back, her liquid hot eyes hitting mine.

"Feeling shy, honey?" she asks, palms settling on the tops of my thighs.

"My cock was just hitting the back of your throat, baby." My mouth curves. "I think we're way past shy by now."

Her nails dig in and she leans close, words brushing over the head of my cock again. "Then"—she flicks her tongue—"I think it's way past time for you to fuck my mouth until you're coming down the back of it."

And there goes the last of my control.

I push between those pretty pink lips...and I fuck her mouth until I'm coming down her throat.

"Fuck, baby," I groan as she swallows me down then licks her lips, mouth curving into a sexy smile.

"My turn," she whispers.

I grin, pick her up, and toss her on the bed.

Luckily, I don't tear any stitches.

And luckily for Dee, even after I've had an orgasm that threatens to split me in half, I still have enough energy to make sure she has one too.

"Diana!"

I still at the semi-familiar voice, but Dee goes ramrod stiff.

"Jason," she whispers on a groan.

"Go into the arena," I mutter. "I'll take care of this asshole."

But before she takes more than a step, she's jerked back so hard her head whips around and she winces.

And *that's* when I see red.

"Don't you fucking touch her," I growl, ripping him away from her and slamming him back against a car.

Since it's Pat's, I don't really give a fuck that the driver's side door is now sporting a Jason-sized dent.

"Let me go," he cries, grabbing at my hand, trying to dislodge me.

"Diana made it clear that she's done with you," I say, squeezing more tightly. "*I* made it clear that I'm done with her having to deal with you, so why *the fuck* are you here?"

He chokes, probably because my hand is gripping the neck of his sweatshirt and I haven't let up.

"You need to leave, to not come back. *Fucking ever.* Do you get me?"

He's turning purple, still choking, but I don't release him.

"You don't need to speak to nod your fucking head, asshole."

His nods are akin to a bobblehead, but I think I've made my point.

"Problem?" I hear.

Jean-Michel is standing there, a smile on his face that is nowhere near amused.

I've seen the man in the midst of the team's playoff battle. I've seen him with his daughters. I've even seen his tolerating a gaggle of cats chewing on his shoelaces.

But I haven't seen the icy edge of what made him a billionaire before the age of thirty.

That edge is in sight right now, though.

And because of that, I don't hesitate to throw Jason under the bus.

"This is Jason," I say. "Diana's ex."

"That, I'm aware of," he replies, making it very clear he's not a fan. Still, he asks, "Is there a reason you're choking him out?"

"He's been harassing Dee." I scowl. "Even though she's made it more than clear that she doesn't want anything further to do with him."

Swear to fuck, but the temperature around us drops a half-dozen degrees.

And if I thought Jean-Michel was scary before, his expression is fucking terrifying now.

"Pascal." He nods to the right, and draws my attention to a man—almost my size, a fearsome expression on his face, and his manner military in a I'll-fuck-you-up-and-stash-you-in-unauthorized-black-site-location-never-to-be-seen-or-heard-from-again way.

"I'll handle it," he says quietly.

Jean-Michel nods.

Then glances over at me and flicks up his brows.

Right, the whole still choking the fucker thing.

I force myself to loosen my grip, and Jason falls to the ground, hands clutching at his neck as he gasps for air.

Ignoring Jason, Jean-Michel turns to Pascal and they start quietly talking.

Dee bugs her eyes out at me.

Since my anger is rapidly fading—Jean-Michel's cool demeanor washing over me and taking it away—I draw Dee into my side, murmur, "It's all good, sweetheart."

"I—" A shake of her head. "How is...*that*"—a nod at Jason —"all good?"

"It's all good," Jean-Michel says as he calmly steps over Jason's body, "because Pascal is going to make certain Jason never bothers you again."

The words have gone from cool...to bitingly cold.

Yup. The man is definitely going to be spending the next decade in a black site.

"Now"—he jerks his chin in the direction of the arena— "shall we?"

THIRTY-SEVEN

Diana

IT'S the next day while I'm sitting in an office at the Gold's practice facility, wrapping up some administrative work with Jean-Michel beside me doing the same when I bring up the whole Jason thing.

"We need to talk about—"

"Nope," he mutters.

Right. Well.

That may be his answer, but it's not the one that will satisfy me. "We *need* to talk about it."

He shrugs. "There's nothing to talk about."

I lean in and drop my voice, thinking about the quiet man who'd told Jean-Michel he'd *handle it*. "Is he... Did Pascal..."

Jean-Michel's head of security is seriously scary and while I'm pissed at what Jason did and how he won't go away, I don't exactly want him to...disappear permanently.

Disappear from my life? Yes.

Be fitted with concrete shoes and dropped in the Bay? Not so much.

Jean-Michel just stares at me as I trail off.

"He's not dead," he says and let it be noted that he waited a while to put me at ease on that front.

I exhale.

"Jason is, however"—he leans back in his chair, steepling his hands in front of his chest—"very motivated to move back to Baltimore."

My eyes go wide.

"And to not come back." Jean-Michel's tone is deadly when he adds, "*Ever.*"

"Oh," I whisper. "You, uh, you know you didn't have to do that."

"I *know* that I won't have someone who's under my protection dealing with an asshole ex-fiancé—"

"But—"

"Same as I know," he goes on, talking over me, "that I don't want my head coach having to deal with the same problem."

I sigh and sit back, something unpleasant churning in my stomach. "I bet you didn't have to deal with this with Auclair."

"You're right," he says. "I didn't."

Ouch.

But I don't get the chance to sit in that bit of hurt.

Because he's still talking.

"But with Auclair, I didn't have someone who cared about our players like you do. I didn't have someone build a system around our talent instead of forcing square pegs into round holes. I didn't have someone who works her ass off to get the best out of the team."

My heart squeezes.

"We're building something special here," he says. "And I'm going to have your back—and it's not because you're a woman or that you're making friends with my daughters. It's not that you adopted a cat or fell in love with one of my players. It's not even because you're a great fucking coach." He bumps his arm against mine.

"Then why?" I whisper.

"It's all of that. And more," he adds. "From the moment you showed up at our first meeting ready to kick ass all the way to the Cup, I knew you were fucking special. So, there's no question of why in my book. You're you, DeeDee"—he smiles as he uses Huddy's nickname for me—"and that means you're stuck with the annoying, nosy, sometimes dysfunctional family that is the Eagles. So you'd better get used to it. We take each other's back. We gossip like fiends. And we don't let *our* people face shitstorms alone—not ones that are already here nor ones that are incoming."

I blink, the unpleasant thing gone. Sort of.

Because that's sweet.

But there's also the whole shitstorm thing he keeps mentioning.

Now," he says, clearing his throat and closing his laptop. "I think it's time to call it a day."

I frown, thinking it's still early and I have a lot of work left to do. "Why?"

"Because I think someone wants you."

"Who?" I ask, confused. Because I'm also thinking that I knew Jean-Michel could be sweet, but I never figured he'd be sweet with me.

So...I'm touched.

And a little terrified.

But mostly touched.

Because it'll be nice to have a family again, even one that can be slightly dysfunctional and nosy.

I glance at Jean-Michel when he doesn't reply, see that he's not looking at me.

His eyes have gone over my shoulder.

"I think someone wants you," he repeats, amusement in his voice.

So much that I table my tangle of emotions (including the terror) and follow his gaze.

It takes me a second to realize what he's looking at.

No. *Who* he's looking at.

Hudson is standing in the open doorway, his stare fixed on me. *Fixed.*

As though I'm the only person on the planet aside from him.

As though I'm some delectable treat he's desperate to devour.

Hell, considering the foreplay—if rounding third base and engaging in oral sex and making out like teenagers for nights on end can be considered foreplay—of the last few weeks, I can't pretend to be in a different mindset.

Clearly seeing that I'm right there with him, his mouth curves up into a sexy half smile.

God, he gave me that smile the other night.

After the towel had "fallen" to the floor and I'd taken his cock in my mouth and he'd—

Heat engulfs me from head to toe, and I shiver—and it's not from the cool air of the rink seeping down the hall and invading the office Jean-Michel and I are using.

Nope.

That shiver is a combo of the need on his face and that sexy smile and...

Because it's (hopefully) Stitch Removal Day.

I know—both because I'm the coach and know these things

but also because this man is mine and he shared his check-in was today—that Huddy has just come from Doc.

And that heat, that smile...they both seem to be pointing at good news.

"I'll just leave you to it," Jean-Michel says.

But I'm barely hearing him.

Because the heat in Hudson's eyes...

Holy hell, how am I not going to be burned to ash by it?

And why am I eagerly anticipating every minute of the conflagration?

Just...tie me to the stake and let him have his way with me as the flames grow.

"See you at the game tomorrow," Jean-Michel says distantly.

Or maybe it's not distant, exactly. More like I'm not processing anything aside from the fact that Hudson is striding over to me, making my lungs hitch and my thighs press together.

Jean-Michel could have revealed he's wearing a tutu and is going to give me a tabletop performance, and I wouldn't care.

He's leaving—that's all that's pertinent.

"Bye," I say distractedly.

Because Huddy has gotten close, so close he's wrapping his fingers around my wrist and drawing me to him, plastering me against his chest.

"Hey," he mutters.

"Hey," I breathe, probably sounding like an idiot, but not caring.

When I'm in his arms, held tight like I'm the most precious of cargos, I don't give a damn about much aside from staying here...and maybe finding some way to do it naked.

"Work's done for the day," he says.

"I—"

He reaches behind me and shuts my computer with a quiet *click*, head bending to my ear, words an erotic caress. "I said, *work's done for the day.*" And he pairs that delicious statement with a press of his pelvis against my front—

I shiver.

Because...*holy hell.*

He's bossy. Turned on (something I'm intimately familiar with at the moment considering the hard length of his cock is pushing against my belly). And...he's all mine.

Total fucking fantasy.

Something he clearly sees on my face because he drops his arms, shifts around me, and starts shoving my stuff into my bag. In an instant, I'm distracted by the play of muscles over his chest and shoulders, the way his shirt lifts slightly in the back, giving me a glimpse of bare skin and taut flesh and—

Mine.

Just...*mine.*

Which is why I rise on tiptoe, press my body to his, and murmur, "Please tell me Doc cleared you."

He jerks, probably because along with the words, I also can't resist darting my tongue out to taste his earlobe. That flick has his packing intensifying and he basically ends up shoving everything into my backpack without any of my usual carefulness, papers and pens going loose, my laptop not in the padded sleeve, my water bottle barely making it into the pocket on the side. Then he's yanking at the zipper, fighting to bring it around to the other side of the canvas.

But he does it.

And in less than ten seconds, I'm packed up and his gaze is locking with mine again. "Doc cleared me."

I shiver again.

Only three words and yet they manage to convey a full night's worth of fantasies.

In a second, I'm wet and aching and searching for another shadowy alcove to start acting out those fantasies...or maybe to just take the edge off ten days' worth of foreplay, but I don't so much as get a chance to even suggest that the space behind the partially closed door may have enough privacy for us to do what we need to do before he's slinging my backpack over his shoulder, grabbing my hand and hauling me out through the corridors.

Thankfully, they're mostly empty, but I don't miss that Cam and King are in the hall, that they definitely clock Hudson's hold on me and the urgency with which we're high-tailing it out of the rink because their smirks are ridiculously huge.

But they don't say anything aloud as Huddy drags me out, and we don't meet anyone else on our way to the parking lot.

Still, I have no doubt that our journey will be discussed.

That's a problem for another day, however.

Right now, I'm wondering the best—read, *quickest*—way for us to get through the afternoon commute traffic so Huddy and I can get horizontal.

Or vertical.

Or really any kind of -*al*.

"Tell me," I demand as we peel out of the lot.

A heated look in my direction but he only holds my gaze for a second because then he's weaving through traffic, eyes focused on the signals and obstacles and other cars around us.

Probably for the best.

Especially when he starts giving me the update on what Doc said—basically that Hudson is completely healed and can return to his normal activities, albeit with measured intent and extra attention from the training staff.

Woohoo!

Because I have all sorts of thoughts on *my* measured intent.

And how long he'll let me keep it up before he takes over.

I grin, staring out the window as the road flies by, thinking it won't be all that long.

Thinking how fun it's going to be to get to the point where my measured intent has his control splintering and I get to enjoy an out of control hockey player in my bed.

In fact, I'm thinking about it so hard I don't realize that we're already pulling up to Hudson's house.

Fuck, yes.

I reach for the handle, start to pop the door, but he snags my shoulder, tugs me back.

Eyes going wide, I look at him. "Wh—"

He leans over the console and kisses me. It's short but no less deep or intense than any of the kisses we've shared over the last few days.

"Let me."

I blink, breathing heavily. "Let you what?"

His mouth hitches up. "Let me give you the night you deserve."

And as I'm absorbing the impact of those words—and how damned much they mean to me—he gets out of the driver's side, rounds the hood, then opens my door, holding out his hand for me to take.

"Let me?" he murmurs again.

I take a deep breath, having the feeling that tonight is going to change everything.

That my life is never going to be the same.

Because I'm not falling in love with this man.

I'm already gone for him.

THIRTY-EIGHT

Hudson

I'M STRANGELY nervous as I unlock the door and lead DeeDee into my house.

The anticipation actually aches, prickling through every cell and nerve.

The preparations I took because of all that anticipation feel over the top.

"Maybe we should go to your house instead," I say, halting in the mud room, realizing that I've likely passed *over the top* and headed straight for *insanely over the top*.

She bumps into my back—likely because I've stopped so abruptly. "What are you talking about?" she asks, pressing herself closer to me. "We're already here, honey."

Christ, I love the feel of her breasts against me.

Almost as much as I love her hand sliding down along my front, slipping beneath the waistband of my sweats—

Until she freezes.

"Is that...music?"

It *is* music.

A playlist I set up to go on repeat so it would be playing softly as we came home.

I have—had?—plans and no little amount of certainty (or maybe hope) that Doc would clear me.

But now...

"And is that garlic?" she whispers.

I inhale even though I know exactly what's in the crockpot.

A freezer meal that I didn't make, except to toss it in the pot and turn the dial to low. But another part of my plan—wine and food, some frozen rolls thrown in the oven to warm, and...

Dee slips by me, too fast for me to corral her, and definitely moving too quickly for me to intercept her and take her back to her place, fuck her senseless, and forget the fact that I'm playing eighties hair bands on repeat not because I necessarily like them but because they're her favorite.

"Oh," I hear and something inside me shrivels up.

Because I can't tell if her tone is full of laughter.

Or if she likes it.

Still, I'm a hockey player.

I stand in front of hundred mile per hour pucks, get into fist fights to protect my teammates. Not to mention, I put my heart on the line for a woman who could have just as easily turned me down.

And I'm more scared of her reaction in this moment than *any* of that.

Because this is important, and it means a lot, and—

"Honey," she whispers, striding back out into the hallway. "Come here."

I just...I can't make my feet move.

Luckily, she doesn't force me to.

Instead, she walks over to me, wrapping her hand around mine, and drawing me forward. Drawing me into the kitchen.

Drawing me into the scene I set up.

It has all the usual suspects—candles, the crockpot full of a delicious-smelling meal, a large bouquet of flowers, her favorite dessert from Molly's in the robin's egg blue box on the counter. But it's the board with the printouts I've been working with that has my stomach knotting.

Because it's important she see it.

That she know she helped create it.

A combination of low tech tools—translucent sticky tabs on the paper, a square ruler with a clear window in it, pages printed in special fonts, and high tech—my therapist making a verbal recording of the drills, voiceover of reports.

Put together?

I'm making progress.

That's the cherry on top of all this.

"Is this—?" she asks.

I nod. "It's not perfect, and I still have a long way to go. But DeeDee—I can read the reports, I can understand the videos, and I think I can make my way through the drills without faltering. And...hell, I'm actually excited about learning in a way—"

My voice cracks and her hand tightens around mine.

"In a way I've never been before." I tug, drawing her into the circle of my arms. "Because of you."

Her exhale is shaky. "You're the one doing all the work, honey."

I touch her cheek, hold her gaze, needing her to understand how big this is for me. "Thank you."

"Baby—"

I press my lips to hers. "Thank you," I repeat.

Another shaky exhale has my heart squeezing, but my determination to take our evening toward a less emotional direction takes over and I heft her up onto to the counter.

"Now," I say, handing her the box. "You're going to eat dessert first while I—"

"No, honey," she says, setting the box aside.

I blink. "I know this"—I sweep a hand out—"is a lot, but I just wanted—"

She opens her legs, wraps them around my hips, pulling me toward her. "I know what you wanted, and I need you to know how much it means to me." Her eyes go damp. "Sharing that"—a nod to the board—"the candles—and I'm glad to see they're battery-operated—"

I touch her cheek. "We live in a fire-prone area, sweetheart—"

"I know. Same as I know you considered exactly that when you put them out." I open my mouth, shut it. Because she's right. And anyway, she's still talking. "What I'm saying is you care. And—" Her hands settle on my shoulders and she leans in, pressing her forehead against mine. "You think about the small details and you look out for me and your heart is so damned beautiful that seeing these glimpses of it almost hurts, it's so gorgeous."

"DeeDee baby—"

"So, I need you to know that I see the flowers and I see the care and I see *you*," she says, pressing even closer, "but—"

My heart thuds hard again.

"*But*," she says again, "what I really would love is for you to fuck me, baby. And then when we're both satisfied we can eat whatever smells so good *and* Molly's dessert and—"

I don't wait for her to go on.

I just...give us what we both want.

Not the romance that I thought she needed, the romance she saw and liked but seriously *doesn't* need tonight.

That doesn't mean I'm not going to give it to her again in the future.

I'm just...

Well, we get to have *this* too.

So, I slant my mouth over hers.

And because her lips are parted on those words, I don't hesitate to take advantage.

Same as I don't hesitate to scoop her up and carry her up the stairs.

THIRTY-NINE

Diana

HE DROPS me on the bed and even as I'm gasping in surprise at my sudden change in position, he's on me.

Oh God, he's never kissed me like this before.

Never.

Like I'm his breath, the only thing keeping him alive.

And since I feel the same—so fucking desperate to taste him, to weld him to my tongue, my body, my *soul*—I push him over to his back, clambering on top and kissing him until my lungs positively scream for oxygen.

And then I kiss him some more.

Thankfully, he's on the same page, lips firm against mine, tongue stroking deep.

Then he flips us and I'm on my back again. But only for a second.

A tug has me upright and then he whips my shirt over my head, tosses it to the side.

"Yours too," I rasp as he reaches for the button on my jeans.

Hot eyes hit mine.

They hold as he reaches down and tears off his tee, sending it sailing through the air in the direction of mine.

This time, when he reaches for the button of my jeans, I don't stop him.

I don't *want* to.

And a moment later they're gone, along with my panties. But when I go to demand the same of him, these last weeks of foreplay meaning I want him inside me, deep and fucking me hard and fast, he kisses me.

Fucking perfect.

Later we can go slow.

Later we can savor.

Later—

He pulls back, breathing heavy. "Open up, sweetheart."

I still. "What?"

"Spread those legs for me."

My breath hitches.

Then I do as he orders.

"Fuck," he growls, crawling between my thighs and trailing his fingers through the slick heat of me. "You have the prettiest pussy I've ever seen."

I choke, hips jerking, eyes going wide.

And then I'm gasping his name as he pushes a finger inside me.

His mouth curves and he bends his head, tongue flicking through my labia, stroking me inside and out.

"Hudson," I groan as he licks me, as he slips in another finger and fucks me slow and deep and steady.

God, that feels good.

But it's not what I *want*.

"Hudson," I groan again as my orgasm starts gathering inside me.

It's going to be big.

It's going to destroy me.

I just...

I don't want to have it alone.

"Hudson," I say again, plunging my hands into his hair and tugging him away from my clit—and seriously, the man never misses, never falters in his rhythm.

Case in point?

Those fingers still fucking me.

The stream of warm air he blows on my pussy has me shivering before his eyes hit mine and he asks, "Yeah, DeeDee baby?"

I smooth his hair back. God, he's pretty. "I love it when you call me that," I whisper.

He smiles and it's sexy as hell. "I know. But baby?"

"Yeah?"

His fingers flex inside me and my head falls back, a moan tumbling from my lips. "You got my attention, sweetheart," he says, amusement in every syllable. "What'd you want?"

I lift it, try to focus. "You."

His smile widens.

"Inside me."

It fades, heat taking its place, his eyes full of thunderstorms...and God, I've never wanted to be struck by lightning.

Until now.

But I watch him temper his need, control that storm. "Let me take care of you first, baby. Let me make it good for you." He curls his fingers and sweet Christ, that feels incredible.

Let me.

And seriously, this man is killing me.

But somehow I manage to stay focused. "We've had weeks of good," I tell him. "Weeks of *incredible*, really. So..." I tilt my hips. "Let's go fast now, honey. And later we can go slow."

His gaze locks with mine.

And I hold my breath, thinking that as serious as I am, as much as I want this, I won't push it further.

Because I want him to want what I want.

But not at the expense of what *he* wants.

"God, I like you," he mutters.

"I like you too," I whisper. "So much."

The storm clears from his eyes.

And then his fingers are out of me, and his pants are off, and—

"Oh, God," I groan as he slides inside me, so hard, so thick, that he's stretching me wide. He's gentle. He's deep.

But he's not slow.

Not the first time anyway.

But that's okay, the second time, after apple muffins and crockpot chicken and hot crunchy rolls doused liberally with butter, is slow.

So slow that he leaves me limp and sated and all but unconscious by the time he's finished with me.

But that's okay too—

Because he holds me tight as I drift off to sleep.

And when he wakes me in the morning for more fast—although this time with a side of hard and deep—he does it by first holding me close.

―――――

"Why am I nervous?" I mutter, Huddy's big hand wrapped tightly around mine as we walk toward the team's plane.

He flicks a glance my way and draws us to a halt. "Because this shit is nerve-wracking?"

"Maybe," I say. "But we talked about this with Jean-Michel.

We talked with the rest of the coaching staff and HR. We're not going to be making out in the hallways—"

"Anymore," he teases, flashing me a smile that has my heart squeezing.

"Anymore," I agree, lips twitching. "But we're also not hiding us."

His fingers brush over my cheek then trail up to my ear, tucking an errant strand of hair behind it. "No," he murmurs, "we're not."

We're not hiding.

We're standing strong, no matter the shitstorm(s) coming our way.

And step one of that is coming out—officially—with the rest of the team.

Oh, my God. The *team*, which includes Pat and Duncan and Kane and—

"I'm going to puke," I mutter.

Huddy's expression is soft and sweet. "No, you're not."

"I am."

He cups both of my cheeks in his palms. "This isn't just a fling or a fuck. This is *us*, remember? And that's special enough we don't give a fuck what anyone else thinks."

"Right," I agree, trying to keep those words close. Because I've said them.

I've meant them.

I just...didn't think about having to abide by them while boarding the team's plane.

"And you're a badass who can handle stubborn, annoying hockey players," he says gently. "The razzing will come. You know that's part of the deal and you'll take it for a bit and then you'll put a stop to it with those drills that kick our ass and everyone will go back to business as usual."

Razzing. Drills. Coaching. Business as usual.

I can do that.

I can *do* that.

"You're right." Exhaling, I push the nerves away and lift my chin, walking across the tarmac. "I just need to channel Coach Dee." My lips twitch. "*And* those drills."

"Since I give you orgasms, do I get out of the super shitty ones?"

"Absolutely not," I say as we climb the stairs and step aboard.

He bursts out laughing and I'm so distracted by the gorgeous sound of it, I'm not worried anymore, or paying attention to the plane's occupants.

I'm just me.

And Huddy's right by my side.

His laughter fades and he leans close, lips at my ear. "I don't think we have to worry about favoritism, DeeDee baby." He kisses my temple and I'm suddenly aware that we're inside the plane.

And it's silent.

And that there are so, so many eyes on us.

My body tenses, but Hudson doesn't retreat. He just whispers. "Should we make out and really give them something to talk about?"

I still.

Then I start laughing. "I think making out on the plane is worse than a shadowed corridor, honey."

"Maybe you're right." A tug of my ponytail before he bends and brushes his lips over mine. "I'll see you on the other side of the flight, DeeDee baby."

And with that, he leaves me, heading to the back of the plane to join the rest of the players.

And I'm sitting down next to my coaching staff.

"Oh my God," Kaitlyn—my assistant coach—says, her eyes

wide but her smile wider. "I love him for you. He's so dreamy and—"

"*I'm* not interested in discussing Diana's love life," Tom mutters.

Kaitlyn's nose wrinkles, but she takes Tom's cue—a cue I'm thankful for—and focuses. "Should we talk about the Sierra's top line then?"

I glance back at Huddy, who's settled in next to Rhodes.

"Yes," I say. "Let's get to work."

FORTY

Hudson

"I HEAR you're fucking that sweet piece of ass who's our coach."

The locker room—that I've just walked through the door of because we have a game tonight and I need to, you know, get my gear on—falls silent at Pat's asshole statement.

Yeah, getting on the plane yesterday morning hand-in-hand with Dee wasn't exactly flying under the radar when it comes to Pat and his merry band of assholes knowing about us, but since we decided we're not going to hide our relationship, them's the breaks.

We'll deal with whatever ridiculous press comes our way, ignore the typical hockey shit-giving (because relationship with Dee or not, my teammates would just find something else to give me shit about), and keep building what we've been building.

Because it's new.

But even if it is new, it's important.

And I can handle teasing and annoying news stories.

I just...

Well, in the time I've known him, I've done my best to not think about Pat, not under any circumstances.

Something that was a fucking mistake, if his smirk is any indication, the poison in his soul shining through his beady, snakelike gaze.

He thinks he's found a weakness.

And he's going to keep poking and prodding at it until we're bleeding out on the floor.

I should have known better, should have kept a wary eye on him, found some way to keep him in line when it comes to Diana and my relationship.

Like blackmail.

Or punching him repeatedly until he sees reason.

Because he's clearly delusional.

And needs to be punched.

Case in point?

He takes my annoyance and ramps it up to murderous rage with his next words.

"I bet Coach is a wildcat in the sack," he drawls, smirking at me as his idiotic teenage bully like sidekicks, Kane and Duncan, cackle like the dumbasses they are.

"Shut the fuck up," Cam growls.

Pat ignores him, meandering my way—and fuck me, but he's within arm's reach now and seriously testing my control.

Especially when his smirk grows and he leans in, poking me in the chest. "She's so controlled. *Fuck.*" He groans and pumps his hips through the air, demonstrating exactly what he'd do to Dee.

To *my* woman.

"—What I wouldn't do to have a go at making her forget herself."

"Not cool, man," Rhodes mutters.

"What's *not cool*," Pat says, "is Huddy tapping that ass of hers and not sharing all the sexy, behind the scenes details."

Motherfucker.

I open my mouth, but King's suddenly at my side and he shoves Pat, sending him skittering back several paces. "You're not funny, dumbass. And no one wants to listen to your bullshit, so keep your thoughts to yourself." He settles a hand on my shoulder, glances down at me and I don't miss the message in his eyes.

Keep cool.

Don't get sucked into Pat's special brand of asshole.

I grind my teeth together and nod.

Pat rights himself, seemingly nonplussed about the push. Instead, he smirks at me and taps a finger against his bottom lip. "Or maybe I'd rather lay back and let her boss me around like she does on the ice while she rides my cock."

Right.

And now I'm going to *kill* this motherfucker.

I brush off King's hand—or maybe he's so pissed that he releases me and shoves me forward. Either way, I take a step toward Pat, hands clenching into fists at my sides, my eyes narrowing, retort bubbling up.

Before it can escape, I pause, claw at the edges of my control.

Because I don't want to make trouble for DeeDee.

I inhale deeply. Then exhale.

"Cat got your tongue?" he asks with that ever-present smirk.

God, he's such a fucking asshole. A poison on the roster, one that slowly eats away at all the good, erodes the camaraderie and teamwork.

"Or maybe you were too busy using it last night."

Red hazes my vision.

"Fuck. *Off*," West snaps.

"Fuck her," Pat says. "I think that's what you mean. Because we all want to."

I growl softly.

"Huddy," Rome warns quietly.

I grit my teeth together so tightly a bolt of pain shoots through my jaw.

Because I know what my captain is reminding me of.

Yes, Pat is head asshole, and he deserves to have his ass handed to him but—

Christ.

I can't to start a fight in the locker room, can't create even more of a mess for DeeDee to clean up when she'll already have enough to deal with when our relationship goes public.

Or *more* public.

I keep grinding my teeth together and this time I pair it with turning on my heel and moving to my stall.

Get dressed.

Get on the ice.

Take this rage out on the other team.

Lake Jordan won't mind if I lay him out mid-ice—or attempt to since the man's a big fuck and at best odds, I have a fifty-fifty chance of successfully checking him. But he can take it, can handle my anger.

Hell, he'd probably be more than happy to dish it back.

And our fans would enjoy that far more than reports of me beating Pat to a bloody pulp before the game, thus taking one of our top scorers off the ice before an important game against one of our top rivals.

Fuck.

Why do I have to have logic pouring through my brain?

No, it's not logic. It's *love*.

And it's...because I will do anything for Diana—eat shit, twist myself into knots, endure whatever torture I have to.

So long as she's safe.

And protected.

And *mine*.

"Ignore him," I mutter to King, who's still glaring at Pat. I tilt my head toward our gear, laid out by the equipment guys. "Let's just focus on the game."

"And after we take down the Sierra, you and me will take turns tagging Coach." Pat grins, thrusts his hips again. "God, I can't wait to fuck that hole."

Right.

Fuck the bad press.

I'm going to kill to him.

I move before I'm really processing it, closing the distance between us and grabbing him by the throat. And if I wasn't so pissed, the fear in his wide eyes as I slam him against the locker room wall would have been hilarious.

As it is, I'm not feeling all that jolly.

"Don't you *ever* say another word about Diana," I growl. "Or you'll be dealing with me."

"And me," King says, tone deadly.

"Me too," Rhodes growls.

"I can't wait to punch out this motherfucker," West mutters.

"I'd rather use Attie's gun." Cam's eyes flash.

"Maybe Chrissy's vet will neuter him," Rome moves to my side, my captain no longer warning me off, not in the least.

"You!"

I jump and, no joke, twenty heads whip toward the open door.

To see Dee standing in the open door.

"My office," she snaps, eyes locked onto Pat. "Now."

FORTY-ONE

Diana

MY HEART IS POUNDING as I lead Pat down the hall and I've never—*ever*—wanted to go all Jason Bourne and stab someone with a pen more than right now.

I exhale silently, strive for calm.

Calm. Calm. *Calm.*

And still, by the time I make it to the door of my makeshift office here at the Sierra's arena, I'm no closer to calm.

I still want to commit murder.

I heard...well, I think I pretty much heard *everything*—or enough to know that a big chunk of what I was worried about in taking this dive with Hudson is coming true.

Enough to know that I need to decide right now.

Here and fucking now.

Am I in or am I out?

Only there's no decision, is there?

I'm in—I've been in for weeks now.

So now it's a matter of digging my heels in and not giving in to this asshole who thinks I'm a *hole* to fuck.

My fingers clench on my iPad and I swear I hear the screen groan in protest.

A screen that's displaying the lineup I'd gone to the room to announce.

And instead I got to hear...

Calm.

I gesture with a hand toward one of the chairs. "Sit," I say.

He leans back against the open door, arms and ankles crossed. "I'd rather stand."

Of course he would.

The better to torment me.

Stifling a sigh, I move to the desk, lean back against it, and stare at him.

For a long, long time.

It's a game of chicken, one that's going to determine who the fuck is in charge here.

And I'm not going to lose.

So yeah, it goes on a long, long time.

Eventually—thank fuck—he cracks. "What do you want, Coach? At some point I need to get dressed for the game."

"Do you?" I ask quietly.

That gets to him, and I see a flicker of emotion—of uncertainty—in his eyes.

I tick that victory onto my side of the board. I don't think I've ever seen him anything but cocky.

So I press my advantage. "I will not tolerate sexual harassment on my team—in any form—between players, directed toward my staff, or toward me."

His mouth curves into a smirk, cocky snapping right back into place. "Oh, but it's okay to fuck one of your players?"

That urge for murder by pen comes roaring back.

"My relationship with Hudson is none of your business," I grit out. "Except to say—and this is the *only* thing I'll ever say to you about it—it's between two consenting adults and management is aware of it, so we can put systems in place to make sure it's fair for you and the rest of the team."

"You mean so your boyfriend doesn't get preferential treatment?"

They're sharp words, still intended to piss me off.

Yet, for the first time, I feel like I'm finally seeing a glimpse of the man beneath all that asshole.

Another victorious tick on my side of the board.

He's just an insecure bully.

And he's scared.

"Right now I'm more worried about why you seem so determined to blow up the team when it's the first time in your career that you're on the roster of a contender for the Cup. A career I don't think I have to remind you is on its leeward slide, so you may never get another chance at winning it all."

His brows drag together, but I see the venom in his eyes.

And I get in front of it.

"You're not dressing out tonight," I tell him.

He pushes off the wall, anger flashing across his face. "What the fuck?"

"Think about what you're doing," I say calmly. "Think about where you want to be. If that's hefting the Cup by my side then you need to get your fucking head in the game. If it's continuing to do this same shit time and again then it won't be with this team—I don't care how many concessions I have to make to get you off my roster."

"This is bullshit," he snaps, moving toward me.

"Bullshit or not"—I shrug carelessly—"I have the power to do *exactly* that."

He stops in front of me, breathing heavily, fury in every line of his taut body.

Even though my pulse speeds up, I just stare up at him calmly. "We're done here."

A long furious look, a microscopic shift of his body that has me tensing.

Then he's spinning on his heel and storming from the room.

Sighing, I rub my forehead, waiting for my pulse to steady, and when it does, I look up and see Jean-Michel leaning against the opposite wall, eyes full of rage, his jaw clenched.

"You good?" he asks tightly.

I know he's here because someone alerted him and those protective instincts of his were triggered.

Same as I know and register—a good thing because my already hanging-on-by-a-thread temper doesn't snap—he didn't interject himself into the conversation with Pat because he knows I'm good at my job and can handle myself and he was giving me the space to do exactly that.

Same as I know, if Pat had gotten physical, he *would* have stepped in.

I'm just glad he didn't need to.

And because of all that, I give him the truth.

"Am I good?" I mutter. "No. But I'm more than ready to go win a fucking hockey game."

His mouth quirks up. "Now that's the best thing I've heard all day."

BEING DOWN one our star forwards less than an hour before game time isn't ideal.

But there are always a few players who travel with the team

253

in case of injury or family emergency, so I looped in Wilder, one of our young guys.

It's a good opportunity for him to get some playing time in the big leagues.

And it's a great opportunity for us to see the skills he's been working so hard to develop in the AHL.

"That's it, kid!" King shouts, jerking me out of my thoughts and sending my focus to Wilder.

And, damn, King's right.

Wilder is carrying the puck up along the far side of the boards and he's just deked around Lake Jordan.

That's right.

Lake Jordan.

With a move that is so damned wicked it should be illegal... with a move that pisses off Lake because he digs in his edges, sending up a spray of snow as he rapidly changes direction and takes off after Wilder.

But Wilder is at full speed and he's got those wicked moves and—

I whistle softly as he gets around one of the Sierra's defenseman, Riggs Ashford, and closes in on the goal.

He lifts his head, looking to dish off a pass—

Or...never mind.

It's a fake, and even I bite for a second.

The Sierra's goalie does too, shifting off his post and giving Wilder space to shoot.

And the kid's got some hands.

Hands he uses to shoot...and slip that puck into the top corner.

All without looking.

I whistle again, and Kaitlyn glances over at me, our hockey coach hearts expanding three sizes at the joy that shot brings us.

I look back at the ice, see that Lake's furious. That Riggs is even more so.

Wilder won't get that much space again, won't have so clear a lane at the net again, not now that they know what he can do.

But given the determination in his hazel eyes as he exchanges fist bumps and nods back at me when I tell him, "Nice work," I have no doubt he'll keep bringing that to his game and upping the ante.

Fuck yeah.

Pat Franklin might have officially just lost his starting spot on the roster.

And the Sierra better watch out.

We're coming for them.

Hell, we're coming for everyone.

FORTY-TWO

Hudson

I DON'T LIKE the way Pat looks at Diana as he boards the team plane, but he doesn't do more than glare before heading to the back of the plane.

"I'll catch you later," I tell DeeDee as she sits down with her coaching staff.

I'll be napping after a game that kicked my ass in a way that had me feeling every minute of the two weeks off.

Meanwhile, since it's fresh in their brains, Dee and her coaching team will be going over the matchup against the Sierra for the first time tonight—looking for all the ways we can improve.

And yeah, I know there are *always* things to clean up, but for tonight, they'll be looking at small tweaks.

Because we killed them.

Fuck, I don't think I've ever seen that much of a blowup against the Sierra. And definitely not on their home ice.

Certainly *I've* never been part of one.

And yeah, we're going to have a battle on our hands the next time we play them, that's for damn sure, but I'm still grinning as I stride down the aisle and plunk my ass in an empty seat.

Because that's the game.

That's the sport.

Every play, every shift, every game a battle. The season long and intense and, sometimes, surprising. You never know when the hockey gods are going to smile down on you so you throw every bit of effort into soaking up each and every moment—good, bad, or otherwise.

Because who knows how long the ride will last.

And *that's* why I love what I do.

Hockey's in my blood, it speaks to my soul.

And it feels fucking great to be back.

"No, honey," I hear and glance up to see Rhodes striding down the aisle, his cell pressed to his ear. "Olive and Pear don't need clothes. They're cats. They have fur."

I bite back a laugh.

Apparently not very well considering the dark look he tosses my direction as he sinks down into the seat next to me.

"And anyway," he mutters, dropping his bag and shoving it under the seat in front of him, "you really should be in bed. It's late. Where's Finn?"

He goes ramrod stiff and I straighten, amusement gone.

"She's sick?" he says. "How sick?" Then he shakes his head, like he realizes that's a ridiculous question to ask a four-year-old who can't possibly discern the difference. "Listen, baby"—his voice goes gentle—"I'll be home in a little over an hour."

Luckily we're in Tahoe and the flight time isn't long.

"Can you do me a favor and be an extra big girl?" He pauses, waiting for her to answer. "Oh, good. Thanks, baby.

Now can you go in Finn's bedroom and keep an eye on her for me?"

I stop, considering that. Because it doesn't make any sense.

She's four.

Finn's an adult.

Then I realize that stubborn, precocious Chloe likely wouldn't go back into *her* bedroom, not just because her dad told her to. But recruit her to his side—being a big girl, looking out for one of her favorite people?

Damn, the man's good.

I file away the parenting note, know that I'm working toward a future where there's a strong possibility I'll have stubborn, precocious daughters just like Chloe.

Or a certain stubborn, badass hockey coach.

"Great," Rhodes says, "tell me when you're there." A pause. "She's sleeping? Oh, good. Can you climb in next to her, make sure she doesn't get cold?" More silence. Then, "You're there? Great job, honey. I'll be home in an hour."

"You good?" I ask when he hangs up.

He's pulled up a camera app on his phone, is scrolling through the screens and I see he's tracking Chloe through the house and upstairs. Then down a hallway where she disappears through a door.

Rhodes exhales, but I notice that he leaves the feed open to the hallway, even though the forward doors are closed and the flight attendants are starting their checks. "I'm good."

I don't say a word—and neither do they.

Minutes later we're in the air.

And not all that long later we're back on the ground.

And, no surprise to anyone around us, when Rhodes is the first one off the plane.

"Meow!"

I blink, see that sunshine is pouring in through the windows and groan.

Even with the short flight, we were home late.

Late enough that I don't want to think about dragging my ass out of bed—not for hours yet.

"*Meow!*"

Apparently more sleep isn't going to happen.

Groaning softly, I slide out from beneath the covers and scoop up Lola.

"You're a pain in the ass," I murmur, both meaning it and not—mostly because Lola is cute as fuck and also currently butting her head against my jaw, purring like a madwoman now that I've picked her up and held her close.

Her purring doesn't stop as I move from the room and head downstairs to make her breakfast.

Lucky for me that means opening the lid on a can of cat food and dumping it into a bowl.

"Meow," she says by way of thanks then gets on with chowing down.

Since I'm awake, I take stock of the fridge.

I have a hankering for French toast, and considering it's one of the few things my mom took it upon herself to teach me how to make, I'm good at it.

So, I start gathering ingredients—bread and cinnamon, milk and vanilla, eggs...

I freeze, my head halfway in the fridge, eyes searching the shelves.

Damn.

No eggs.

I guess I'm heading to the store.

I grab my keys, slip out the front door, making sure it's latched and locked before heading to my car.

"Hey, boy!"

Freezing, I glance over the top of my car, see Ernest on his porch.

Damn.

He's using the cane today.

Which means he's not feeling good.

"Where are you off to?" he calls.

"The grocery store. We're out of eggs."

"Whatcha using eggs for?" he asks and even across the yard, I see his face light up. "Is Diana making her frittata? Because, boy, that frittata will have you falling in love."

"Too late for that," I tell him.

He grins. "Thatta boy."

"Anyway, she's not making her frittata, I'm making her French toast."

"I love French toast."

Christ.

"Me too," I say and then add because I know that DeeDee would offer the same, "Want to join us for breakfast?"

"Oh no, I couldn't." He tilts his head to the side. "Though, I do *love* French toast."

A throb in my temple. "Right," I mutter. "Come over in an hour. I'll be back from the store and ready by then."

I tug open the door to my car. "Boy?"

"Ernest," I say, clinging to my patience, "I really should get going."

"Didn't you want some eggs?" He hitches a thumb over his shoulder. "I have some inside."

FORTY-THREE

Diana

"DEEDEE BABY," I hear from a distance.

But I don't want to wake up.

I'm tired and cozy and it's too damned early.

Unfortunately, the voice doesn't go away.

"No," I groan, burrowing deeper into my pillows. "More sleeping. Less talking."

"Hmm," I hear, and unfortunately it draws me closer to the surface of wakefulness. "Normally, I would love you sleepy and naked in bed. But we have a senior citizen chaperone." I frown, processing that as a hand ghosts over my cheek, my neck, down along my side, taking the blankets with them.

"Hey!" I cry as cold invades, my eyes flashing open.

"I made breakfast," Huddy murmurs, trailing his fingertips over my belly.

Which growls. "You did?"

He nods, mouth twitching. "French toast, sausage, and eggs."

My stomach rumbles again.

"Get dressed," he says, wrapping his fingers around my wrist and tugging me out of bed, nudging me toward the closet.

"Bossy," I mutter.

"Gotta compete with my stubborn badass girlfriend," he says, swatting me lightly on the ass.

"Rude." I mock scowl.

"DeeDee baby?"

"Mmm?" I ask as I reach into a drawer and pull out a pair of sweats.

"Ernest is eating with us."

I still, heart squeezing. "He is?"

Suddenly, Huddy is there, body close, hands cupping my cheeks. "He loaned us the eggs." His mouth hitches up. "Couldn't leave him to his own devices. Plus"—he settles his forehead against mine—"he's using his cane today, so I figure he can use a good meal and a couple of underlings to boss around."

There my heart goes again. "Honey," I whisper, covering his hands with my own.

"If you want to stay up here while I pull weeds or wax his car or whatever he orders me to do, you can." He brushes his lips over my forehead. "I'll bring you up a plate and you can—"

"I love you!" I blurt.

He rocks back on his heels and my heart convulses again—this time painfully.

Shit.

I can't believe I said that out loud. It's too much. Too soon. Just too *much*.

"Forget I said anything," I whisper. "I, uh. I'm just hungry and really love French toast. Clearly, that's gone to my head."

"Baby," he says, his voice so damned soft it almost hurts. "Look at me."

"Go on downstairs," I order. "I'll be right behind you."

"*Dee.*" His fingers come to my jaw. "Please look at me, sweetheart."

My throat is tight, my pulse hammering through my veins, but I manage to bring my gaze back to his.

And God, but his eyes are beautiful.

Like a thunderstorm is just beginning to clear on a warm summer day.

He takes my hand, presses it to his chest. "Feel that?"

"Feel what?" I ask.

"My heart," he murmurs.

I nod.

"Baby, it beats for you."

I suck in a breath, my knees going weak as relief surges through me. But he's got me—of course he does. His arms band around my waist and he draws me close, and then...he's kissing me.

And it's a different kind of kiss.

It's not hot and deep, full of lips and teeth and tongues.

It's not gentle and slow, lazily tasting me on a morning off.

It's...a promise. The promise of forever despite the shit-storms. The promise of a future that may not be perfect but will be perfect for us. The promise of—

"Let's go, kids!" Ernest calls up the stairs, making us jump apart, chests heaving. "Breakfast is getting cold!"

The promise of smiles shared and lives intertwining and love growing strong and sure.

Hudson presses his forehead to mine, sighs.

I laugh softly. "I'll get dressed and be right down."

"Okay, sweetheart," he murmurs. Then his eyes sparkle with mirth. "But don't think you telling me you love me means that you're getting out of weeding."

More laughter, this time mine *and* his.

Then he kisses me briefly before slipping out of the room.

I get dressed, brush my teeth, put up my hair—the better for that forthcoming weeding. Then I head downstairs.

Ernest is sitting at my kitchen table, a plate in front of him that he's going to town on.

Huddy looks up as I stride into the room, eyes warm. "Coffee, baby?" he asks, holding up a mug.

I nod, whisper, "Thanks."

He cups my cheek then jerks his chin toward the table. "Your plate's ready for you."

"What about you?"

He picks up another plate. "Right behind you."

"Thank you."

His brows drag together. "Why you thanking me?"

"For taking care of me," I murmur. "For making me breakfast." I touch his cheek. "For loving me."

Gentle fingers on my cheek, telling me how much he likes to hear that.

And how much he'd like to *show* me how much he likes to hear that, if only we didn't have that senior citizen chaperone.

"Later," I murmur.

"I'm going to hold you to that." His lips twitch and he hands me my mug of coffee—with two sugars and a dash of vanilla creamer.

"I sure like having you around much more than that Jason asshole," Ernest says as he saws off a huge hunk of his French toast. "He never cooked." He shoves it in his mouth, talking around the bite. "Never even so much as waved hello." He swallows, cuts off another piece. "He definitely never invited me over for breakfast or offered to help clean out my gutters."

I glance at Huddy, my lips twitching.

He just shrugs.

"Hell," Ernest says around another bite. "He never did much of anything except be useless. You on the other hand"—

he waves his fork in our direction—"appear to be a halfway decent sort of man."

Hudson snorts and shakes his head, topping off his own coffee.

"The highest of compliments," I say dryly as I take my mug to the table and sit down across from Ernest. "And anyway," I tell him firmly as I pick up my own fork, "there's no need to talk about Jason any longer. He's out of my life, which means none of us will have to worry about seeing him ever again."

Ernest frowns, setting his fork down, eyebrows drawn together.

"But, missy, I saw him on TV this morning."

And even though I knew the shitstorm was coming...

I'm still not prepared.

FORTY-FOUR

Hudson

SO MUCH FOR the day off.

I'm currently sitting in the chair across from Dee's desk at the Gold's practice facility, thinking this shit would have been much easier to undertake if the Eagles' rink was back up and running.

Mostly because I wouldn't have to temper the urge to put my fist through the wall.

This space isn't ours. I can't start punching sheetrock and throwing chairs.

Jean-Michel is sitting on the edge of the desk, Diana is behind it, her head in her hands, and our social media team is talking about the best course of action to get ahead of this.

Only...there's no *getting ahead* of it.

Because the scene that Diana told me about—Jason wrapping his arms around another woman and kissing her as Wings (the team's mascot) ran through the back halls intent on crowd entertainment has hit the internet.

And it's gone viral.

Mostly because someone found the full video feed—of both Jason *and* Diana.

And spliced them together.

I shouldn't have watched.

But seeing the wide shot of Jason sucking face with a random woman as Wings ran by transitioning right onto Dee, her face tilted up to the screen, her eyes filled with hurt...

Yeah, that was what really triggered my wall-punching and chair-throwing urges.

Or maybe it was the *other* video that is starting to rack up views.

Me and Diana walking hand-in-hand toward the plane, me smiling down at her then tucking a strand of hair behind her ear combined with that original video, the news of our relationship fanning the fires of social media virality to epic proportions.

Dee's old and new.

Add in the beleaguered Eagles who've been in the news far too much of late.

The firing and criminal activities of the last head coach.

Chrissy and Rome.

Rory and King.

Jean-Michel and Tiff.

The earthquake.

And—oh yeah—my taking a hit from the ceiling for Dee is making its rounds thanks to some of the patients at the hospital.

I wish it was a nurse or doctor so they'd get their gossiping asses fired.

Unfortunately, I don't get everything I want.

So yeah, I'm pissed.

But, fuck, the look in DeeDee's eyes during that first game.

Her *first* game coaching in the NHL.

How could Jason do that to her?

"...is there something in the water the training staff gives the Eagles' players?"

I blink, narrow my eyes at the social media team who are scrolling through videos and playing them on a portable screen for us to see.

This line is spoken by a slender brunette who's fanning herself. "I didn't think they could get hotter, but sweet baby Jesus, I think I need to move to the Bay Area and throw myself in front of one of their cars."

"Or beneath a collapsing ceiling," her friend says with a smirk.

Diana groans and thumps her head against her desk.

I really don't think the team needs to show us every single video that's trending.

"They are *hawt*," another influencer says. "Have you seen the way he looks at her?" She grins. "It's a real-life hockey romance. The head coach with her hot hockey player boyfriend. I'm in *luv!*"

DeeDee groans.

I shove out of my chair, round the desk, and crouch beside her.

"I should step down," she whispers. "Should take the train wreck of my life far, far away from the team. Let the guys focus on hockey instead of who I love."

Most of those words piss me off.

The last three keep my temper in check.

They don't do the same for Jean-Michel.

"You're not quitting," he snaps, plucking the words out of my brain and saying them far more sharply than I would have dared to at this moment in the proceedings.

I was thinking soft and gentle, coaxing.

And barring that technique, digging my heels in and outstubborning her.

Jean-Michel, apparently, is choosing the nuclear option.

"Come on," she says. "You know better. This is—"

"Brilliant!" Toni, one of the social media girls, exclaims.

"No," Dee murmurs. "I was going to say this is a disaster."

"The internet is on your side," Toni says, ignoring her.

Stephanie nods, adds, "Do you know how rare that is for women?"

Dee glances at me then closes her eyes. "I know," she says morosely. "Same as I know it never lasts. Soon enough someone is going to have an opinion about Hudson and me, and that's going to catch fire. Then there will be more bad press for the team, more talk of inappropriate conduct." She opens her eyes, locks gazes with Jean-Michel. "The team doesn't need that."

Fuck.

I hate that she's right.

Almost as much as I hate the expression on her face right now—the one that's resigned and worn down.

Like she's already given up.

Accepted that the world will turn on her.

"You're not quitting," I say. "If there ever comes a time when one of us has to go, that person will be me."

"No, Huddy—"

I cup her jaw. "It. Will. Be. Me."

Her eyes fill with tears and I can't take it anymore. I drag her out of her chair and into my arms. "I love you," I whisper. "And I've lived my dream. I'm not letting you give up yours."

"How could I live with myself if you—"

"It's not going to happen," I promise. "Because neither of us are going anywhere."

"And we actually have an opportunity here if we play it right," Toni says gently.

Dee pulls out of my arms, sinks back into her chair, and

sighs. "I don't want to have to think about playing things right or wrong. I just want to live my life."

"Tough shit." More sharp words from Jean-Michel.

Right.

One sharp rejoinder was bad enough.

A second is two too many.

A third...isn't going to happen.

"You need to give us the room," I tell them. "And you"—I hold Jean-Michel's gaze—"need to watch your fucking tone."

The girls fall quiet.

Jean-Michel glares at me.

I hear a surreptitious snap and whip my head around, glaring at Stephanie.

She puts her hands up, palms out. "Just in case we want to use that later."

Toni nods, and I transfer my glare to her. "The protective boyfriend. Those thunderstorms in your gray eyes. Total chef's kiss." She glances at Stephanie, who holds up her phone. "If this man doesn't score a brand deal from this—"

Brand deals.

Influencers.

TikToks.

Fuck my life.

Yet, even as I'm thinking that, something shifts in my mind and a memory surfaces. Of a very different sort of video by a very different kind of influencer.

And suddenly the pieces start coming together.

I just need to get DeeDee on board.

"Out," I tell the room at large. "Now."

Stephanie and Toni are talking shop so they don't mind taking it into the hall. Jean-Michel, on the other hand, doesn't look happy to be kicked out.

Or maybe it's because I basically threatened him—my boss's boss.

Jesus, talk about living dangerously.

But I don't stop.

"Don't expect an apology," I mutter. "I won't tolerate any disrespect toward my woman."

His mouth hitches up. "You know there will be guys on other rosters who'll use that," he points out, and not wrongly.

"If you just let me—" Dee begins.

"No," Jean-Michel and I say together.

"She's one of us," I say—to him and to *her*. "We'll have her back against whoever seeks to hurt her." I fix him in place with a glare. "No matter what it takes."

He studies me.

Then nods, and I don't miss the approval in the gesture. He tilts his head in Dee's direction. "Make sure she gets we *all* feel that way."

"All except Pat," she mutters.

"After his scene the other day, I've already decided that Pat's getting traded at the first opportunity, and Duncan and Kane are right behind him if they don't get their shit together," Jean-Michel proclaims before striding from the room.

"Honey," she begins, shaking her head. "I don't think—"

"I say this with complete and total love, but baby, you need to shut the fuck up."

Her brows drag together, anger in the deep green depths. "Didn't you just get on Jean-Michel's case—not smart by the way—about respect?"

"Why?" I ask shortly.

She frowns. "Why what?"

"Why won't you fight for us?"

Her mouth is open, the fury in her eyes flaring.

Then she seems to process exactly what I said because the fury fades and tears fill her eyes. "Huddy," she whispers.

"You know I didn't have much growing up," I say softly. "You know precisely how little that *much* was. So you have to know how much you being in my life means to me, and how much it means that you love me."

Her exhale is shaky. "I—"

"But you also have to know that I would never do anything to hurt you—and that extends to what you're building here, the dream you're living." I cup her cheek. "You're not leaving," I command. "So stop fucking offering."

"Hudson!"

"No," I say. "No *Hudson*. No arguments. No bending to the will of some asshole who threw away the most precious gift the universe could give him."

Tears slide over her lashes, drip down her cheeks.

I wipe them away. "And I meant what I said before. If there ever comes a time when both us being on the same team is too much then *I'll* be the one to go."

"I can't ask you—"

"And *I'm* telling *you*." I rest my forehead against hers. "I've lived my dream for years now, baby. If me having you means stepping back so you can be free to live yours, then I'll do it in a heartbeat."

Her lungs hitch. "D-dammit!" she cries.

"Sweetheart," I murmur, drawing her against me, holding her tight. "What's the matter now?"

"Well, aside from you being so wonderful and sweet it's impossible to resist you"—she tilts her head back and scowls at me—"you're also right." She sighs and drops her head forward, resting it against my collarbone. "I'm sorry. What we have is more important than a video or some hard questions. It's even more important than my job."

"Baby—"

"But I hear you," she says. "I hear you and I don't think it'll come to that. But if it does..." She brushes her lips over my jaw. "I *hear* you, honey."

Relief ripples through me. "Glad to hear that."

We stand there, holding each other for a moment. Then she sighs and wrinkles her nose. "Do we have to let everyone back in now?"

"Probably." I grin at her disgruntled expression. "But it won't be so bad."

"Why do you say that?"

"Because I have a plan."

"A plan?"

"Yup," I tell her and tap her adorable nose. "And it's one I think you're going to like."

Her brows shoot up in question.

"We're going to let everyone back in—"

"Somehow I don't like *that* part," she mutters dryly.

I just grin before I finish.

"—and then we're going to set up an interview with Eva Moreno."

She stills. Then the tension leaves her frame and a smile curves her lips.

"What do you think?" I ask softly.

"Oh, my hot hockey player boyfriend..."

I laugh when she quotes one of the videos.

"...I think I need to kiss you now," she finishes, ad libbing in the best possible way.

The good news is that she's finally smiling.

The better news?

She does exactly that.

And *keeps* kissing me until Jean-Michel and the social media team get impatient and come back in to the office.

"That's hot," Stephanie says, snapping another pic before we break apart.

I sigh, glare at her then...focus.

Because we've got work to do.

FORTY-FIVE

Diana

I NERVOUSLY ADJUST the microphone that's attached to my lapel while trying to appear calm and serene and, well...

Not nervous.

"Breathe," Eva murmurs, gently batting my hands away. "I promise I'll be gentle."

Okay, so maybe I'm not hiding my nerves well.

I glance up at her, and she smiles. "I know our paths didn't much cross at the Breakers," she says quietly. "But I know something about falling for a hot hockey player boyfriend"—her mouth quirks—"at the absolute worst possible time." She finishes fixing my mic and leans back. "But I promise to be gentle."

"As gentle as the Eagles' social media team?" I ask dryly.

Her lips twitch. "Okay, how about more gentle than a mammogram and less gentle than say..."

"Walking over flaming coals?" I quip.

She snorts. "I was thinking stepping on a Lego."

I laugh...

And that's the moment I start giving my first—and last—interview on my love life.

It's live and it's raw and it's far from my favorite experience, but...it's me.

And that's all I can be.

"We have one final question from one of our viewers," Eva says, glancing down at a laptop as she scrolls through the comments. "Are you—"

I still when she doesn't finish, and something about her demeanor has the hair on my nape prickling. "Am I what?" I ask lightly, trying to get her focus back, to wrap this up. "Am I in awe of Hudson's abilities on the ice almost as much as I'm in awe of his big, generous—"

A throat clears and I glance over at the man I've been lucky enough to fall in love with, my lips twitching.

"I was going to say heart," I tell him.

And the world.

He swoops in and kisses me lightly, earning sighs from Eva's crew...and lots more pings from the comments coming in on the chat.

It's not until he's off-screen again, and no teasing has come from Eva that I realize something is seriously wrong.

I flick my eyes to the camera then back to her.

And finally, she looks up at me, her eyes shrouded, her expression serious. "I don't think this is where you'd choose to hear this news, but considering you're here, I think this is likely the best space for you to make a comment on it."

My stomach twists, but I lift my chin, straighten my shoulders. "Lay it on me."

Eva's mouth hitches up and then she turns the laptop in my direction.

I frown, not getting it.

Then she hits play.

And Pat's face comes on the screen.

"I figured the best thing I could do at this juncture is offer up my experience as a player on Coach Connors' roster."

"Right," I say, tapping the keyboard and pausing the three-minute video—or likely the three-minute long rant about my abilities. "I don't need to listen to any more of that."

Eva tilts her head to the side, blond ponytail swinging behind her.

But I don't miss the approval rippling across her face.

"Pat Franklin is a very talented hockey player, but I don't think I'm being remiss in saying that he's problematic in the locker room. We disagree on a lot of things—his work ethic, how he treats his teammates, the way he interacts with the Eagles' support staff."

"That's...quite a list."

"It is," I agree. "But here's the thing—I never give up on my players. If he showed up at the rink tomorrow ready to work hard, ready to be a team player, I would be all over that. He's talented. He's the second leading scorer on the roster."

"But you benched him before the last game."

"Yes." I nod and just...go for it. "Because he said some pretty reprehensible things while trying to start a fight in the locker room. I don't want my players breaking hands when they fight on the ice, but I sure as hell don't want them cracking bones before they even make it onto the rink."

"Were those reprehensible things about you?"

I inhale. Then exhale slowly. "Yes," I say. "This time they were about me. And, I can ignore awful comments about me made by online trolls, but I can't ignore them—whether they're directed at me or someone else in my organization—when they come from a player on my roster. That's not the team I'm trying to build, and it's not something I'm going to tolerate from this point forward."

"I think that's commendable," she says.

I shrug. "I don't know about that."

"I do." She reaches over and squeezes my head. "Working for the Breakers has given me plenty of insight into how good it feels to be part of team like that. And I think, if anyone can build it here in Oakland, it will be you."

"Thanks," I murmur, and I mean it.

Because I can tell by her words that *she* means it.

She straightens then gets back to business, dropping one final bomb on me when she says, "Last thing before we let you go, would you like to comment on Pat's admission that he released the initial footage of your ex cheating on you?"

I suck in a breath, my gaze locking with Hudson's. His expression is furious, and Jean-Michel, who's standing next to him, is equally as pissed.

I want to lean into that anger.

But I also know that's not me.

I'm better than that.

I can be smart and thoughtful and...*real.*

"That...that doesn't feel great," I admit, returning my focus to Eva. "Because I know he wasn't coming from a place of sharing that I've found someone better, someone who loves me and will treat me right."

She snorts. "It's pretty obvious he was trying to hurt you—either personally or professionally."

"I think you're right, but that intent aside, I also know it was probably the kindest thing he could have done for me." Her brows fly up in surprise. "I was agonizing over Hudson and my relationship coming out," I explain. "Knowing I would fight for it, same as I would fight for Huddy's place on the team and for my job, and yet also knowing I would step away from the team if I had to."

Hudson jerks like he wants to say something.

Jean-Michel actually opens his mouth.

Eva notices both of those and grins. "I'm guessing the team wasn't willing to let you go so easily."

"No," I say, glancing over at them again. "Lucky for me, they weren't. So really"—I turn toward her again—"Pat saved me weeks or months of angst. The world knows about Hudson and me, we're in love and have the team's blessing, and now we can move forward and play some really great fucking hockey."

"And I think that's the perfect place to end for today," Eva says, grinning at me before she gives her signature sign-off and then the live feed ends. "You did great," she murmurs. "Thank you for trusting me with this."

"Thank you for—"

Which is all I get out before Hudson tugs me into his arms.

And as he and Jean-Michel lead me to the door, I hear Eva chuckling.

But I hear it as her own hot, hockey-player boyfriend brushes past us.

So I do some chuckling of my own.

Because...

I fell for a hockey player.

How could I not?

And, despite my best efforts, the world found out every juicy detail.

Mostly because I shared them.

Isn't it great?

EPILOGUE

Hudson, Six Months Later

"READY?" I ask as we stand in the hall, the crowd roaring.

Tonight is game one of the Stanley Cup finals.

And we're here because of the woman standing next to me.

Diana Connors is well on her way to being a fucking legend.

And she's all mine.

"Do you think Ernest is okay?" she murmurs, teeth nibbling at the corner of her mouth.

I know Ernest is okay.

Because he's sitting up in the owner's box alongside Jean-Michel, Chrissy (and Chrissy and Rome's daughter Jessie), Rory, Belle and Quinn, Attie, and Smitty and Kailey.

The last because DeeDee did some poaching.

Kailey has brought her scouting goodness to the Eagles.

She's not just ours—the Grizzlies make a claim, along with the Breakers—but she's still ours.

So fight us for it.

So yeah, Kailey's here and Smitty and his booming voice.

The Grizzlies didn't make it to the finals. All five of the top teams in the conference—us, the Gold, the Sierra, the Vipers, and the aforementioned Grizzlies had a brutal battle leading up the playoffs. Ok, well really, it was all six since the Hawks brought some serious intensity thanks to their captain, Ace Ambrose.

Points were close.

Series were intense.

And eventually the Sierra ended up knocking the Grizzlies out.

We inched out our series against the Hawks by the skin of our teeth.

And now we're here.

Game one. The Cup in sight.

My woman on the battlefield beside me.

And a surprise on the horizon.

Because DeeDee may not need romance, but I've still taken every chance over the last six months to prove it to her.

So, even though I know what's coming, even though I want to find a shadowy alcove and kiss her senseless, I just bump her shoulder with mine and murmur, "Ernest is probably ordering Jean-Michel around and consuming his bodyweight in popcorn. He's good."

She glances up at me, bouncing nervously. "You're right. He's good. I'm good." A nod. "*We're* all good."

The warmup music starts playing and she jerks, teeth pressing into the corner of her mouth again.

"We're all good," I agree.

And the team is.

Dee and Jean-Michel—thanks to some help from Kailey's

magical scouting program—were able to move Pat not long after he went public with his "grievances."

Suffice to say, he didn't endear himself with the public.

And he definitely didn't make it easy on his new teammates.

If he secures another contract after this one runs out, I'll be really fucking surprised.

What *has* surprised me?

Duncan and Kane. They're not perfect team players but Pat's trade threw them for a loop and they've really pulled it together.

I hate to say I'm proud of them.

But...I'm proud of them—most especially of their contributions on the ice.

I'm also proud of myself.

I may not be a young kid with a fuckton of neuroplasticity (a fun term I learned during my occupational therapy sessions), but I'm managing my dyslexia.

I'm reading. I'm learning strategies and techniques to make it easier.

And most importantly, I'm not giving up.

The lights come on, the music rises to a crescendo, and the line of players in front of me starts to move, the guys rushing out onto the ice, their jitters and excitement mingling, hyping everyone up further. I don't immediately follow them and Dee, fidgeting in the suit her grandmother bought her, is standing right beside me, lost in thought again, her nerves practically palpable as she .

I get it.

This shit is the pinnacle.

And Dee is the one who's going to lead us through it.

But she's also wound so fucking tight, she's not enjoying it, not at all.

Hence the romance—just a little dash of it.

"DeeDee baby," I murmur, catching her arm before she and I fully exit the tunnel.

She stops, eyes coming to mine. "Are you ok—" She gasps.

Probably because I'm slip the ring I bought her onto her finger.

"Huddy," she whispers.

I touch her cheek. "Even when I'm out there"—a nod to the rink—"you're in here"—I tap my chest and wink. "Now you just have the diamond to prove it."

Her mouth opens. Closes. Opens again. "Are you seriously asking me to marry you right now?"

"No, baby. I know I don't need to ask. Because you and me forever is an inevitability." I grin. "This is just to show the assholes on the other team you belong to me."

She freezes.

Then shakes her head.

Then she does what she always does—she powers through.

This time she does it by lifting on tiptoe, slanting her mouth over mine, and kissing me senseless.

"I like the ring," she says, dropping back down onto her heels. "But don't think me wearing it means that you're getting out of a real proposal." Then she tosses a pointed look over her shoulder and marches out into the arena.

Cheers ring out.

And I know my job here is done.

With a little dash of romance—literally a *little*—Dee's nerves have faded away and she's right here.

In the present. In the moment.

Ready to kickass in the game.

And she just happens to be doing it wearing my ring.

I follow her out, wink again, and then hop on the ice, shifting into hockey mode.

But even as I do that, I can help by smile.

Because I cannot wait for the *real* romance that's waiting for her at the house.

Because she may be already wearing my ring...

But I plan on kicking ass in the real proposal too.

After we win this game.

RHODES

I SLIP INTO THE HOUSE, pausing only to drop my shit on the counter, before I'm hurrying upstairs to Finley's bedroom.

Finn's bedroom.

Because don't let her hear you call her Finley.

Normally, that thought has me smiling. Finn's fun and smart and beautiful. She's also a spitfire who has no compunction about calling me on my shit.

And with a dead wife and a four-year-old determined to turn my hair gray—or, I suppose, if Chloe could manage it, *pink* —I have plenty of baggage.

Finn, I think has some of her own.

Not that she shares it with me.

Fun and smart and beautiful and calling me on my shit doesn't come with a side of whatever secrets are locked up in that gorgeous brain of hers.

They come with taking great care of Chloe, with making sure my daughter is safe and healthy and fed, dropped off to preschool on time, bathed and her hair taken care of, her clothes clean, her playdates kept.

They also come with her making sure my daughter gets enough sleep.

Or *normally* they do.

Because tonight after a game against the Sierra, Chloe called me. I'm used to odd hours, what with games that don't start until seven-thirty at night and travel and changing time zones and morning skates. I'm even used to my daughter pushing her bedtime routine, mostly when she comes to a weekend home game to watch me play.

But she doesn't normally do that shit with Finn.

Still, the call didn't immediately tweak me, not until I put the pieces together, not until Chloe said that Finn was sick.

Then I realized my daughter, my precious, stubborn, smart as a whip daughter was basically home without supervision, considering Finn was too sick to provide it.

And *I* wasn't home.

I was on a fucking plane, counting down the seconds to make it back here.

I'm still feeling that urgency, that stress, that anxiety when I push into the room and see my daughter in bed with Finn, totally out, her arms and legs akimbo, her head on Finn's belly.

Finn...

Who's awake.

And looks to be at death's door when her head jerks my way.

"Fuck," I whisper, knees wavering in a way that has nothing to do with my legs being tired after the game and everything to do with the relief pouring through me.

"I couldn't lift her to put her back in bed," Finn rasps.

Yup. Rasps.

"I've got her," I say, striding forward and scooping her up into my arms.

Chloe doesn't so much as stir. But then again, my baby girl is a deep sleeper, and once she's out, she's *out*. It's only when she's really trying to push it on the bedtime that she pulls shenanigans like tonight.

"I wouldn't have gone to sleep if I knew there was a possibility that she was awake," Finn says, or rather rasps.

"I know," I tell her. "Don't worry about it. It's why we have the child locks on the doors—this isn't her first nighttime wandering rodeo."

"Right." She nods, but guilt is slicing through her expression. "I still wouldn't have slept, Rhodes. You have to believe me."

I frown, cuddle Chloe closer.

Which has something else slicing through Finn's expression.

Fear?

"I *do* believe you."

"I—"

"It's okay, Finn. I'll bring you some medicine. You can get some rest, and if you're really worried we can talk more in the morning, okay?"

She nibbles at her lip.

But eventually she nods.

"I'll be back." I slip from the room, carrying Chloe over to hers, tucking her in and closing her door.

Then I move into my bedroom—well move *through* it—not stopping until I'm in the bathroom and surveying the contents of my medicine cabinet.

I grab some overnight cold relief tablets, make a pitstop in the kitchen for a couple of saltines and a glass of water then make my way back into Finn's bedroom.

She's slumped down, eyes closed, her head on the pillows, her cheeks flushed with fever.

Damn.

"Finn," I murmur, sinking down onto the edge of the mattress.

"Rhodes."

For a second, I freeze, thinking she's heard me come in or felt the bed shift.

But no, her eyes are closed.

"Finn," I say again, just a little bit louder, hating to wake her but knowing she'll be a lot better off if she takes the medicine.

"*Rhodes*." It's a whisper...and it's full of agony.

But not because she's ill, I realize as her words keep coming.

Because they're full of longing.

Because they change *everything*—at least for me.

Because they're the words I've been desperate to hear for months now.

"Kiss me, Rhodes," she says on a soft sigh, her head burrowing into the pillows. "Please kiss me."

And also because...

When she wakes up in the morning, Finn doesn't remember say them at all.

THANK YOU FOR READING! I hope you loved Huddy and Dee's journey to happily-ever-after as much as I enjoyed writing it! The final full-length book in the Eagles Hockey series is FOREVER LACED. **She's the nanny. I shouldn't be in love with her. But then she begs me to kiss her...**

CLICK HERE TO READ FOREVER LACED NOW>

And are you curious about Jean-Michel, grumpy billionaire and team owner with a protective streak a mile wide? Check out a sneak peek of his happy ending below in BOTTLES & BLADES. **I fell for a billionaire...I just didn't know it.**

CLICK HERE TO READ BOTTLES & BLADES NOW>

Tiff

"Your total is $23.26," the cashier says, tapping on the register's keyboard, the computer screen above it changing as rapidly as her fingers move.

Clickity-click. Clickity-click. Clickity-click.

She pauses, glances up.

But not at me.

At the man she's currently ringing up, the man just in front of me. The man who reacts after a brief moment, jerking as though jarred from his thoughts and reaching into his pocket.

He's wearing a pair of jeans stained with so much dirt that I pity his washing machine, and his tee isn't much better, filthy and sweat-covered, plastered against a broad, well-muscled chest.

His forearms and hands are stained with something dark.

Clearly coming from some sort of hard, physical work, and on a day like today, summer clinging to the edges of a sunny spring afternoon, I envy him.

Not that I don't love my job—I'm a nanny, and my charge is awesome, and I love that it gives me the freedom to pursue my degree.

But sometimes I wouldn't mind playing hooky and getting out on one of the many trails around us on this side of the Bay, all rolling green hills and old-growth oaks and spring wild-flowers.

"Sir?"

I blink, realize that while I've been daydreaming about poppies and blue lupines, the man in front of me has been searching his pockets.

And coming up empty.

"Your total is $23.26," the cashier repeats, a little sharper now.

"Right," the man says, patting his pockets in turn. "Just give me a second. I know my wallet—"

"If you can't pay, I'm going to have to ask you to step aside and let the others behind you have their turn."

Her tone is brusque and cold and—

Filled with disdain.

It slices through me, even though it's not directed at me.

Because I've lived that life.

Because even today, I calculated my own spread on the conveyor belt—sitting behind the plastic divider—to a precise degree. I know that I have exactly the amount in my account to cover my food for the week.

Food and tuition. Medical debts and gas.

All of my expenses carefully worked out.

The man keeps searching. "I know I have—"

Someone sighs behind me—a sharp, irritated sound that zips through the air, stinging as it flies by me.

The man looks up, mid pocket-pat, and I almost gasp at the startling blue of his eyes.

They're as bright as the cloudless sky outside the store and filled with embarrassment that has my heart squeezing.

"If you'll just give me a moment," he murmurs, eyes narrowing as they drift behind me, presumably toward the impatient sigher and the line that's growing by the moment. "I have—"

The cashier starts tapping on her keyboard again, this time angrily. "I'll have to cancel the transaction, sir."

It's the condescension in her tone that unsticks me.

I double tap the side of my cell, take a step toward the man with the dirt marring his strong chin, clinging to the salt and pepper beard on his jaw, his cheeks. I slip between his strong, obviously hardworking body and the payment kiosk, avoiding those bright blue eyes as I say, "I've got it."

That brilliant cerulean gaze comes to mine. "No, that's—"

But I'm already waving my phone at the machine, and it doesn't so much as have to make contact to solve this problem.

Bleep-beep.

And it's done.

"There," I say softly, giving him a small smile. "Enjoy your meal."

His expression...

Well, I'm not sure I can discern the flurry of emotions—annoyance and surprise and embarrassment and...

Gratitude.

"Thank you," he says softly, snagging the sandwich, soda, and bag of chips from the counter.

"No worries," I reply, turning back to the cashier, taking the receipt she passes over.

He waits there for a moment, big body still, eyes on me, so I turn and hold it out to him.

"Did you need this?" I ask, careful to not get lost in his eyes, careful to not notice how handsome he is, all strong muscles and brutal features and those gorgeous blue irises.

"No," he says.

But doesn't move.

Just stares at me like I'm a puzzle to be solved.

And well...no puzzle here.

Just a woman who's barely holding her life together.

"Right, okay." I nibble at the corner of my mouth. "You have a good day."

Another hesitation from the big man next to me.

"You're all paid, sir," the cashier snaps as she starts scanning my items. "You can go now."

I see him stiffen out of the corner of my eye, but he doesn't snap back, and...he doesn't linger.

Just gives a slight nod and walks away.

Some part of me is disappointed.

The rest...is relieved.

Beep. Beep. Beep. Beep—

"Wait," I tell the cashier, as she reaches for the bottle of wine. It's a discount brand, but I'll have to do without it after that $23.26. "I'll pass on the wine," I say softly.

Her eyes come to mine and she rolls hers, silently setting it to the side before reaching for the next item.

A block of cheese.

"And that too," I murmur, doing some mental math. "And the bread," I add when she puts that aside, starts to scan.

More eye rolls, but my math proves to be on point because by the time she finishes scanning—minus the cheese and bread and wine—I have enough left in my account to cover everything else.

I click the button on the side of my phone.

Do another wave of my cell, hear that *bleep-beep.*

And ignore the surly cashier as I bag my items, gather up my receipt, and head out of the store.

I'm putting my bags into my trunk when I feel a presence behind me.

I slam it closed, spin around, and—

See the man from the store standing there, eyes flashing, body big and broad and giving more than a few Daddy vibes.

My heart skips a beat.

Warmth blooms in my belly.

Lower.

He's too old for me.
But my mind is running away with itself anyway.
"Can I help you—?" I begin.
"Come with me," he mutters.
Before I can protest, he wraps his fingers around my arm.
And drags me away from my car.

Hate missing Elise's new releases? Love contests, exclusive excerpts and giveaways?
Then signup for Elise's newsletter here!

www.elisefaber.com/newsletter

And join Elise's fan group, the Fabinators (https://www.face book.com/groups/fabinators) for insider information, sneak peaks at new releases, and fun freebies! Hope to see you there!

If you enjoy my series, considering supporting me on PATREON! Get access to early releases, bonus content, character art, audiobooks, special edition covers, swag, and much more!

CLICK HERE TO SUPPORT ME>

I so appreciate your help in spreading the word about my books, including sharing with friends! Please leave a review on your favorite book site!

EAGLES HOCKEY SERIES

ALSO BY ELISE FABER

Broken

Boldly

Breathless

Ballsy

Bewitched

Blowout

Breathe

Blazed

Sierra Hockey Series

Over the Line

Caught from Behind

The Big Skate

On the Fly

Eagles Hockey Series (all stand alone)

Broken Laces

Lace 'em Up

Knotted Laces

Loaded Laces

Lucky Laces

Oak Ridge Vineyards

Bottles & Blades

Beauty & the Boardroom

Rush Hockey Trilogy #1

Big Puck Energy

Filthy Puckboy

So Pucking Over It

Rush Hockey Trilogy #2

Love, Pucks, and Other Stories

All's Fair in Pucks and War

No Pucks Lost Between Us

Rush Hockey Novellas

Puck and Make Up

Billionaire's Club (**all stand alone**)

Bad Night Stand

Bad Breakup

Bad Husband

Bad Hookup

Bad Divorce

Bad Fiancé

Bad Boyfriend

Bad Blind Date

Bad Wedding

Bad Engagement

Bad Bridesmaid

Bad Swipe

Bad Girlfriend

Bad Best Friend

Bad Rebound

Bad Romance

Bad Business

Bad Billionaire's Quickies

Love, Action, Camera (all stand alone)

Dotted Line

Action Shot

Close-Up

End Scene

Meet Cute

Love After Midnight (all stand alone)

Rum And Notes

Virgin Daiquiri

On The Rocks

Sex On The Seats

Life Sucks Series

Train Wreck

Hot Mess

Dumpster Fire

Clusterf*@k

FUBAR

Perfect Storm

Free Fall

Lost Cause

Roosevelt Ranch Series (all stand alone, series complete)

Disaster at Roosevelt Ranch

Heartbreak at Roosevelt Ranch

Collision at Roosevelt Ranch

Regret at Roosevelt Ranch

Desire at Roosevelt Ranch

Phoenix Series (read in order)

Phoenix Rising

Dark Phoenix

Phoenix Freed

Phoenix: LexTal Chronicles (rereleasing soon, stand alone, Phoenix world)

From Ashes

In Flames

To Smoke

KTS Series (all stand alone, series complete)

Riding The Edge

Crossing The Line

Leveling The Field

Scorching The Earth

Cocky Heroes World

Tattooed Troublemaker

ABOUT THE AUTHOR

USA Today bestselling author, Elise Faber, loves chocolate, Star Wars, Harry Potter, and hockey (the order depending on the day and how well her team -- the Sharks! -- are playing). She and her husband also play as much hockey as they can squeeze into their schedules, so much so that their typical date night is spent on the ice. Elise is the mom to two exuberant boys and lives in Northern California. Connect with her in her Facebook group, the Fabinators or find more information about her books at www.elisefaber.com.

f facebook.com/elisefaberauthor

a amazon.com/author/elisefaber

BB bookbub.com/profile/elise-faber

O instagram.com/elisefaber

♪ tiktok.com/@elisefaberauthor

g goodreads.com/elisefaber